c.1

Sherburne
   Way to Fort Pillow

We who served with the black troops have this peculiar satisfaction, that, whatever dignity or sacredness the memories of the war may have to others, they have more to us . . . We had touched the pivot of the war. Whether this vast and dusky mass should prove the weakness of the nation or its strength, must depend in great measure, we knew, upon our efforts. Till the blacks were armed, there was no guarantee of their freedom.

— Thomas Wentworth Higginson
Army Life in a Black Regiment, 1869

CONTENTS

THE WAY TO
FORT PILLOW

I

———•—•———

School's Out

I<small>T WAS TWO DAYS</small> after Christmas when they drove us out of Berea. The year was 1859, and the college was twenty-three months old.

The Committee formed two lines along the side of the road. They sat their horses silently, watching us as we passed between their lines. They were all armed. Nobody spoke; even the horses were quiet. It was a gray day, with a rime of frost spread over the dead grass and brush. You could see your breath.

The hand-carved cherrywood box — the wanga — was wrapped in a square of flannel, and carefully packed at the bottom of my saddlebag.

We twenty Bereans walked our horses single file down the frozen mud track. The irregularity of the ground forced us to glance down often, but in between times we held our heads high. In front of me Dr. Rogers stared rigidly ahead, but I looked into the eyes of the gunmen to the left and right. I knew most of them by sight, and a few had once been my friends, as well as my neighbors in Madison County for a quarter of a century. Some stared back, angrily or defiantly. Some looked away. One spat at my boots. One smiled broadly as if he were watching a comic turn at a music hall. That was Danford Ranew.

It took us five minutes to pass down the road between the lines. When we were past the Committee, we drew together in a group to mount. I held Ellie's stirrup and helped her into the saddle — the sidesaddle she hated, and only used that day because she didn't want the Committee to see her in the worn jeans she customarily used for riding. Then I swung up on my horse, and we all rode together toward Richmond in silence.

In Richmond we separated. Ellie and I were going to Hazelwood, my family's home on the Kentucky River. The other Bereans were bound for Cincinnati by train. The train was waiting when we reached the station, and the engineer gave a blast on his whistle when we came in sight.

"I guess they can't hardly wait to get shut of us," said Ellie, straightening her back and raising her chin a little higher.

I dismounted and shook hands with each of the exiles individually. Last I said goodbye to Dr. Rogers. "You'll be back soon, Doctor, I know you will. We'll all be back soon!"

He gave me his quiet, affectionate smile. "God's will be done, Hacey," he answered, and climbed up the steps into the coach. The whistle blew again, wheels began to turn, and the train moved out, away from the South, toward the Ohio River.

My name is Hacey Miller. I was born and bred in the Bluegrass, and my life was entirely unremarkable until, at the age of thirteen, I chanced to fall under the influence of Cassius Marcellus Clay. Clay's passionate belief in emancipation, together with his propensity for settling disputes with a bowie knife, made him an almost Godlike figure to me. I was a fascinated onlooker, and then a secret partisan, as he challenged Kentucky's slavery power with his newspaper, *The True American,* and then carried the fight to the hustings.

It was Clay who first suggested to me that I go to Harvard, where I became totally dedicated to emancipationism. And it was Clay who brought me to Berea.

The Berea adventure had lasted a grand total of six and a half years, counting from the time Cash Clay had persuaded Reverend John G. Fee to come to a little settlement at the edge of the mountains called "The Glades" and preach a series of antislavery sermons there. That was the summer of 1853. The next year Fee returned to make The Glades his permanent home, living on land given him by Clay, in a cabin built mostly by me. (The building of log cabins is an art for which my expensive Eastern education had done little to prepare me, I soon discovered.)

In 1855 Reverend Fee agreed to open a one-room schoolhouse at The Glades, which he named the Berea School. I taught there and combined my pedagogy with carpentry chores, while Fee widened the audience for his antislavery preaching by riding a circuit through two hundred miles of the Cumberland Mountains. He made Berea a magnet for young people from the mountains — the proud, independent, often ornery, and heretofore isolated folk who, Clay and Fee believed, would become a powerful force for emancipation in Southern politics.

The more influence Berea gained, the more fury it generated in the slavocracy of the Bluegrass. All of us, teachers and pupils alike, were threatened by night riders, insulted and provoked on our trips into town, and harassed in small, spiteful ways. Reverend Fee was "accidentally" fired upon, my fellow teacher Bill Lincoln was beaten by Richmond bullies, and on one terrible occasion I was tied to a tree and whipped into unconsciousness. But the level of persecution never quite rose high enough to swamp us; more and more children came in from the lonely hollows to the south and east; and, at the beginning of 1858 we changed our name again, this time to Berea College.

When the fall term began that year, we had better than a hundred students, and there were eight of us on the faculty and staff. We added a second large room to the schoolhouse, and hung tarpaulins to subdivide it into recitation areas. Twenty students slept in the loft, and we built another large cabin to serve as a dormitory. We wrote a Constitution, elected a Board of Trustees, and — thanks to the mechanical genius and tireless dedication of Fee's cousin, John G. Hanson — built ourselves a sawmill. The lumber went into new houses, and soon the Berea Ridge was bristling with them.

But as Berea grew in size, our expenses grew also, and in September of '59 Reverend Fee went east to raise money. He was in Brooklyn, preparing to speak at Henry Ward Beecher's church, when John Brown raided Harper's Ferry.

A spasm of outrage swept through the South at this disastrous and futile act of violence. The dread specter of servile revolt rose to haunt the slavocracy and their hangers-on, who in their rage condemned every abolitionist and emancipationist, every radical and reformer, equally.

At that unfortunate moment, Reverend Fee made a speech which was fatally easy to misquote.

Standing in the pulpit of Beecher's Plymouth Congregational Church, his oversized head bobbing from side to side on his stalk of a neck, he cried out in his high penetrating voice, "We need more John Browns! We need men of his boldness and honesty, of his self-sacrificing spirit — *not to carry the sword, but the Gospel of Love!"*

The speech netted a collection of $217.50 — and a crop of headlines in every newspaper in Kentucky, warning readers that "Berean asks for more John Browns!" Of course, no editors bothered to print the second half of the quotation.

Rumors flew through the Bluegrass that Berea was preparing itself to be a second and more ambitious Harper's Ferry — that shipments of Sharps rifles had been stockpiled awaiting the Negro rebels who would use them on their former owners. In the heat and confusion generated by this and other fantasies, meeting followed meeting to determine how Madison County should go about ridding itself of us Bereans.

Life at the college went on almost as usual. We were apprehensive, but resolved not to yell until we were bitten. A few students were withdrawn by their parents, but the rest of us concentrated on showing the world that Berea had no doubt it would continue in the even tenor of its days until the end of time.

In Richmond a Committee selected itself, and gave itself a mandate to remove the most notorious Bereans from the state, peacefully if possible, by violence if necessary. Fee's name headed the list, and I am proud to say my own was not far below his. The Committeemen arrived on the Berea Ridge after dark on the evening of December 17. A powder of dry snow covered the ground and gave it an unreal paleness in contrast to the looming darkness of the trees and brush. Silhouetted against the luminescence, the men moved from house to house. They knew where everybody lived; when the knock came on my door and I opened it, one of the two men on the threshold presented me with a printed document with my name handwritten at the top. "Hacey Miller," he said in a flat voice, "you have ten days to leave. The reasons are all writ down here. If you're not gone when we come back, we'll run you out." He gave a little nod of his head, as if thanking me for my attention, and turned to leave.

I looked past him at the other man standing in his shadow. "Hello, Danford," I said. "Torn the clothes off any more mulatto gals lately?"

He moved into the light, and the fat smile on his face broadened into a grin. "Why, I declare, Hacey, you sound as jealous as a true lover — a true nigger-lover, that is. You better watch that mouth of yours, son. You keep talking rude like that, and somebody's going to call you out. You wouldn't want that, now that your little brother's not here to do your fighting for you."

"I don't suppose you'd like to call me out right now, would you? I'm sure your friend here could handle the formalities."

Danford Ranew laughed. "That's a boat you missed, Hacey, and I reckon it's halfway to Memphis by now. You had your chance — you just didn't have the belly for it."

"Try me again."

"It's too late. You're past fighting duels, with me or anybody else. You're getting the hell out of here, you and the rest of this nigger-stealing scum. You'll be out in ten days, or we'll carry you out. And I'd as lief we carried you."

I looked at him for a moment in silence. Although his face was fleshier and his eyes more deeply sunken into his cheeks than I remembered, he hadn't changed much in the past ten years. It seemed strange that he hadn't. "And to think that once I might have gotten you for a brother-in-law," I said musingly. "God moves in mysterious ways, Danford."

"Oh, you know all about the way God moves, that's for sure."

"I know one thing, Danford. There'll come a time. For us — for you and me. There'll come a time."

"Sure there will, Hacey — you count on it." He turned to his companion impatiently. "All right, he's got his god-damned paper. What are we waiting for?" he snapped, and the two of them stepped back into the darkness.

In twenty minutes the Committee finished serving their papers, and, with a good deal of unnecessary shouting back and forth, rode off the Ridge. As soon as they were gone we gathered at the schoolhouse for a meeting of the faculty and staff. We huddled together on the hand-hewn benches for warmth, and argued back and forth for an hour about whether we should wait out the ultimatum in Berea, or whether our point had already been made for us by the Committee's illegal behavior. One thing we needed to know was whether we could count on any outside assistance whatever. To find out, I was delegated to appeal to Cassius Clay, and two others agreed to take a petition to Governor Magoffin in Frankfort.

About ten the next morning I tied my horse to the hitching post outside White Hall, Clay's home in Madison County. Before I could rap my knuckles on the familiar door, it was opened by Timothy, Clay's half-blind old Negro servant. He must have heard me riding up and dismounting; he certainly couldn't have seen me. "Who that? What you want?" he asked querulously.

"It's Hacey Miller, from Hazelwood, Timothy. Is Mr. Clay home?"

"Why, how you been, Mister Hacey? You over here to get yourself another glass of Mr. Clay's root beer?" It was an old joke between us, going back to my first visit to Clay's

7

home as a boy of fifteen. I answered, as I had a dozen times before, "Not if you've still got some of that twelve-year-old bourbon, Timothy."

"You sure you old enough to drink, Mister Hacey?" he asked, screwing his face up in mock ferocity.

"Why, I'm almost as old as you are, Timothy. And you must be nearly thirty now, aren't you?"

He leaned closer, lowering his voice to a stage whisper. "That's right — but you don't tell none of my gal friends, you hear? They all think I'm only twenty-one." For a moment we laughed together in the comfortable intimacy that old jokes create, and then he led the way to Clay's study and opened the door for me.

Kentucky's most famous emancipationist was working at his desk as I entered, his big, broad-shouldered athlete's body erect in his chair, his shock of black hair falling over his wide forehead almost to his eyes. He rose when he recognized me, and welcomed me heartily.

"Hacey, boy, it's good to see you. It's been twice too long since you visited us."

"Much too long, Mr. Clay," I agreed.

He offered me a chair, dispatched Timothy for cold toddies, asked about my family, made two minutes' worth of small talk and then said directly, "I hope this is a social visit, Hacey."

"No, sir, it isn't. I've come here to ask your help." He didn't say anything and I went on to tell him about the Committee and its ultimatum. "So before we can decide what to do, we have to know who we can count on to stand behind us," I concluded.

Clay rose from his desk and began to pace back and forth, striking one large fist into the other palm. "I'm sorry you

8

came to me. I'm truly sorry. But I can't tell you what you want to hear."

"You're saying that when push comes to shove, we can't count on you?" I cried incredulously. "I don't believe it. Mr. Clay, there wouldn't even *be* a Berea College, if it wasn't for you!"

"Hacey, listen. The Fugitive Slave Law is the law of the land. Rebellion is against the law. John Brown broke the law. When John Fee set himself and Berea above the law, the fat went into the fire. Since that newspaper story about him saying we need more John Browns, why, hell — he couldn't find a corporal's guard in all of Kentucky to stand beside him."

"But he was misquoted! You've been a newspaper editor yourself — you know how misleading it is to quote out of context."

He sighed and brushed his hair out of his eyes with an automatic gesture. "Oh, of course I know, boy. But that's not the point, don't you see? The question's not what Fee really said. It's what people think he said, and what they *want* to think he said. Since he set himself above the law, they *want* to think he's planning a slave revolt. And there's nothing you or I or anybody can do to convince them otherwise."

"Then you'd suggest — what? Doing nothing? Packing up and leaving? Letting that trash close down Berea? *Giving up,* for God's sake?" My mouth was dry, and I could hear my voice rising.

"Hacey, believe me, I know how you feel —"

"I expect you do, Mr. Clay. Anyway, you should, since it was you who persuaded Reverend Fee to come down in the first place, and got me to go in with him and build those

9

buildings with my own damn hands. If anybody knows how we feel, it ought to be you!"

His eyes flashed angrily, and he hunched his broad shoulders as if preparing for physical combat. "Yes, I know, you bet I know! How do you think I felt when I lay half dead with typhoid while a mob of boors and poltroons suppressed my newspaper? Or when those Turner whelps held my hands and drove a knife into my lungs? You think I haven't heard those thousands of curses and sneers from the fine ladies and gentlemen of Lexington, just because I've kept my face turned away from them?" His deep voice thundered in the small room. "Do you people think you invented the antislavery movement in Kentucky? Why, I was risking my life and my honor for it every day, before you stopped sucking your mother's tit."

"I know that, sir," I cried. "That's why I can't understand why you won't help us now."

His anger left him as suddenly as it had come, and his shoulders slumped. "Hacey, can't you understand? There's nothing anybody can do. It's too late for Berea. It's a lost cause. You have to accept the fact, and go on from there."

"I don't see how I can do that," I answered stubbornly. "I can't see anything beyond Berea."

"Well, it's time you did. There are bigger things happening now. You're needed in a hundred other fights — get up and dust yourself off again, and put up your fists."

"I can't write off the college that easily, Mr. Clay."

"You've got to. Look, next year there's going to be a presidential election, and for the first time in history we've got an antislavery party with a chance to win! *That's* the fight you should be getting ready for." Lithe and restless as a caged tiger, he began to pace the room again. His voice became fuller and deeper — it sounded as if he were beginning a stump speech. "Hacey, today, in countless towns and villages all over this country, the lines are drawn. On one side, the beast, the Antichrist — slavery. On the other, the sword — the *legal* sword, Hacey — to destroy it. The time has come to grasp the sword and drive it home." His face was flushed, and he struck himself a blow on the chest. *"Carpe diem* — and let the dead bury their dead!"

I gazed at him with no emotion but the nausea of defeat. For the first time in my life I was beyond the reach of his oratory. He must have realized it, for he stopped his oration and looked back at me sadly. The silence was more eloquent than his words had been. I turned from him quickly and opened the door into the hall.

"Goodbye, Mr. Clay. I — " I wanted to say something, but couldn't think what, so instead I strode quickly from the house. He called after me, but I couldn't make out the words.

When I got back to Berea that night, I found that the governor's response had been as discouraging as Clay's, and more harshly expressed. His feeling was that Berea was an outlaw community and deserved exactly what it was getting.

I left the joyless meeting in the schoolhouse and walked down the Ridge to the Willums cabin, where Ellie had boarded for the past few months. She was reading a Bible lesson to the three Willums children when I arrived. Her soft black hair accented the thinness of her face with its high mountain cheekbones, and her eyes shone in the lamplight. She added a quick "Amen" to the verse she was finishing, slipped on her coat, wrapped a scarf around her head, tucked her small hand under my arm and went with me to walk through the still, cold darkness.

"Clay won't help us, Ellie," I said.

"Nor the governor either?"

"Nor him either. No help's going to come for us. Nine days from now we're finished."

She was silent a moment, then sighed and said, "Well, at least we know what's coming, if we never see the back of our neck."

"We've got to start thinking ahead, Ellie. What are you going to do when they close the school? Will you come home to Hazelwood with me?"

"Hacey, you know that wouldn't be right. What would folks say if you was to bring some ignorant mountain girl to live at your house with you?"

"It's not as if we'd be living in sin," I said exasperatedly. "We'd be getting married, for God's sake!"

"I keep telling you, I'm not about to marry you now."

"Ellie, I wish you'd be sensible."

"I *am* being sensible, and you know it," she said fiercely. "I'm not about to marry you till I've got my education. I'm still bone ignorant. You think I'll sit myself in your rich house and let your folks look down on Hacey Miller's ignorant wife?"

This was our old argument, and we'd been having it for a year now, practically since Ellie had arrived in Berea. I thought her idea of the importance of education was inflated, but I couldn't seem to deflate it to reasonable proportions. After all, I remembered, that idea was what had brought her out of the Big Sandy country and into my life in the first place.

But now the situation had changed, as I was quick to point out. "Ellie, you're sure not going to get any more education here at Berea for a while. What are you going to do? There's no point in staying here with the Willumses and slopping their hogs for them, with no more school to go to. You know you don't want to go back home to Head of West

Hollow — you don't want your family to see you again till you graduate, you told me that. You just can't go off by yourself to Lexington or Cincinnati or someplace — you don't know anybody, and you don't have any money. Isn't that right?"

"I reckon," she replied in a small voice.

"And look here," I pressed on. "You're going to marry me sooner or later anyway, so why not sooner? And furthermore, I'm the best teacher you'll ever find, and I won't charge you a cent for my services. So what the devil are we arguing about?"

We walked side by side over the rocky ground, watching our step. She said, irrelevantly, "It's as dark as a yard up a black cow."

"Now, come on, Ellie. Everything I said is true. Admit it!"

"Oh, all right, Hacey. But that ain't all of it. There's still your Ma and Pa, and your brother Boone and that fancy wife of his. How are they going to feel, you bringing me into their house without so much as a by-your-leave?"

"I've told you and told you — they'll love you as much as I do. They won't be able to help themselves, any more than I could. Ellie, honey" — I put my hands on her shoulders and turned her to face me — "will you please stop arguing for a minute?" I kissed her, and her lips were warm and her cheeks were frosty cold. After a while I said, "You're coming with me to Hazelwood. You hear me?"

She answered in a voice that was more the caress of her breath than a sound, "I hear you."

By Christmas almost all of the students were gone. The few who remained joined the faculty and staff in the schoolhouse for a service on Christmas morning. Ellie sat beside

13

me as we sang the beloved carols. Dr. Rogers read the familiar lesson from Luke, and John G. Hanson led us in the Twenty-third Psalm. The sweetness of the music and the eternal hopefulness of the Christmas message contrasted cruelly with our situation.

I raised my eyes to the blackboard at the front of the room. There, printed in white chalk, in almost the same place where Reverend Fee had first written it in 1855, was Berea's motto: "God hath made of one blood all nations of men."

I clutched Ellic's hand as if I were drowning.

The next day I set out my few possessions on my bed, and prepared to pack them in my saddlebags. I took up the little cherrywood box, and began to wrap it protectively in soft flannel. Then I stopped and stared at the curious design carved on the lid, remembering that the man was called Papa Legba, the woman was Maitresse Ezille, the great coiled snake was Damballa — and the boy who stood with his feet in the serpent's coils had no name. It was a fetish — what the Negroes called a wanga. I had owned it for fourteen years. I wrapped it very carefully and packed it away.

The following morning the Committee came back, and we said goodbye to the college for what none of us believed, but all of us feared, would be the last time.

II

DOMINOES

THE TIME Ellie and I spent at Hazelwood before our marriage seemed out of joint — some things were ending before they should have ended, and other things were starting before they were supposed to start. I found myself spending a good share of my waking hours alone, as Ellie and Mother cautiously laid the groundwork for their approaching relationship. Mother's attitude toward Ellie moved from incredulity to disdain, to ironic acceptance, to cautious approval, to furious partisanship, ending with her emphatic decision to outfit her daughter-in-law-to-be in her own wedding dress, suitably altered to the fashion of the time. Ellie accepted each mutation of attitude with grave courtesy.

I occupied myself during most of January by riding my little mare Jenny Lind over the winter-stricken hills that overlook the Kentucky River. I was oppressed by a sense of purposelessness, much, I imagine, as a priest is when, for whatever reason, he leaves the Church. I had never known how deeply committed I was to Berea until the Committee expelled me from it; the labor I had contributed and the joy that came with it had combined to prevent introspection.

Now that the labor and the joy were both gone, I felt like one "who treds alone some banquet hall deserted."

About the time I became aware that not only was I talking to myself, but that also I had stopped listening, my old mentor, Josh Brain, sent word he wanted to see me. Almost ten years had passed since I had given up reading law with him, but the fat little lawyer had kept in touch with me by correspondence during my years in Boston and Berea. He had never had a family of his own, and enjoyed assuming a parental role with me.

"So you're finally making the hymeneal plunge, eh, boy? You're a bit long in the tooth for it, but I don't suppose you'll be any more miserable than most other wretches in the double-blessedness game." He was permanently bedridden, and lay propped up on pillows. His skin, which had always been rosy pink and stretched as tight over his fat as the casing on a sausage, hung in folds and wattles down his cheeks and throat.

"Sometimes I wonder what the connubial estate is really like," he mused. "No bachelor ever sees more of it than a blind Hindu feeling up an elephant. But I reckon it's a little late for me to find out."

"I wouldn't be too sure of that, Mr. Brain," I said with bogus cheeriness. "You have an infinite capacity for surprising people."

"I fear I've about exhausted it, Hacey. And to tell you the damn truth, I'm just as glad. I think all of us will run out of time together."

"You mean the war? You think it's really coming?"

"As sure as God made goldfish."

"How soon, Mr. Brain?"

"I'd say about a year, give or take a couple of months."

"You don't think there's any chance of avoiding it?"

"You think there's any chance of avoiding the sun rising tomorrow? You think there's any chance of — " He was interrupted by a spasm of violent coughing, and he held a handkerchief over his mouth. After a few moments the coughing stopped. He took the handkerchief away and his lips were bright red in the corners. I rose in alarm, but he waved me back to my chair. "Sit down, I want to talk," he rasped.

I sat down again. I waited a moment for him to speak. When he didn't I prompted him. "How can you be so sure there's going to be a war?"

"Been sure of it since Abe Lincoln made that speech in Freeport in 'fifty-eight. That was like knocking over the first domino in a line. From then on, everything goes like clockwork."

"I remember the debates between Lincoln and Douglas in Illinois, but I don't understand why Freeport was the first domino."

Brain propped himself a little higher on his pillows, and a touch of color came to his cheeks as he started to expound an intricate argument with a lawyer's zest. "Now pay attention, Hacey," he began brightly. "When the U.S. Congress passed the Kansas-Nebraska Act, both Northern Democrats and Southern Democrats supported it, and Stephen Douglas was their hero. Northern Democrats liked it because it promised that new states could come into the Union either free or slave, depending on what the people themselves wanted. Popular sovereignty. But the Southern Democrats liked it because it offered them the chance to expand slavery north of the old Missouri Compromise line that had them painted into a corner — and also because never in their fondest dreams had they ever expected to get a law even half as favorable to their 'Peculiar Institution.' Are you following me?"

"Yes, sir — you say all the Democrats like the Kansas-Nebraska Act — but for different reasons."

"That's right — and it's that discrepancy that Lincoln played on at Freeport. You see, once they got used to it, the Kansas-Nebraska law suited Southern Democrats like a homely old wife who's good in the kitchen — just fine, until something young and pretty wiggles her ass at you. The pulchritudinous posterior I have reference to, as you have no doubt guessed, was the Dred Scott decision."

"Mr. Brain," I said honestly, "never before this moment have I ever thought of any law case resembling the female derrière."

"Lamentable lack of symbolic imagination. The great thing about the Dred Scott case, from the slaveholder's point of view, was that it officially reduced the slave to the status of mere property, with no human rights whatever. No different from a chair, or a house, or a bank account. It didn't take the South long to figure out that if slaves are only property, then the Fifth Amendment to the Constitution covers them: No person shall be deprived of life, liberty *or property* without due process of law."

I began to get an inkling of the direction his argument was leading. "And the old Missouri Compromise didn't count as 'due process' in the Constitutional sense?"

"Of course not — not any more than if the Congress had passed a law confiscating the homes of everybody in Vermont!"

"Then that means the Missouri Compromise and Henry Clay's Compromise of eighteen-fifty were illegal to begin with!"

"Hacey, all evidence to the contrary notwithstanding, sometimes I think you are a loss to the Law." The little lawyer gave a chuckle which threatened to turn into a cough, but which he suppressed. "Now let's move on to the Freeport debate. The year is eighteen fifty-eight, and Abraham Lincoln is running against Stephen A. Douglas for the office of U.S. senator from Illinois. Lincoln knows he's the underdog in Illinois, where most folks think the 'Little Giant' hung the moon. He also knows that in two years — in eighteen-sixty — there will be a presidential election, and Stephen A. Douglas is almost sure to run for the Democratic nomination. And he knows that Douglas is *the only possible Democratic candidate* who would be acceptable to both Northern and Southern Democrats.

"Hacey, that Lincoln is some lawyer — and it takes one to know one. At Freeport he asked Douglas a question that started knocking over the dominoes. He asked him if he believed that territories had a right to exclude slavery *before* they were formed and admitted as states. Douglas leaped for it like a trout, because he knew the answer the people of Illinois wanted to hear. Certainly the territories can exclude slavery if they want to, he said. The enforcement of slavery depends on police power, and the territory can set up its police power so as not to protect slavery.

"Cheers and huzzas from the Illinois apple-knockers. Dancing in the street. Douglas preens himself like a peacock. The election is in the bag. Nobody notices Lincoln watching from the wings like some slab-sided prairie Iago.

"Because Stephen A. Douglas may be a U.S. senator, Hacey — but he is *dead* as a presidential candidate! The South is bristling like a constipated porcupine. The Dred Scott case had reassured them that nobody could ever outlaw slavery in the new states, and here is their own friend in the North — their *only* friend in the North — siding with the abolitionists to open up the whole mess again. Just goes to show you can't trust anybody north of the Ohio River! What's the solution? Why, nominate a presidential candidate from the South, of course. The only problem is, there ain't any Southern candidates that the Northern delegates will nominate — so the only way out is to have two conventions, and nominate two Democratic candidates, one Yankee and one Southern. And the Democratic Party will split down the middle as cute as a baby's butt!"

"Hold up a minute, Mr. Brain. You really think Lincoln set out to drive a wedge into the Democratic Party, and sacrificed his chance to win the senatorial election in eighteen fifty-eight to do it?"

"No doubt about it. Of course his chances of winning were mighty slim even before Freeport — but just the same, that tall ugly drink of water drew a bead on the Little Giant and blasted him out of the tree as slick as a whistle, and he knew exactly what he was doing."

"All right, let's get back to the dominoes, and see if I follow you. To begin with — "

"Hacey, my boy, could I prevail upon you to hand me one of those cigars on the table? And splash me a smidgen of bourbon into that glass there? It will help me get through the considerable amount of talking it takes to put these simple ideas across to you."

I poured him a drink, but refused the cigar, as I had been instructed to do by the Negro woman sitting outside the door. He grumbled, but I soothed him with an extra ounce of sour mash.

"About those dominoes, Mr. Brain. The first one was the Freeport debate. It knocked over the second one, which is

Stephen Douglas's chance to be nominated by the whole Democratic Party. Then the second one knocks over the third one, which is the presidential election this year — "

"Which will be won by a Republican. Can't tell which one yet. It might be Seward, or Chase, or even Lincoln, if we're lucky — after all, he *is* married to a Lexington gal. But whichever, the result will be the same."

"Secession?" The word had been in the mouths of Southern firebrands for years.

"Secession — that's the next domino, the second-to-last one." He took a swallow of bourbon and coughed. We sat in silence for a moment.

"And the last one is war?" I asked.

"Yes, the last one is war. A war which I truly thank a merciful God I will not see." He reached a wasted hand toward me, and I clasped it in mine. "But you don't have any choice, son," he said in a hoarse whisper. "You'll see it — you'll see it all. So take your little gal and love her and bed her down and make yourself a family — families are good, families are better than no families. God bless you, Hacey Miller." His fingers squeezed mine. "Is there a drop more of that bourbon?"

That was the last time I saw him before he died.

Ellie and I were married the 1st of February, 1860, in a small ceremony at Hazelwood. Falk Padgett, Ellie's brother, was my best man, and a Berea girl named Cassie Lomax was maid of honor. Also in attendance were my mother and father, and my younger brother Boone and his wife Robin. The Miller slaves, 'Shach and Aunt Hessie, Jubal, Pierre and Opal, watched silently from the back of the room, their presence seeming to mock everything I believed in.

The ceremony was performed by Reverend Hapgood, a

Campbellite preacher from Richmond, a dim and pious man who tended to mumble his Scripture as though the wedding service was a confidential dialogue between himself and the Lord.

Ellie was as pale as death, and when I kissed her after the pronouncement she was trembling like a wet puppy. After the ceremony, as we drank sherry and ate cake, she had little to say to me or anyone else. The only person who did much talking was Mother. Falk and Cassie seemed intimidated by their surroundings; Father was ill, as he had been for some months, and looked as though he should have been in bed; Boone was simply silent; and Robin watched Ellie and me with an arched eyebrow and a slight twist to her upper lip that was no doubt meant to remind us that her name had been Ledyard before she married into the Miller family. Mother tried to make up for everybody else single-handed. She was indomitable, but not successful. I was glad when Ellie and I could make our adieus and begin our trip to Louisville and the first night of our honeymoon.

We stayed at the Galt House, in an airy room with a handsome brass double bed. I threw myself down on it while Ellie stood at the window, looking out at the distant lights that glimmered in the black waters of the Ohio.

"Lordy, it's big and scary out there," she said.

"Don't you worry your head, honey — I'll wrap it all up in a ribbon with a bow and give it to you for a wedding present."

She turned her big, uptilted eyes away from the window and looked at me worriedly. "Hacey, you don't reckon this is a dang-fool mistake, do you? You ain't going to wake up tomorrow and say, What in Tophet did I ever tie up with an ignorant thing like her for?"

"If you keep talking foolishness like that, I might." I got

up and walked over to the window behind her, and put my arms around her waist. She leaned her head back against my shoulder, and we looked out at the mirrored lights together. After a moment she said, "That's the Ohio River there, ain't — isn't it?"

"That's right, honey."

"And those lights on the far side — that's the North?"

"That's Jeffersonville, Indiana. Yes, it's the North."

"And it keeps going on, and on, and on, out there behind that blackness — don't it? For thousands of miles, with millions of people in it — all sleeping now, but they'll all be getting up tomorrow morning for their chores, eating their breakfasts, going to schools, going to work —" Her voice trailed off as she marveled at the thought of those millions of invisible people. Then she twisted in my arms and pressed her cool little hands against my cheeks. "Hacey, is there going to be a war between the North and the South?" I pulled her closer and tried to kiss her, but she held my head away. "No! Now tell me, I want to know!"

"Some people think so."

"What do you think?"

I sighed and loosened my hold on her. "Yes, I think there will be a war — probably in a year or so."

"Over the slaves?"

"Mostly over the slaves."

"You reckon you'll be in it?"

"Ellie, sweetie — " I pulled her closer again and buried my face in her soft, fragrant hair, but she would have none of that yet. She pushed me away again.

"Now tell," she said severely.

"Yes, damn it! Yes, I think I'll be in it."

"And on the North side, too, I warrant."

"Yes, if I go in, it will have to be on the North side. If

what I've done with my life so far means anything at all, I'll have to go with the North. I can't fight to preserve slavery."

"Even if your own folks is on the other side?"

"Even then."

"I knowed that was the way you felt." Her great dark eyes searched mine, and there was sadness in them. "We've got a ways to go, Hacey," she whispered, and then raised her lips to be kissed.

Then we got into that fine big bed with its cool white sheets, our first time together. We lay hugging each other and enjoying the new feeling in our bodies, and talking a little, and kissing a little. When our blood rose, and I entered her, she gave a gasp of pain, then wrapped her arms and legs around me as if she wanted to hold on to the pain, and mix it with the joy, and keep it inside herself forever.

From Louisville we went down the Ohio and up the Mississippi to St. Louis, on the stern-wheeler *Queen of the West*. We stayed a week, then began a leisurely trip back to the Bluegrass overland, by way of Paducah, Bowling Green, and Danville. We returned to find my father's illness more grave than when we'd left. Ellie and I moved into a small rented house in Lexington, and I took over the management of the family store.

Presiding over the affairs of Miller's Feed and Dry Goods was something I had never in the world expected to do, and which I had precious little talent for. But there wasn't any choice. My brother Boone's medical practice was growing at a great rate — he seemed to be on excellent terms with John Hunt Morgan's clique of blue-blooded bravoes, who could certainly afford to pay well to have their dueling wounds patched. Old Elam Yates, who had been Father's assistant for more than thirty years, was suffering from an exotic combination of ailments, and was only able to work irregularly. My brother-in-law, Falk Padgett, though honest and diligent enough on the job, felt there were many things in his life more important than keeping books and taking inventory. And in all candor I had to admit to myself that the closing of Berea had left me with nothing of much importance to do, at least until I could find a teaching position in the fall.

Ellie and I had barely gotten ourselves settled in our little rented house on West Short Street, and I was just beginning to remember the first names of a few of our better customers, when John G. Hanson took it into his head to come back to his sawmill and cut some logs.

Hanson was a cousin of Reverend Fee, and his sawmill had played an important role in the building of Berea. Hanson loved that sawmill with his whole heart, and after he was expelled from the college with the rest of the exiles, as he was sitting out the dismal winter in Cincinnati, he couldn't help remembering that there were three hundred uncut logs back at the mill. And blades were rusting, belts were rotting — it was more than he could stand. Without telling anyone his plans, in March he returned to Berea Ridge to cut the lumber.

I heard about it when I was in Richmond one weekend, from young Andrew Swinglehurst, whose family still lived in the village of Berea. His voice emerged excitedly from under a luxuriant mop of red hair. "That Hanson's got everybody in Berea helping him cut them logs, Mr. Miller, and he ain't about to leave till he's cut them all."

This was serious; of all the Bereans who had been driven from the college, Hanson was probably disliked the most by the citizens of Madison County. It was easy to see why. His religious and political views were dogmatic and humorless, and at work he was a harsh and tireless taskmaster. There was a broad strain of kindliness in his character, but often it didn't surface for days at a time.

"Does anybody here in Richmond know he's come back?" I asked.

"Shucks, *everybody* knows. That's all they're talking about, down on the courthouse lawn."

"What are they saying?"

"Saying that they're going over and get him, and burn down the whole blamed place, like they should have done last Christmas!"

I scribbled a note to Ellie, telling her I might have to stay overnight in Richmond, and gave it to Andrew with instructions to deliver it to Hazelwood, where we were spending the weekend. Then I pointed my little mare's nose down the road to Berea.

I could hear the whine of the saw blade a half mile out of town. Hanson, his big body stripped to the waist under a leather apron, was working furiously in a blizzard of sawdust, which stuck to the sweat on his chest and shoulders and made him look like a huge and furious cinnamon bear. He was swinging a stack of twenty-foot boards and shouting directions to the two boys who were helping him. When he saw me, he dropped the boards on the floor and seized my hand, shouting something that was drowned in the screech of the blade.

"Hello, John, it's good to see you," I shouted back. "Listen, you've got to get away from here!"

He smiled and nodded, his sawdust-caked eyebrows rising and falling dramatically as he pantomimed his pleasure at our meeting. I raised my voice and screamed, "John, you've got to get out of here! They're coming to get you!"

He nodded and smiled some more. He couldn't hear a

word I said over the shrill whine of the saw. It took me a minute of gesticulation before I could get him to turn the thing off. When the silence came it was startling.

In the ominous quiet I tried to persuade him that his life was in danger. He wanted to believe I was exaggerating. "But Hacey, my friend," he argued, "if I'm in such mortal peril, how is it you can keep living right here in Madison County with nobody ever laying a finger on you? You were on the Committee's list too, if I remember."

"It's different with me, John. My family's lived here for years. We're kin to all sorts of people. My mother and father are proslavery, and so's my brother. I'm safe as in church. But you — why, if they get you, they'll string you up in a minute!"

"Oh, I can't believe that," he said in his low, rumbling voice. "I'm sure you mean well, Hacey —"

My patience ran out. "God damn it, John, it you want to get yourself lynched, it's all right with me. But for Christ's sake at least send these boys away from here before they get their necks stretched too."

"Taking the Lord's name in vain don't make your argument no stronger," he said, rubbing his bushy beard abstractedly and creating a miniature snowstorm of falling sawdust. "Howsomever, if you think my presence here puts these lads in jeopardy . . ."

"Believe me, I *know* it does! Saddle up, and don't waste a minute. They're probably right behind us now."

But it was half an hour before we were able to put distance between ourselves and Berea, because Hanson remembered some college records that had been overlooked during the hegira the previous December and insisted on packing them in saddlebags and taking them with us. That half an hour was almost too much. We weren't five minutes from the set-

tlement when we heard a large body of horsemen coming toward us on the Richmond pike. We pulled back into the
bushes as they passed at a gallop. There must have been
sixty men in the party, and they were loaded for bear. Leading the way were three men I recognized from John Hunt
Morgan's coterie — Danford Ranew was one. After they had
passed I looked at Hanson ironically. "Now what do you
think?" I asked.

"Well, I swan," he said mildly.

Later I heard what the Committee — all mobs seemed to
call themselves Committees in the Bluegrass — did in Berea
that evening. They forced their way into house after house
at gunpoint, searching for Hanson. Finally they hit a barred
door that didn't open for them. That made them mad, so
they broke it down and pistol-whipped the man they found
inside it, a poor old consumptive named George West. For
good measure they slapped and abused his daughter, too. I
understand Ranew played a part in that. When two neighbors tried to intervene they were beaten severely.

But in spite of the pious best efforts of John G. Fee during
his ministry in Berea, there were still some residents of the
settlement who didn't share his pacifist beliefs. As the
Committee began to remount outside West's cabin, shots
were fired from cover, and one of the horsemen was
wounded. This set off a brisk flurry of answering gunfire, as
the Committee milled around shooting at everything and
everybody that wasn't on horseback. After a few moments
it dawned on them that they were exposed to fire they
couldn't answer effectively, and with a ragged shout they galloped down from the Ridge and disappeared up the Richmond road.

That wasn't the end, of course. That night the Committee
sent for reinforcements, and before sunrise the next morning

they returned. There was no gunfire to greet them this time, so they went unhindered through their appointed tasks; they sacked the school and the homes of all the exiles, and burned John Hanson's sawmill to the ground — three hundred logs and all.

Meanwhile I had taken the fugitive by a route of back roads and trails that skirted Richmond, and we reached Hazelwood unseen by human eyes. I decided to put Hanson in Star's cabin — a ramshackle hut on the bank of the Kentucky River which had been occupied, until he abandoned it fifteen years before, by a freed Negro with a five-pointed scar on his forehead, whom I had many reasons to remember.

The cabin was still reasonably weathertight, and Hanson insisted his comfort would be complete. "Don't worry about me, Hacey," he rumbled. "If you want to worry about something, worry about the low-down, miserable souls of those wretches in that posse back there. They need all the Christian worrying they can get!"

Up at the house, I found my mother and Ellie concerned. They had heard rumors of the trouble at Berea and had guessed that I had ridden there. "What happened, son?" Mother asked abruptly.

I told them how I had persuaded Hanson to leave the sawmill and ride with me, and how we had missed the Committee by minutes. "He's down at Star's cabin now," I finished. "He'll be all right there for a day or two, until this blows over a little. Then I'll get him out of the Bluegrass. He's got some friends in Jackson County who'll take care of him."

Mother and Ellie looked at each other, and something unspoken passed between them. Then Mother said crisply, "Hacey, you've got no more manners than a hungry shoat. Go tell your friend that if he's staying with the Millers, we expect him to stay up here, not in an abandoned nigger shanty. We'll put him in the guest room. Ellie, will you tell Aunt Hessie to see that the bed's made?"

I said apologetically, "I thought it would be safer if nobody saw him at the house, Mama —"

She raised her chin and looked down her thin nose at me severely. "Hacey, the only person who might tell tales out of school about your Mr. Hanson is Robin, and she and Boone are staying in Lexington this weekend. Even though I may not approve of your friend's politics" — her mouth puckered involuntarily — "I expect we can extend him the same hospitality we would grant any other guest in our home. Now run along, son, and let us get something hot on the table."

Hanson stayed with us until Monday night, when I judged it was safe enough to travel. We left about ten, and rode southwest in an arc that paralleled the river and kept us well east of Richmond and Berea. I left him about 2:00 A.M., and was back at Hazelwood by dawn, where I slept the sleep of the dead.

III

BETWEEN PEACE AND WAR

TRUE TO JOSH BRAIN'S PREDICTION, the national Democratic
Party found itself unable to agree on a candidate or a platform, and so split itself right down the middle, the Northern
Democrats nominating Stephen A. Douglas, and the Southern Democrats choosing John C. Breckinridge of Kentucky.

In May the Republican Party met in Chicago. Cassius M.
Clay announced his support of Abraham Lincoln, carrying
most of the Kentucky delegation with him. Lincoln was
nominated — but Clay failed to receive the vice-presidential
nomination he hoped for, largely because of his efforts on
Lincoln's behalf. If Clay had made a deal with, for instance,
Montgomery Blair, who wanted his support, he might well
have had the vice-presidential nomination in return. Then it
would have been C. M. Clay, not Hannibal Hamlin, and
later Andrew Johnson, who stood second in line of succession
to the presidency.

If Clay had succeeded Lincoln as President, what would
the history of the Reconstruction have been? Speculations
like that fill the empty hours of old men.

For the first time in my life, I took an active part in the
election process. I became secretary of the Lexington Lin-
coln-Hamlin Society, an organization of some twenty mem-

bers, and scarcely burgeoning. Nobody took us seriously; if I had been on the other side I don't think I would have taken us seriously myself.

But feeble though we may have been in the Bluegrass, we were mighty in the North. Lincoln was elected, with almost all of the 40 per cent of the national vote he received coming from north of the Ohio River.

A sudden, unbelieving pall of shock and outrage fell over the South.

Visitors from the Cotton States talked openly of secession in the Phoenix Hotel taproom, and the bloods and bravoes of John Hunt Morgan's Lexington Rifles claimed they'd be damned for Boston nigger-lovers before they'd take orders from a black Republican baboon.

Ellie and I spent Christmas at Hazelwood in an atmosphere of foreboding. Father was still bedridden, Mother was distracted and irritable, and Boone and Robin had little to say to us, spending most of Christmas Day with Robin's family at Redbird, the Ledyard house, a few miles from Hazelwood. Three days before, South Carolina had seceded from the Union, and it was expected that most, if not all, of the Deep South states would follow suit immediately after the first of the year. Governor Magoffin was expected to convene the Kentucky Legislature sometime in January for the same purpose.

After dinner on Christmas Day Ellie and I were alone in the sitting room. "I reckon we'll see a lot of changes next year," she said pensively.

"I reckon," I replied, staring into the fire.

"I bet I know one you don't know, Hacey."

"Oh, what's that?" I asked.

"No, on second thought, it's not rightly a *change*. You might say it's more of an *addition*."

32

"All right, honey," I said with a touch of irritation, "change or addition, or whatever — what is it?"

"I hope you don't mind too much — even if it's a kind of contrary time for it."

"Ellie, whatever it is, will you please spit it out?"

Her eyes shone in the firelight. "Why, we're going to have us a baby," she said.

It took me a second or two to realize what she had said. Then, thoughtlessly, I replied, "I've heard of things timed better."

The smile left her face and she straightened herself in the chair. "I'm sorry if I've disappointed you," she said coolly. "I guess I should have asked your permission first."

"I didn't say that. I'm not blaming you, Ellie —"

"Thank you! That's real generous of you!"

"— but you've got to admit this is one hell of an inconvenient time to have a baby!"

"Nobody ever told me what was a *convenient* time! If I'd known, maybe I just could have slid it in some Sunday afternoon, when it wouldn't have bothered anybody!"

"Ellie, honey, listen to me. I shouldn't have said that. I love you. I'm glad you're having — *we're* having — a baby. It's wonderful. It's what I've wanted for us more than anything." I got down on my knees beside her chair and put my arms around her waist and my head against her breast. "It's going to make me the proudest man in the world."

She stiffened and tried to pull her body away from me, but I held her tightly. After a moment she relaxed, and I felt her fingers gently touch my hair. Then she said, in a voice from which the prickliness had departed, "I *do* see how it would distemper you, Hacey. Really I do."

"Nonsense!"

"— but I bet you'll get to like the idea once you give it a

33

chance." I looked up into her face and saw she was smiling. I kissed her and went back to my own chair, and we watched the fire in silence for a while.

"You know what I think, Hacey?" Ellie asked.

"What, honey?"

"I think there isn't really any such thing as a *convenient* time for having babies. Because when everything's nice and easy in the world and you'd like a baby to break the monotony, why, you don't need it any more than another mosquito in summertime. But when it seems as if everything's so chancy that it would be plain cruel to bring a baby into this world, that's the time it's the most needful to breed good men and women. So, in a way, the best time is the worst time, and the worst time is the best time."

I looked at her, admiring the play of shadow around her cleanly drawn chin-line, and below her almost Asian cheekbones. "For our children, Ellie, there will never be any worst times," I said.

The day after Christmas, filled with my great news, I paid a call on Cassius M. Clay at White Hall. During the year since the expulsion of the Bereans, Clay and I had resumed our old knight-and-squire relationship, up to a point.

He pushed a cup of milk punch into my hand, slapped me on the back and voiced two or three pleasantries appropriate to the occasion. Then, abandoning the subject of my prospective entrance into the estate of fatherhood, he launched into Lincoln's cabinet, which was then in the process of being selected.

"It could be Secretary of War for me," he said in an intense and anxious voice, as he began to pace the room, "but I've heard that Simon Cameron's friends are pressing Lincoln to choose him for the job. Simon Cameron — dear God! What military experience did he ever have?" He kicked at the rug irritably. "Secretary of State? Possible, possible — but Weed is working to get it for Seward, and no doubt he will. Navy? Don't want it!" he said accusingly, glaring at me as if I were urging the unwanted portfolio on him. "Attorney General? Probably will be Bates — I wouldn't want it anyway. Treasury? Possible again — although chances are it will go to Chase. No, all things considered, I should think it will either be War or Ambassador to the Court of St. James. I don't believe I need consider anything less."

"Have you heard anything from Mr. Lincoln about it?" I asked.

"To tell you the truth, I haven't, and I'm beginning to suspect my enemies are working behind my back. There's nothing some of them wouldn't stoop to if they could deprive me of my just deserts, you know. Contemptible, whining curs! Where were they when I was fighting slavery single-handed!" His heavy features twisted in anger. He brushed the shock of hair back from his eyes with a hand that trembled. I noticed that the hair wasn't solid black anymore, but streaked with gray, and that his face had become florid.

"Surely Mr. Lincoln would never take the advice of anyone else against you, Mr. Clay — not after what you've done for emancipation over the last twenty years!"

"By the living God, he better not!" Clay cried furiously. He struck one fist into the other palm in his familiar gesture. "There are a lot of people who remember which of us is the Johnny-come-lately who came down from Illinois to be cosseted by his father-in-law's slaves, while the other lay between life and death with a knife wound in his lungs!"

His sudden unbridled anger startled me, and I tried to

35

soothe his feelings. "Between the two appointments — War and St. James — which would you prefer, Mr. Clay?"

His face cleared, and he clasped his hands behind his back and resumed his pacing at a more moderate rate. His deep voice was melodious as he answered. "No doubt my military experiences during the Mexican War would stand me in good stead in the administration of the War Department — and yet I must admit I'd enjoy cutting a swathe across the croquet fields of the British aristocracy. And glory — wouldn't my wife love it!" He made a face as if he had bitten into something sour, then laughed as delightedly as a boy with a new kite. "Oh, it's a difficult choice, Hacey — one in all fairness I should let Mr. Lincoln make for me. The needs of the country should be our first consideration, after all. Here, your glass is empty, boy — that will never do!" He took my cup from me and filled it from the small cut-glass bowl on the sideboard. "To Abraham Lincoln and the Republican Party," he toasted, "and confusion to our enemies!" Then as an afterthought he added politely, "And to the newest Miller, who's knocking on the door of Life. May he, too, find admittance to the cause of emancipation!" We raised our glasses and clinked them together, and I took a deep drink, trying to calm the sense of unease I felt about the man who, until the past year, had been the polestar of my life.

Ellie and I were at home one evening, making lists of children's names, when my brother Boone knocked on the door. It was the first time he had called at our West Short Street house, and I welcomed him warmly and asked him what he would drink. He refused anything, and sat down on the front six inches of a chair, with a purposeful straightness to his back.

"Hacey, I don't know if you know the truth about Papa," he began. "He has a carcinoma at the base of his skull. It's pressing on the brain, and in six weeks I expect him to be dead. Mama doesn't know yet, but he does, and I think you should too."

I sat silent for a few moments and then said inadequately, "I knew he was pretty sick."

"He's beyond the skill of any physician. The only thing anybody can do to help him now is to give him peace of mind." He looked at me gravely from under level brows.

I could see this was going to be a conversation I would have avoided if I could. "Of course," I said.

"Hacey, I'm not going to beat around the bush. You know the best way you could bring Papa peace of mind would be to prove to him that you were loyal to your people and your state and that you had given up all this abolitionist craziness of yours once and for all."

"How would you suggest I prove that, Boone?" I asked quietly.

"Last week John Hunt Morgan asked me to serve as regimental surgeon for the Lexington Rifles. While we were talking I brought up your name and asked whether you'd be acceptable, in case you wanted to enlist. Well, as you can imagine, Hacey, your record over the last few years could easily be held against you —"

"I should hope so."

"— but Captain Morgan said he was prepared to overlook many things, as long as a man was willing to do his duty to protect Kentucky against a Yankee invasion."

"Boone, I think I'm going to have a drink now, before we go any further with this, and I'd be obliged if you'd join me." This time he agreed, and I asked Ellie if she would have one with us. She nodded assent. Boone looked shocked as I came back from the kitchen with the three drinks. I don't imagine his Robin had ever tasted bourbon in her life.

I took a long pull on my toddy and asked, "Have you actually joined the Rifles, Boone?"

"I have. I'm to receive the rank of first lieutenant."

"And now you think I should join too, and wipe out all my dishonorable past with one brave stroke?"

"That's your language, Hacey, not mine. What I think is that supporting your own people is the right thing to do, and that Papa would die happier if you did." It was typical of Boone that he neither added emphasis to the word "die," nor hurried past it.

"I expect you're right about Papa, Boone," I answered slowly. "If he thought I'd had a change of heart and had become a good Democrat, it probably would make him happier. But I wonder how he'd feel if he knew I was doing something I didn't believe in, just for his sake?"

"Hacey, can't you see it wouldn't be *just* for his sake? It would be for the sake of our people! The only way we can protect ourselves in the South is to stand together. Seven states have seceded from the Union already, and it looks like eight more will join them in the next month or two. That's thirteen million people, Hacey! Thirteen million people ready to spit in Abe Lincoln's eye! If we all stand united, they'll never dare to attack us. It's the only possible way to prevent war."

"You talk about 'our people,' Boone — but I'm not sure *your* people are the same as *my* people. Your people are the Morgans and the Wickliffes and the Danford Ranews, and my people are Cash Clay and John Hanson and little Andrew Swinglehurst from Berea."

"But we're both Millers!"

38

Ellie spoke for the first time. "I reckon what Hacey means is that you're not the same kind of Millers. You're a Miller who married a Ledyard — and he's a Miller who married a Padgett. That's not hardly what you'd call peas in a pod."

Boone flushed. "I've got nothing against the mountain people, Ellie. But blood is blood, and it ought to stand for something."

"It stands for a lot, as far as I'm concerned," I said. "It stands for the way you and I used to feel about each other when we were children. That was good. I hope we can go back to it one day."

Boone emptied his glass and set it down with a rap. "About the Rifles — I take it this is your final word?"

"I'm afraid so, Boone."

"It wouldn't do me any good to quote you John C. Breckinridge or Simon Bolivar Buckner or Jefferson Davis either, I suppose."

"I'd be obliged if you didn't."

He rose to his feet briskly, and his face was expressionless. "Then I won't take up any more of your time. Thanks for the drink, Hacey. Your servant, Ellie." He gave a jerky little bow and left the house.

I returned to my chair and finished my toddy in silence. Only after I let out a long, hopeless sigh did Ellie speak. "I'm mighty sorry about your Pap, Hacey."

"He's a good man," I said.

"So's Boone," she said.

"I know that."

Neither of us spoke again for a few minutes. Ellie took up her pencil and the list of children's names she had been compiling when my brother arrived.

"Honey, if the baby's a boy —" she said shyly.

"Yes?"

"You reckon you'd rather name him Sheldon, after your Pap — or Boone?"

"Put them both on the list, Ellie. I suppose it would be a way of showing we care about our people."

Lincoln was inaugurated on the 4th of March. He found himself facing seven states which had combined in a Confederacy, elected a president and vice-president, and seized the U.S. Government arsenals within their borders. Four more states had not yet seceded from the Union, but had indicated their intention to do so. The Kentucky Legislature was swinging toward a position of neutrality between North and South, Governor Magoffin failed in his attempt to stampede the legislators into secession, but the Unionists were equally unsuccessful in passing resolutions of loyalty to the United States. Kentucky neutrality couldn't last long after the fighting started — we all realized that — but, for the moment, it offered the antislavery forces their best hope of saving the state for the Union.

President Lincoln wrote his friend Orville H. Browning, "I think to lose Kentucky is nearly the same as to lose the whole game."

Then, on April 12, South Carolina troops fired upon Fort Sumter. Five days later Virginia seceded, and the next day Cassius M. Clay either did or didn't save Washington, D.C., for the Union — depending on which newspaper you read.

Clay had not been offered either the War Department or the Court of St. James. In fact, for an agonizing two months, he wasn't offered anything at all. He finally wrote the President-elect in January, reminding him of his services to the Party and demanding to know what appointment was reserved for him. A number of letters were exchanged between Springfield and White Hall, and the upshot was that Clay finally agreed to accept the appointment of Minister to the Court of the Tsars. In March he left for Washington to receive his instructions from Secretary of State Seward.

Clay was still in the capital when Virginia seceded from the Union, bringing the Confederacy to the shores of the Potomac. Virginia had thousands of troops under arms, and there were no Union troops at all in Washington. A near panic swept the city, as everyone asked everyone else what would prevent the Rebel army from marching across the Long Bridge and right up Pennsylvania Avenue?

The question was answered the next day, when Cassius M. Clay led the "Clay Battalion" in its first parade. Hastily raised the night before, and equipped early in the morning from new government stores, the battalion probably contained more U.S. senators, congressmen and civil servants than any other military organization in history. They couldn't keep step, but they carried rifles and cartridges, which they all knew how to use. Clay, who had recruited them, and had been elected their major, wore a cavalry saber buckled to his belt and a bowie knife strapped under his arm. Crowds along the street cheered him wildly.

During the week of its existence — it was disbanded when regular troops arrived by boat from New York — the Clay Battalion and its commander doubtless spent as much time in the taproom of the Willard Hotel as its critics charged. But it also patrolled the streets at night and guarded the Navy Yard and the bridges. No fires broke out in the city while it was on duty, and no Confederate troops crossed the river. When the immediate emergency was past, Lincoln called Clay to the White House, thanked him warmly for his services, and presented him with a handsome Colt revolver. Two weeks later Clay and his wife embarked for Russia.

Both the Union and Confederate governments had guaranteed the neutrality of Kentucky, but that didn't prevent them from sending officers into the state to recruit. By early June two or three new Kentucky regiments had already passed through Lexington, heading south. Major Robert Anderson, the defender of Fort Sumter, and a native of Louisville, arrived to raise troops for the Union army. My brother-in-law, Falk Padgett, and I talked about it one day during a slack period at the store.

"Hasty, what do you think about this Major Anderson, and these Yankee regiments he's raising up?" he asked, scratching his nose.

"What do you mean, what do I think about him?"

"I mean, do you think he's the kind of feller a man ought to go along with?"

"You mean, do I think you should let him enlist you in the Union army?"

He winced, as he always did when I blurted out an unpleasant statement without what he felt was sufficient circumspection. "Well, yes — I reckon that's more or less what I mean."

"Hell, Falk, that depends on the way you feel about the war. If you feel like you should be in it, then I guess you ought to join up. If you don't, don't."

"No, but this Anderson worrits me a mite, you see."

"How so?"

"Well, you couldn't hardly call him a born winner, now, could you?"

I laughed. "It's sort of hard to be a winner when you're sitting out on a little island in the middle of a harbor, with hardly any food and powder, while a whole army is shooting cannons at you from the shore."

"Maybe so," he replied judiciously, "but I'd as lief not

42

hang around the kind of man who get himself into scrapes like that."

"I don't know what you're worrying about Anderson for, anyway. He won't be in command of any of the regiments he's raising."

He looked dubious. "There's another thing that don't sit too well with me, to tell you the truth. Them regiments is all infantry."

"Well, what's wrong with that? Here, you want an apple?" He nodded, and I handed him one from the barrel beside the counter. He bit into it with a sound like the distant report of a rifle. "Obliged. Do you happen to remember old Lem Howlett?"

"The one-armed man that used to work at the livery stable?"

"That's him. Old Lem lost his arm at Buena Vista, fighting under Zach Taylor. He was in the infantry, and I'll always remember something he said to me once."

"What was that?" I asked through a mouthful of partly chewed apple.

"He said he'd never seen a dead cavalryman."

"Oh, that's just an old infantry saying. You shouldn't take it seriously."

"Well, I don't know. *I've* never seen a dead cavalryman. Have you?"

"Well, no. But I've never seen a dead infantryman, either. And neither have you."

"Maybe not what you called dead — but old Lem Howlett wasn't in the best shape in the world the last time I seen him!" He took an impressive bite of his apple, and reflected a moment. "Then there's all that walking they do in the infantry," he said. "I ain't never been real strong on walking."

"Somehow I get the feeling you'd just as soon wait for

somebody to raise a cavalry regiment before you join up."

"You know, Hace, I believe you've put your finger right on it!" He smiled sweetly. "So I don't reckon there's any point in thinking about it now, is there?"

But in July we had to start thinking about it again, and seriously. Another Union officer came to Kentucky to recruit — a brigadier general, a tough ex-naval officer named Nelson, who was called "Bull" — and he was authorized to raise a cavalry regiment.

Right about then we heard the news of the disaster of First Bull Run. It came as a profound shock to all Union sympathizers in Kentucky. No longer could we hope for an easy victory; we were committed to a long and bitter struggle against an opponent who was at least our equal in military ability, and quite possibly our superior.

"Falk, I hear this Bull Nelson will be in Madison County to recruit a regiment of cavalry next week." Ellie's brother had joined us for dinner, and the three of us were sitting in the parlor with our coffee. "I've thought it over, and last night Ellie and I talked about it half the night, and I've decided to join up. I'm afraid that means I'll either have to find a new manager for the store, or sell it. Either way, your job will be affected."

"That's all right. I don't aim to keep that job for more than another week anyhow."

Ellie lowered her knitting and eyed Falk quizzically. "You wouldn't be figuring on joining the same troop, would you?" she asked.

"Well, hellfire, Little Sister, now that old Hasty here has got you wearing your apron so high you can't hardly see over it, you don't think I'm going to let anything happen to him, do you? I can't hardly support myself, let alone some widder lady with a brand new baby!"

"Then what say we ride over to Richmond together next Monday?" I suggested. "You come out to Hazelwood on Sunday, and we'll put you up for the night and get an early start next morning."

But I wasn't destined to ride to Richmond with Falk that Monday. When Ellie and I arrived at Hazelwood on Saturday afternoon, we found my father in a coma, not expected to live through the next twenty-four hours. Boone and his partner, old Dr. Miles Renfro, were both in attendance.

"It's just a matter of time now, Hacey," Boone told me quietly. "There's no need for you to go upstairs to see him, unless you want to. He can't recognize anyone, not even Mama."

"Just the same, I'd like to be with him for a while, if it's all right." He shrugged and stepped aside, and I climbed the curving staircase to my father's room.

Everyone's first impression of a dying man is that he seems to have shrunk as the life force leaked out of him. Father had never been a big man, but his bulk had been ponderable and well-proportioned. Now there was an appearance of weightlessness about him, like a cocoon after the chrysalis has flown. I took one of his hands and squeezed it; there was no answering pressure. His eyes were closed, and his nose was more prominent than I remembered it — as though the rest of the face were receding from it, like an ebbing tide receding from a rock.

"Forgive me if I've disappointed you, Papa," I said softly. "You never disappointed me my whole life long." His breathing was hoarse and shuddering. I remembered how he had come to my room just before I went east to Harvard, to embrace doctrines which were anathema to him. "I believe you are old enough and smart enough to know the difference between good and evil," he had said with embarrassed

45

abruptness, "and I'm prepared to back your play." Tears welled up and blurred my vision.

"Papa, I'm going to join the Union cavalry. I think it's the right thing to do. I know Mama won't think so, and Boone won't, and I guess you wouldn't either, but I do." For a moment it seemed that his fingers trembled slightly in my grasp, but otherwise he was motionless, except for the erratic heaving of his chest. "I love you, Father," I whispered, then placed his hand back on the quilt, and bent to kiss him on the forehead. As I turned away, I saw that Ellie was standing beside me. I hadn't heard her come in. She looked at my father's face gravely and seriously, like a student memorizing a fact he never wants to forget. Then after a moment she turned her eyes to mine, and we looked at each other for the space of a dozen heartbeats. There was nothing that needed saying.

He died that night. The next day they came for his body and carried him over to Richmond to the funeral home. He was buried in the Richmond Cemetery on Wednesday. Mother remained calm through it all. Ellie was a great comfort to her, especially since my sister Rosalie, who lived in Georgia, was unable to get to Hazelwood in time for the services.

Wednesday night after the funeral, Mother, Ellie, Robin, Boone and I had a glass of sherry together in the sitting room. For the first time since Father's collapse, Mother wanted to discuss our future.

"What do you think we should do about the store, Hacey?" she asked. "Will you want to keep it open, or should we sell it?"

"I think we should sell it, Mama. If we tried to hire a manager to run it for us, there wouldn't be anybody around to keep an eye on him."

"What about you?" She fixed me with a sudden penetrating look.

"I'll be gone. I'm riding to Richmond tomorrow to enlist in the Union cavalry."

Nobody said anything for a second, and then Robin set her wine glass down with a sharp clatter. "Can I believe my ears?" she cried dramatically.

"Why, you been having trouble with them?" asked Ellie in a conversational tone.

"The Union cavalry. You did say *Union* cavalry, didn't you?" said Mother.

"Yes, ma'am. The Union cavalry. There's a general named Nelson down here to raise a regiment. Falk Padgett and I decided to join up. We would have gone over Monday, except for Papa."

Mother looked at Ellie. "Did you know about this, child?"

"Yes, Mrs. Miller. We talked it all over. It's what he thinks he ought to do."

"But what about you, and the baby?"

I answered for her. "I thought Ellie ought to move out here to Hazelwood, Mama. I'd like her to be with you when the baby comes."

Robin had risen from her chair. There were angry spots of color in her cheeks. "I simply cannot believe this is happening," she cried. "A member of my family — my family by marriage — announces he's joining the Yankee army, and everybody just sits around discussing it like the weather!"

"Now simmer down, Robbie," Boone began placatingly.

"Simmer down? When black treason is planned right before my very eyes? When my name is dishonored because my own brother-in-law decides to join a band of cowards and cutthroats?"

47

"Robin," said Mother firmly, "hush up!"

"I'll never be able to hold my head up in Lexington again! The best people will cut me dead on the street!" She turned to Boone and seized his hands. "You won't let him do this, will you? You're his brother! You can make him change his mind!"

"Boone," Mother said, raising her voice slightly, "I think we had better excuse Robin for the evening. See her to her room, please. Good night, my dear."

Boone put his arm around his wife and tried to lead her out of the room, but she turned back to face me. Tears were streaming down her face, but her pretty mouth was distorted by fury, not grief.

"Hacey Miller, you're a freak, a disgusting freak. I detest you, just like every other decent person detests you. You and your la-di-da Yankee education, it hasn't made you good for anything but being a nigger-stealer and a schoolteacher for dirt-ignorant mountaineers!"

"Robin, come *on!*" muttered Boone.

"I *won't* come on! Why shouldn't I tell the truth? You know you all are ashamed of everything he's done! He's been a burden and a disgrace to this family ever since he fell in with Cash Clay." She sobbed once, then cried out in a straining voice, "And what's more, you know his poor old daddy died with shame in his heart because of Hacey's dirty abolitionist ideas!"

Ellie had risen from her chair, and now took a step toward Robin, her open hand moving down and out from her body. But before she could deliver the blow, Mother stepped in front of her. Mother's face was only inches from Robin's as she said coldly, "I'm sure none of us will remember any of this tomorrow. Good night, Robin. *Go . . . to . . . bed!*"

Robin burst into tumultuous sobs as Boone led her from

the room. Mother and Ellie and I stood together in silence for a minute or two. Then Mother looked at me, and a dry little smile flitted across her tired face.

"Life might have worked out easier if you felt different about things, Hacey."

"I guess it might have, Mama."

"Well, maybe the Lord isn't as interested as we are in making life work out easy." She reached out to Ellie and patted her hand. "I'm glad you'll be staying here with me, dear."

That night Ellie and I were quiet as we prepared for bed. She sat before her mirror, giving her hair the hundred nightly brushstrokes that constituted one of her few concessions to feminine vanity. I was lying on my back on the bed, reliving the whole embarrassing scene.

"Hacey," she said softly, "you're not to get all upset worrying about what she said, you hear? It's not as if Robin had enough sense to pour — to come in out of the rain."

I grinned in spite of myself. "I know what you were going to say. You were going to say she doesn't have enough sense to pour piss out of a boot. Weren't you?"

"You have a dirty mouth on you. You know I never talk unrefined that way." She pulled the brush down the sleek fall of her hair purposefully. "Or hardly ever," she amended.

"Ellie, I can't believe it's being a freak to hate slavery and to do what you can to end it. If there are any freaks around, they're the people who believe they have a right to buy and sell human beings like livestock!"

We shared silence for a moment. I remembered the steps that had brought me to the eve of this day when I would leave a pregnant wife to go to war. My mind rattled across fifteen years like a boy's stick along the palings of a picket fence. I remembered Cassius Clay, prostrated by typhoid, defying all the wealth and power of the Bluegrass when they voted to suppress his newspaper, *The True American* . . . the screams of the white mob as they hunted down Negroes on the night the paper was destroyed . . . the blood that splashed out like paint as Clay gutted Cyrus Turner in the fight at Foxtown . . . the proud anger of Frederick Douglass and the roguish irony of Wentworth Higginson in Boston . . . the hot sweat and aching muscles, as I labored with John G. Fee on the Berea Ridge . . . and the firm pressure of Ellie's breasts against my back, as she rode behind me into Berea.

"It's funny, isn't it?" I said. "To begin with, we were going to end slavery by changing the law, peacefully, only fighting in self-defense. Then we decided we had to break the law, with the Underground Railroad — but it was still peaceful — we still weren't going to take up arms against slave owners. Now, we're raising armies and fighting battles to get the job done. We've come a long way for the black man — now we're even fighting other white men for his freedom. I wonder where we go from here?"

"Maybe to the point of letting him help in the fight — you reckon?" Ellie stopped brushing her hair and turned to look at me. For a long second, I felt as if everything that moves in the world had suddenly stopped.

The next morning Falk and I rode to Richmond and enlisted.

IV

Wolford's Cavalry

I ONCE HEARD IT SAID that all first-rate military units take on the characteristics of their commanding officers. This may or may not have been true of Caesar's Legions or Napoleon's Old Guard, but I can vouch that it applied to the First Kentucky Cavalry. To friend and foe alike, all through the war it was never spoken of or thought of as anything but "Wolford's Cavalry."

Frank Wolford was originally commissioned lieutenant colonel and appointed second in command of the regiment, but within a month he was elevated to full colonel commanding, where he remained until March of '64, when he was churlishly humiliated and deprived of his rank and driven from the service without even the courtesy of a court-martial.

He looked like an unmade bed. He couldn't be bothered learning commands from the drill book; he'd bellow out his orders in his own expressive language, which on occasion could be lurid indeed. He ate too much and drank too much. He was a compulsive talker, and that, combined with his prejudices, led to his undoing.

He was also as fiercely and constantly combative as a wolverine, as solicitous of his troopers' welfare as a cat with kittens, and as dedicated to the preservation of the Union as any Republican in Washington.

He passed his vices and his virtues on to his officers in equal measure, and they communicated them to the men, so Wolford's Cavalry soon exhibited the character it was to keep throughout the war — a butt on the parade ground and a catamount on the battlefield.

Falk and I got our first sight of Frank Wolford in Richmond the day we enlisted, and looking at him with the eyes of a civilian, I was not impressed with his military bearing. General "Bull" Nelson was much more what I imagined an army officer should look like, with his tall, broad-shouldered athlete's body superbly set off by his well-tailored and immaculate uniform, with his thick neck and heavy jaw and imperious eye. Nelson had spent most of his military career in the navy, and the spit-and-polish tradition of that service had never left him. Neither had its implicit assumption of superiority.

We were enrolled in K Troop that afternoon, and given a week to conclude our personal business and get our affairs in shape. I cleared out the little house on Short Street and moved Ellie into Hazelwood, made my farewells to the few old friends in Lexington who still spoke to me, and returned to Richmond on the 14th of August. That night we elected our officers, and the next morning we rode to Camp Dick Robinson, the camp Bull Nelson had established on the Kentucky River twenty-five miles south of Lexington.

Our troop commander was Captain Nelson Burrus and our platoon commander was Lieutenant Stephen Sallee — both of Richmond, and both known slightly to me. I was elected a corporal, as a tribute to my seven years of college, no doubt. Falk was a private, and was assigned to my squad.

Colonel Wolford talked to us our first day in camp. This time he looked a bit more martial, probably because General Nelson wasn't there for comparison.

"Boys," he began, pulling the crotch of his britches up between his legs as if to prevent his thighs from chafing, "I'm Frank Wolford. I have the dubious honor of commanding this ill-matched assortment of individualists here. And right now, I don't know if I should be bragging or complaining. Whichever I end up doing, it's going to depend on you.

"Now if this was the same old regiment that fought at the River Raisin or Cerro Gordo, or places like that, why, then I wouldn't have any doubts about what kind of an outfit we were going to be, and neither would you. We'd all just settle down and follow the tradition, just as easy as a mule breaking wind. But it ain't that simple, boys. There was a First Kentucky Cavalry in the Mexican War, but it wasn't *this* First Kentucky Cavalry. We're a new regiment, and we don't have doodly-crap of any tradition. We're going to make our own tradition, you hear me? That means *you* — *you're* going to make *your* own tradition — with a certain amount of gentle encouragement from me!"

He hitched up his belt, settled his pants comfortably in the cleft of his buttocks, wiped his hand across his nose, and continued. "We're a cavalry regiment. That means we ride horses. Most of you come from the Bluegrass, I understand. So when you look at a horse, I expect you to be able to tell his ass from his eyeball." Some of the younger men snickered at this earthiness, but Wolford silenced them with a glare. "I also expect you to be able to take care of your horse. You let him down, and he'll let you down. A horse is a cavalryman's best friend, and God help you if you ever forget it!"

He paused to let his words sink in, and we all glanced at

53

one another, as if each of us hoped for a clue from his neighbor as to how to take our new commander. Then he resumed in a conversational tone:

"While you're here at Camp Dick Robinson, you'll learn as much drill as we can teach you. We'll try to show you something about cavalry tactics, too. You'll be issued rifles today, and you'll have marksmanship practice. Unfortunately the guns you'll get are infantry muskets, which ain't exactly suited to a cavalryman's needs, but we'll get them replaced one day.

"And if you want some advice, you better work your tails off, because there's no telling how long we've got before we go on active duty. Like as not, we'll be riding into Tennessee next week!"

The men cheered and applauded. Any old soldier would have had no trouble identifying them as recruits.

"Just one more thing, and then I'll shut up," Wolford continued. "I want to tell you something about some of the people you'll have to put up with here at Camp Dick. First, there's General Nelson. Now I wouldn't say he was *mean* — but ever since he's been out of the navy he hasn't been able to order any enlisted man keelhauled, and it's like to drive him crazy. He keeps trying to think up some dry land punishment that's equally savage and hideous. If I was you, I wouldn't let him experiment on *me!*"

"My second in command is Lieutenant Colonel John Letcher. Now understand this, boys — no matter what you hear — 'Letcher' is his *name,* not his description. I want that understood, you hear? It's bad enough for a man to have a name like that, without people thinking he's got a personality to match."

There was an appreciative chuckle from the audience.

54

Colonel Letcher was the nephew of a past governor of Kentucky, and his surname was one of the most distinguished in the state.

"And one other man I want to mention is our chaplain, Reverend Honnell. Now, those of you who are God-fearing folks will be glad to know your souls are going to be ministered to by one of the most *fantastically effective* preachers in Christendom!" Wolford leaned forward, lowered his voice confidentially, and assumed an unconvincingly pious expression. "Why, do you know that last Sunday there was a big service here, with all sorts of civilians coming over from Danville for the festivities? Well, Reverend Honnell was preaching and hymn-singing and praying up a storm, and right in the middle of it all a lady jumps up and starts beating at herself with her bonnet, and takes off at a dead run.

"Then, pretty soon, up jumps another lady, whooping and swatting herself, and she takes off too. And this time you can see what's causing it — it's bees! Seems like there's a whole swarm of them in under the speaker's platform, and something's riled them up. And here they come out, buzzing through the crowd.

"Now Reverend Honnell figures he can't expect to hold an audience indefinitely under these circumstances — but on the other hand, it wouldn't be fair to Jesus to just cut and run. So he compromises by sliding into the Benediction, just as slick as you please — and he don't bobtail it hardly a bit!

"And do you know not one mortal human being tried to leave during the Benediction? They just stood there with the bees buzzing around their heads until that last amen — when they parted like the Red Sea in a manner marvelous to behold!

55

"Now I ask you, men — with a preacher who can bring the power of the Lord to bear like that, what do we have to fear from a bunch of Rebels?"

Wolford joined in the laughter for a few moments, then turned to Captain Burrus and told him to dismiss us. Later, I asked Falk what he thought of our regimental commander.

"If he can fight as well as he talks, I reckon he's a ring-tailed bobcat," he answered.

In September the fiction that the North and the South respected Kentucky's neutrality was swept away for good. First, Confederate troops occupied Columbus, in the western part of the state, then Union troops countered by occupying Paducah. There were also reports of a Confederate general with the odd name of Zollicoffer, commanding an army of 10,000 just over the line in Tennessee, and in the eastern mountains Confederate cavalry had entered the state from Virginia. We knew we would be in action soon, and we were still almost completely untrained.

I was corporal of the 2nd Squad of the 2nd Platoon of K Troop, I had six troopers under me, and all of us were green as grass. First, there was Falk Padgett. Then there was a boy of seventeen from a farm near Berea, Cleon Henry. Cleon didn't understand the army way of doing things at all and greeted every order with a look of stark incredulity on his otherwise expressionless face. Then there were two brothers, K.B. and Jason MacCallum, from Valley View, on the Kentucky River. They were both big, silent, black-haired men. K.B. had a pockmarked face, and Jason had a purple birthmark that ran from under his chin almost to his hairline — he looked like he had rested his face on a plate of grape jelly. The last two men in the squad were father and son; Thomas Watson, a wiry little man of fifty or so, toothless as a babe, who was inevitably called "Pap," and Tom Junior, fat and stolid, who faced every problem with a placid smile on his moon face.

We had a long way to go to become cavalrymen, and we all knew it. I think it was due more to Falk than to me that we were able to become an effective fighting and scouting unit. His patience and good-humored irony never faltered. In the evenings he would show Cleon how to disassemble a musket blindfolded, or demonstrate to the MacCallums how to draw a usable sketch map, while I generally lay sulking before the fire, reliving the tongue-lashing I had received from Sergeant Otis, my nemesis, during the day's drill.

My squad started with a few advantages: we were all good shots and good horsemen; I was articulate enough to represent us well with our officers, and the others were grateful; finally, my education soon qualified me as a sort of Resident Scholar of K Troop, and all sorts of people brought questions to me. It wasn't hard to wring certain small benefits for us out of this state of affairs.

On the 19th of September, Union infantry marched into Lexington. I heard about it in the late afternoon, and immediately went to Captain Burrus. He was sitting on his cot with one stockinged foot braced on his orderly's buttocks, while the man struggled to separate the other foot from its boot, which was clasped between his legs.

"Sir, may I speak to you? It's important."

"Pull, God damn it, Jenkins, pull! Well, what is it, Miller?"

"Sir, I just heard that our troops have occupied Lexington."

"Well, what about it?"

"That means John Hunt Morgan's regiment will be pulling out tonight, if it hasn't left already."

He looked at me sharply. "What do you know about Morgan's regiment?"

"Enough to be sure he's not going to sit in his armory and wait for Union soldiers to disarm him. Look, Captain, for the last six months Morgan's supposedly been neutral, because Kentucky is neutral — but he hasn't made any secret of his loyalties. Everybody in Lexington knows he sent a telegram to Jefferson Davis last April, offering to raise twenty thousand Kentuckians for the Confederacy. He may already have left, but if he hasn't he'll be leaving tonight, as sure as fate. He's got to, unless he wants to lose his regiment!"

"Stop pulling on that boot, Jenkins," Burrus ordered. "I've got to put them on again." He looked at me appraisingly. "Have you ever met Colonel Wolford personally, Miller?"

"No, sir."

"Well, you're going to now. And if he happens to have had a drop too much, pay it no mind. He's a better cavalryman drunk than any other regimental commander in the U.S. Army is sober."

But Wolford wasn't drunk. He listened to what I had to say, questioned me tersely, then spread out a map of central Kentucky on the paper-covered table. "All right, Corporal, now tell me this. If you're right, and if Morgan rides out of Lexington tonight, where would he be heading, and which road would he take to get there?"

I hesitated a moment. "Well, Colonel, he'd have a choice of two directions, I think. He might try to make contact with Simon Bolivar Buckner at Bowling Green — that would mean he'd move southwesterly, probably either on the Versailles or Harrodsburg pike. But then again, he could head south, to join Zollicoffer in Tennessee. If he goes that way he can't take the direct road, because he'd have to pass right by us, here at Camp Dick. So his best route would be by way of Richmond."

"Richmond — that's Madison County. Wasn't K Troop recruited from Madison County, Burrus?"

"Yes, sir."

"Then I expect your boys know the ground. All right, Miller — which way do you reckon Morgan will come — Versailles, Harrodsburg, or Richmond?"

I considered my answer carefully. "I'd eliminate Harrodsburg, Colonel — that road passes within five or six miles of us here, too close for comfort. Between Versailles and Richmond, I'd guess Richmond, just because Zollicoffer is closer to Lexington than Buckner is."

Wolford peered nearsightedly at the map and scratched his belly. "That would mean they'd be crossing the Kentucky River right *here*." He pointed with a stubby finger.

"Yes sir — right there, at Clay's Ferry."

Clay's Ferry was less than three miles from home.

Wolford sent scouts into Lexington to determine whether or not Morgan had left, and ordered them to wait for us with the news at the village of Nicholasville, about ten miles south of the city. Then he assembled two hundred men, four troops, had them swap their muskets for the two hundred new Sharps rifles which had arrived the day before, and which had not yet been fired, and then ordered them to mount up. K Troop was among those chosen. We moved out of Camp Dick about midnight.

The scouts were waiting at the crossroads in Nicholasville, and confirmed my hunch. Morgan had left earlier that night, with all his arms packed in wagons. The loading had been accomplished under cover of a noisy drill in the armory, and

59

the Union officers occupying Lexington had suspected nothing.

Wolford had decided to concentrate his available troops at the single likeliest point, rather than to spread them thin over two or three possible escape routes. Following my reasoning, he intended to cross his fingers and try to catch Morgan at Clay's Ferry.

It was a hard ride from Nicholasville, and it was after three when we reached our destination on the north side of the Kentucky River. There was no sign that Morgan's men had passed that way, and the ferryman claimed his sleep had been undisturbed all night.

Wolford placed two troops on each side of the road and ordered them to take cover. Each squad dispatched one man to lead its horses to a meadow on the edge of the water a quarter mile away. I sent Cleon, and he left, pausing only to stare at me in his unbelieving way, as if I were committing some enormity unparalleled in military history. Then the rest of us settled down to wait for Morgan.

Nights along the Kentucky River are always damp, but some are damper than others. This was one of the damper ones. The lowland we lay upon was so saturated with dew that drops of moisture condensed and fell from trees and bushes almost as steadily as rain. Within minutes our uniforms were sodden. The opaque gray mist that rose from the river was simply a rarefied kind of water. Each breath of air we drew into our lungs brought drops of water trickling down our windpipes. Very soon the men started coughing, and by sunup, if Morgan had come down that road he would have heard the sound of our massed bronchial discomfort two miles away.

"No wonder the Bluegrass is so goddamned green," Falk whispered dismally. "It's underwater every night!"

By seven o'clock the sun had begun to burn off the mist, and we could feel its warmth on our faces and hands. Soon our wet uniforms began to steam, and we began slowly to dry out — at least on the upper portions of our bodies; the parts the sun couldn't reach stayed cold and clammy. It was miserable.

At eight-thirty, Colonel Wolford came walking down the road in front of us. When he reached a point about equidistant from all four troops, he stopped and blew his nose into a red bandanna. He looked at the results dispassionately for a moment, then stuffed the cloth into his back pocket and called out in a ringing voice, "Well, boys, I reckon this is a horse on me. I just got word that Morgan and his men went out of Lexington by way of the Versailles pike about two this morning. That means they've gone to join Simon Bolivar Buckner in Bowling Green. So I guess we don't get a crack at them just yet — but don't you worry, we will soon enough! Troop commanders — let's haul ass!"

As the horses were being led back from their night's pasture to the road, I sought out Captain Burrus. I reminded him that my home was only ten minutes' ride away, and that my wife was within a few days of her time, and asked his permission to take my squad back to camp by way of Hazelwood.

He looked at me sourly. "You feel you're so covered with glory from this exploit that you deserve special favors, is that it?"

"Well, sir, I *could* have been right, couldn't I?"

"And pigs *could* fly, if they had wings. All right, Miller, you can go — but be back at Camp Dick by tattoo, do you hear?"

A few minutes later, feeling partly proud and partly foolish, I led my squad up the road and onto the green grounds of Hazelwood. As we neared the house, Aunt Hessie and

'Shach and Opal came out of the kitchen door, and at the same time Mother and Ellie stepped out on the porch. The members of my squad halted more or less at the same time. "Squa — aad, DIS — MOUNT!" I shouted, and swung down from Jenny Lind's back just as the others dismounted. I thought we looked pretty good, considering. Aunt Hessie clapped her hands and cried, "Why, if that don't beat all — it's Mister Hacey!" Mother straightened her back, a tight little smile on her lips. And Ellie ran down the steps and into my arms as lightly as her condition allowed.

Falk, with a significant glance at his sister, suggested that the men would be more comfortable resting outside, underneath the elms, so we put Aunt Hessie and 'Shach to work cooking up a big breakfast for them and serving it al fresco. I saw to it there was a small stone jug to go with the food, then Mother and Ellie and I retired to the sitting room.

"How long can you and your men stay, Hacey?" Mother asked.

"Two or three hours. We've got to be back at camp this evening."

"Oh, I wish it were longer. What brought you here?"

"John Hunt Morgan. He left Lexington last night to join the Confederacy. Did you know about it?" I meant to say, did Boone tell you about it?

She hesitated a moment, considering whether her answer could cause any harm. "Yes, Hacey. Boone was out here yesterday. He told me then he was leaving with the regiment that night. He didn't say where they were going —"

"Bowling Green. We know that now." Briefly I told them of my hunch about Morgan heading for Clay's Ferry, and the resultant fiasco. "So we had four hours of waiting in the wet for nothing, thanks to my bright idea," I concluded.

"Hacey, what if you'd been right, and Morgan's regiment

62

had come down the Lexington pike?" Mother asked quietly.

I knew where her question was pointing, but I pretended to misunderstand. "I don't know, Mama. We would have had them outnumbered and surrounded, so I suppose they would have surrendered. Since they haven't been mustered into the Confederate army yet, we probably would have disarmed them and let them go."

"But what if they didn't surrender? What about Boone?"

"Well, Boone's a doctor, so that makes him a noncombatant. I don't think —"

"Could you tell a doctor from a soldier in the darkness at fifty yards?"

"Mama, don't do this," I said wretchedly. "What do you want me to say?"

"What I always want you to say. The truth."

"All right, this is the truth. I would have fired when I was told to fire. I would have shot at the man who made the best target, and I wouldn't have had the faintest idea who he was! I'm sorry, but that's the way things are in the army."

Ellie rose from her chair and went to the sideboard, where she poured us three glasses of sherry from the cut-glass carafe. Mother looked searchingly into my eyes. "Yes, I see that's the way things are. God grant that your path never crosses Boone's as long as this horrible war continues."

"I pray so too, with all my heart," I answered.

We talked of other subjects for a few more minutes and sipped our sherry. Then Mother abruptly stood up and set her empty glass on the little table beside her chair. "Well, pleasant as this is, I've got too many fishes to fry to gossip away the whole day. Why don't you go up to your room and take a nap, Hacey? I'll call you in an hour and a half or so." Erect as a young poplar tree, she left the room.

I stepped over to Ellie, took her two hands, and drew her

from her chair. I patted the full swelling of her belly. "I see old what's-his-name is coming along like a house afire. He must weigh thirty or forty pounds by now, I bet."

Her big gray uptilted eyes laughed at me, as she pulled my face down to hers. "Oh that's not my baby, that's my calf. I keep my baby upstairs in a bureau drawer. You want to go up and see him?" She kissed me quickly, then took my hand, and together we went up the curving staircase to our room. Inside, she closed the door.

"I expect I'm too far along for real loving, honey — but I'd sure delight to take my clothes off and have you hold me for a while. Would that be all right?" We stripped and got into bed and hugged each other. I fancied I could feel movement inside her. The room was bright and sunny, and there were faint daytime noises outside — a cow mooing, a boy calling a dog a half mile away. It was sanctuary. We kissed, and kissed again. "I love you so much, Ellie."

"I love you too, Hacey — more'n I ever thought to love anybody." She sighed. "When will it all be over and you'll come back again?"

"Next year, I expect. It won't be too long. How are you getting on with Mama? Are you having any problems?"

"No, we get along just fine, ever since Robin moved back to stay with her family last month. Before that, though, it wasn't no bed of roses, I tell you."

"What made her move back to Redbird?"

"Partly it was because Boone figured to be leaving with Morgan any day, and he wanted her settled before he left. And partly it was because of me. I guess she don't cotton to white trash too much."

"You know something, Ellie? *I* cotton to white trash."

"I figured you did."

The time went by too fast. It seemed only moments later

that a discreet tap at the door warned us that the time had come to say goodbye again. We dressed quickly, and joined Mother on the front porch. The squad was waiting beside their saddled horses, and 'Shach was holding Jenny Lind's bridle. None of the men appeared to be noticeably drunk.

"Goodbye, Mother. Take care of Ellie for me."

"Goodbye, son. Come home to us soon."

I looked over my shoulder as we rode off through the trees, and the two women stood on the front porch as long as Hazelwood remained in sight.

V

The Squad Is Blooded

ELLIE HAD HER BABY about two weeks later than expected, on the 15th of September. It was a fine, healthy boy, and she decided his name should be Boone, as we had discussed nine months before. My mother sent a messenger to Camp Dick Robinson with the news, but by then half the regiment was at Camp Wild Cat, and I was with them. It was another week before I found out I was a father.

Wild Cat was a crude improvised camp in the Rock Castle Hills, up Rock Castle River a few miles from the Cumberland. Considering that Zollicoffer might find the banks and bottom of Rock Castle River an easier highway for his troops to travel than the mountainous paths that paralleled it, Wolford began construction of a fortified point overlooking the river. It was finished — or as nearly finished as it ever would be — by the end of September, and occupied by those of the First Kentucky Cavalry who weren't in their beds at Camp Dick or furloughed home because of the epidemic of measles that had suddenly hit us. (We lost considerably more men to the measles than to the Confederates in the fall of 1861.)

Zollicoffer, with between two and three thousand troops, worked his way slowly up Rock Castle River, brushing detachments of Home Guards out of his way like gnats. We had had two or three small affairs of outposts when our two new generals arrived to inspect us at Wild Cat.

Bull Nelson had been replaced by General George Thomas, and Robert Anderson, of Fort Sumter fame, by General William Tecumseh Sherman. We enlisted men of K Troop found the newcomers reassuring. Thomas was a heavy, stolid man with a deep voice and a soft, unhurried Tidewater Virginia accent. He already had his nickname, "Slow Trot," by the time he visited us. Sherman was his complete opposite: thin and taut, with scruffy red hair, angry restless eyes, jerky movements, a high, abrasive voice — he displayed all the characteristics that would earn him the reputation of a lunatic and the loss of his command before the year was out. But it was the civilians in Louisville who would think him crazy, not the soldiers he commanded. Troops were as willing to fight under him then as they were in the battles before Atlanta in '64.

After the generals had inspected our persons and position, and left, we settled down to wait for Zollicoffer. We had been joined by three infantry regiments and an artillery battery, and were now known as First Brigade, Army of the Cumberland. Rumor had it that we were outnumbered by the Confederates, but not badly, considering the strength of our position.

They attacked us late in the afternoon. The shadows were long, and this, combined with many rocks and much dense underbrush on the slopes, gave them good cover. K Troop was holding a section of the perimeter about fifty yards long. Our trenches weren't deep enough to give us adequate protection. Our opponents worked their way to within a hundred feet of us before they charged.

I heard Wolford's voice cry out behind us, "Don't shoot

till you can spit on 'em!" But even as he was shouting some of the men fired, and the sound of their pieces triggered off other nervous troopers, until perhaps one-third of our fire-power was expended at a range too great to be effective.

Of my squad, only Cleon Henry discharged his rifle prematurely. Realizing he had wasted his shot, he gave a little whimpering groan and, drawing his gun to him, began to reload. "Get that bayonet out there, God damn you," I snarled. "You shot your wad, now at least keep your place in the line!"

A few seconds later the Rebels were close enough for accurate shooting. The two MacCallums fired simultaneously, and a moment later the Watsons, Falk and I added our shots to the volley. The whole oncoming Confederate line disappeared behind a pall of sharp, bitter smoke. For a moment it was as if they had been magically exorcised, and were no longer there at all — and then they burst through the smoke with their bayonets leveled.

The boy who charged at me had a face so contorted with fear and hatred it was hardly human. He screamed something in a voice that rose and broke, and slashed at me with his bayonet as if it were a saber. I recoiled and felt myself losing my balance. As I began to fall against the back of the trench, I thrust my rifle forward in an instinctive effort to regain my equilibrium. The point of my bayonet met his body right under the breastbone. He impaled himself on it and slid down the blade until his chest was pressed against the muzzle of my rifle. His hands made a clutching gesture, and his eyes looked into mine for a moment in sudden surprise before they lost their focus. Then he crashed down beside me in the trench.

I pulled my bayonet from his body and looked around. All along the perimeter our men were locked with the Confederates in hand-to-hand combat. In a few places our line seemed in danger of breaking as blue-uniformed soldiers climbed out of the shallow trench and scuttled to the rear. But a great many more gray-clad men were running or crawling back down the slope. All at once everyone realized that the line had held, and a ragged yell went up from the Union ranks. The Confederates who were still engaged suddenly discovered the attack was over and the time to leave had come — and as we cheered and cheered, they retreated down the hill to the safety of their cover.

"Son of a gun, we did it, boys! Didn't we?" cried old Pap Watson. "How about that, boy?"

"Reckon we did, Pap," answered Tom Junior, with a gentle smile on his powder-blackened round face.

My squad was intact. K.B. MacCallum had been bruised on the arm by a blow from a rifle butt, but whether one of our own or a Confederate's, he couldn't say. That was our only injury. There was a dead man on the slope about twenty yards down from our position, and the boy lying in the trench beside me. We had killed two of them for sure, with no losses of our own. Second Squad, 2nd Platoon, K Troop, First Kentucky Cavalry, was blooded.

"Got yourself one of the bastards, did you, Hasty?" said Falk, with unusual excitement in his voice.

I snorted contemptuously to hide the sudden giddiness I felt. "Damned fool jumped right on my bayonet. I couldn't have missed him if I wanted to."

"Gol, Corp — you skewered him like a roasting pig," said Cleon breathlessly.

I turned on him in sudden anger. "And you, you simpleminded hay-shaker, if I ever see you lower your gun to load it during a bayonet charge again, I'll snatch you baldheaded!"

69

Captain Burrus and Colonel Wolford came along the line, inspecting the troop's condition. "You did good, boys," Wolford called loudly. "They got themselves a bloody nose this time. But don't worry, they'll be back. It's nearly sundown, so you better figure on receiving a night attack. You'll probably have an hour, and you better spend some of it digging those trenches deeper. The way they are now, they ain't up to the balls on a midget."

But Wolford was wrong. Zollicoffer didn't attack again that night. Instead, he withdrew his troops down Rock Castle River toward the Cumberland. When we added up the figures, our losses were 4 killed and 18 wounded. General Thomas later estimated the Confederate casualties at 100.

After Wild Cat the Rebels pulled all the way back into Tennessee to regroup. September became October, and the silver maples turned brilliant yellow, reprising the yellow of the springtime forsythia. The air smelled like cold water and dry leaves, and was so clear you could see a circling hawk a mile away. There was nothing much for Wolford's Cavalry to do, and the military life began to seem unexpectedly pleasant.

Then Zollicoffer re-entered Kentucky with a full army of 10,000 men. The Confederates crossed at Mill Springs, and, with the river at their back, built themselves a camp. When he heard the news, General Thomas started down from Louisville to do something about it. Old "Slow Trot" spent a month gathering up the various scattered bits and pieces of the First Brigade, and shaping them into a battle-ready organization.

As Christmas approached, our spirits were considerably raised by a possibly unchristian, but nonetheless deeply appreciated, gift from the War Department — a shipment of

Navy Colt revolvers. For the first time we were armed to fight in the saddle with something other than sabers. There still weren't nearly enough Sharps carbines to go around, but everybody at least had a pistol. Very few troopers ever became expert enough with one to hit the Fayette County Courthouse from ten feet on a clear day, but we all happily burned powder at a great rate.

Christmas came. There were no furloughs; we all knew that a battle was imminent. There were, however, boxes from home, and roast goose, and splendid programs of Christmas music in the nearby churches. Christmas night, 2nd Squad was sitting on the cot and floor in my tent, eating fruitcake and passing around a jug. I had a fire going in a ten-gallon tub, and it was snug and warm and not smoky at all. Pap Watson passed the jug to his son and took his mouth organ out of his shirt pocket. He ran a scale and settled down to play. First he played "Camptown Races," and we all joined in boisterously, even the usually quiet MacCallums. Then he started "Lonesome Dove," and the rest of us hushed up and let Cleon Henry sing it alone, in his clear, sweet tenor voice.

> Oh, don't you see that lonesome dove
> That flies from vine to vine?
> He's mourning for his own true love
> Like I will mourn for mine.
>
> Like I will mourn for mine, my love,
> Believe me when I say —
> You are the darling of my heart
> Until my dying day.

As the last plaintive note died away there was a long moment of silence. Then Falk Padgett asked jokingly, "You sure enough got a darling of your heart, Cleon?"

Cleon looked at the floor and kicked at one of the legs of my cot. "Well, maybe not exactly," he said, "but I've known plenty of girls, and someday I'm going to get me one of my own."

"What do you reckon you'd do with a girl if you had one?" Falk asked.

"Just never you mind."

"Sit around the kitchen pulling taffy," suggested Pap Watson.

"Trying to work up the grit to hold hands with her," contributed Jason MacCallum.

"Who's going to want to hold hands with him when he's all sticky from that taffy?" asked Falk.

Cleon glared at us all with an expression compounded of outrage and uncertainty. "You all may just as well shut up — you ain't making *me* mad! I'll get me a girl when the time comes, you just wait and see if I don't. And then I'll know what to do with her — better than any of you could, you big windbags!"

I judged it was time to intervene. "Cleon, take a drink out of that jug and pass it here. Then suppose you sing something else — how about 'Lorena'? Can you play 'Lorena,' Pap?"

He could, and did, and so the Christmas evening passed.

Three weeks later Thomas was ready to move on the Rebels. He sent word to General Schoepf, commanding our brigade, to join him just north of Mill Springs. Schoepf planned to reach the rendezvous on the 19th of January, and he did — but he arrived in the afternoon and almost missed the battle.

The Battle of Mill Springs, which really was the Battle of Logan's Cross Roads, was a small but very important engagement. Together with the capture of Fort Donelson by Ulysses Grant a month later, it threw the Confederate armies of the west into a defensive posture from which they were able to return to the offense only twice during the remainder of the war, and then only briefly and clumsily. Just as Donelson broke the Confederate line at the western end, Mill Springs broke it at the eastern end. The Rebels had to move south — and there was no place to stop short of Corinth, Mississippi.

It was a foul day, rainy and cold, with a raw wind. Our little army had been on the move for three days, and all of us were sore and wet and muddy. The infantry was the muddiest, but the cavalry was the sorest; we were equally wet.

About eleven in the morning we thought we heard firing, oddly muffled by the sodden air. In a few minutes we were sure of it, and then a messenger from General Thomas arrived to confirm the news that the battle had started.

Thomas urged us to come as quickly as possible. He had met what he believed to be the major part of Zollicoffer's army at Logan's Cross Roads, about four miles north of Mill Springs. His pickets, our fellow troopers of the First Kentucky Cavalry, had been driven in, and almost immediately the body of his brigade was attacked by the Confederates. The fighting was furious and the outcome in doubt.

Since both our cavalry troops could make better time than the infantry — although not much better, considering the condition of the road — Schoepf sent us on ahead, following as quickly as he could with foot soldiers and guns. It was after two o'clock when we reached the field.

We dismounted and formed into platoons, carrying our clumsy muskets and big new Navy Colt revolvers. Our two captains marched us at double time toward the firing. We passed through a swarm of men from an Ohio infantry regi-

73

ment heading for the road, some wounded, some not. The air was almost beyond breathing — the stink of burned powder lay on the ground like a rotten blanket, prevented from dispersing by the clammy atmosphere.

We ran and slipped and stumbled in the mud, chests heaving with our need for air, coughing and hacking from the putrid air we breathed.

We deployed and moved up between Wolford's three companies and an Indiana infantry regiment. We were on both sides of a narrow road that extended into the battlefield. From the bodies that lay like gray laundry bags along it, it was clear the Confederates had already attacked down it and would probably do so again.

They did, five minutes after we took our positions in the mud. For the first time I heard their high, yipping battle cry. "Jesus Christ, what's that?" asked Pap Watson.

"That's the Rebel Yell," Falk replied. "Ain't you never heard of it? It's supposed to make strong men despair."

"It does a right good job of it, for a fact," said Pap thoughtfully.

The Rebel charge broke thirty yards from us. The difference between this and Wild Cat was our firepower; those big Colt revolvers laid out such a storm of lead that only the most resolute attack had any chance of succeeding.

"Good enough, men," said Captain Burrus as he paced back and forth behind our line. "But they'll be back directly. It's a long day, and there's still a passel of them out there. I know you can't dig in, but see if you can't at least squinch down a little."

We found that by rolling our bodies from side to side, and digging down with our knees and elbows, we could hollow out shallow depressions for ourselves in the slippery muck. This

74

put our guns almost flat on the ground, and lowered our heads the two or three inches that can be very reassuring during an attack.

It wasn't long until we heard the yip-yipping start again, and moments later they broke out of the gloomy murk in a bayonet charge. The line may have thinned a little since the last charge, but not so you could notice it. Officers on horseback were with them, urging them on.

"Them damn fool officers must want to get killed," Falk marveled.

Burrus yelled behind us, "Get the men on the horses!"

We all began to blaze away at the riders and their mounts. One older officer stiffened in the saddle and went over backward, one foot caught in a stirrup, the other pivoting stiffly over and down, as he fell on his face in the mud. His horse swerved and began to run parallel to our lines, the rider bouncing after him like a broken toy. Two of the other mounted officers spurred after the runaway horse; the other three wheeled and cantered back toward the Confederate lines.

We kept up a rapid fire against the approaching infantry. Some of their starch went out of them when they saw their mounted officers disperse; their yipping died down, and here and there in the approaching line men hesitated, turned away or fell to the ground.

"Pour it on them, boys," shouted Burrus. "We've got the bastards, God damn it, we've got them!"

The Confederate line came to a complete halt. For a long second they stood out there in the rain and mud and stinking air, peering through the curtain of smoke, trying to see us and decide if they should continue the attack. But once stopped, there could be no new beginning. First singly, then all together, they retreated. In a few moments all those who could still walk had disappeared.

The two mounted officers continued their pursuit of the fear-crazed horse and the man he dragged behind him. One of them took a bullet and slipped jerkily out of his saddle and onto the ground, but the other reached the runaway and dragged him to a trembling halt. He flung himself off his own horse and began to wrestle the boot of the wounded man from the stirrup. His own horse was between him and our line, preventing any accurate shooting.

"We must have winged us a colonel," Falk cried excitedly. "They wouldn't take on so much over bringing back a wounded lieutenant."

Then the intervening horse moved to one side, and we had a clear shot at the two men in the field, the one tugging and lifting, the other limp, heavy, almost unrecognizable as a man under the slimy casing of mud that covered him from head to toe.

"Shoot!" screamed Burrus, and twenty pistols crashed, almost in a single report. Both officers were slammed to the ground as though by a fist. They sprawled, side by side, motionless.

Then a silence fell on the battlefield. We lay in our shallow depressions, chilled by the inch or two of water that had already collected under us, staring at the two still figures on the ground and the two riderless horses that fidgeted nervously in their unexpected freedom. For a half minute nothing happened. Then a man moved forward from our line, reached the dead men and bent over them. It was our chaplain, Reverend Honnell. As we watched, he wiped mud from the face of the older man and uncovered the insignia on his collar. Then he rose to his feet and called to us in a voice that seemed to be traveling a distance over water.

76

"Men, let me have some volunteers to carry in the body of General Zollicoffer."

There was a great sigh as all of us in the line exhaled the breath we hadn't realized we were holding. Then half the troopers in Wolford's Cavalry sprang forward to bring in the bodies. All my squad was on its feet and hurrying out to see the real, honest-to-God dead general — all but Cleon Henry.

"Cleon," I called, "don't you want to see Zollicoffer?"

But Cleon didn't want to see Zollicoffer, or anything else. Sometime during the Confederate attack a Minié ball had pierced his forehead, just above the eyes, and made its exit from the back of his head, leaving a hole the size of a man's fist. He was lying with his head on his hands, his revolver pointed toward the enemy. His eyes were open and his face was composed; at his moment of supreme outrage, he didn't look outraged at all.

What a pity, I thought — Cleon would never get that girl of his own now.

General Schoepf's infantry came up then, attacking through our positions, and the Confederates began to retreat. The retreat turned into a rout. They paid the price for placing their camp with the river at its back; they had to swim the swollen, icy Cumberland, and many of them never made it. The First Kentucky Cavalry remounted and harried the retreating Rebels all the way to Mill Springs and the riverbank. It was butcher's work, and I'm just as happy that the rain and gathering darkness prevented us from doing it effectively.

So that was Mill Springs — the first time in the war we killed their commanding general in a battle. Their losses were over 500 killed, wounded and captured — better than one out of eight men engaged. We lost forty men killed —

one of them Cleon. That night, as I tried to remember how he looked when we were joshing him at Christmastime, his face kept getting mixed up with the young Confederate who slid down my bayonet at Wild Cat.

VI

Rendezvous in Lebanon

One result of the Battle of Mill Springs was a third chevron for my arm. My joy at this promotion was not due to any lust for the power and prerogatives of the first sergeant's position; I would have welcomed any change that removed me from the authority of the current first sergeant, Sergeant Otis — of whom it could truly be said, in the words that John G. Fee had once quoted from the Acts of the Apostles, that he was a "lewd fellow of the baser sort."

Sergeant Otis had received a bullet in the buttocks, painful enough to disqualify him for further duty, yet trivial enough to absolve me from a guilty conscience when I heard I was to succeed him.

"So you're moving up to top kick," Falk said when I told him the news. "And poor old Otis leaves the regiment. It seems like you're a right unhealthy man to be on the wrong side of, Hasty."

"All my enemies get it in the ass sooner or later," I replied darkly, "and don't you forget it."

"You won't think it's disrespectful if I make it a point to stay sitting down when you're around, will you?"

"You can't thwart destiny that easy, you poor fool. You got any more of that awful stuff left in that jug?"

After Mill Springs, we were ordered to Bardstown, to a camp previously occupied by infantrymen. There we acquired an active army of "graybacks," a singularly repellent kind of louse that digs in and clamps on to the hairy parts of the body like the Stonewall Jackson brigade on Henry Hill, defeating any method of eradication short of shaving the affected area. There were so many of these little brutes in camp that Falk said if you took a swipe at them with a quart jar, you'd catch a gallon of them.

It was in Bardstown that I first heard the name of Champe Ferguson.

The First Kentucky Cavalry was ordered to Nashville, and Wolford was told to detach 300 troopers and lead them by a different route, through that part of Tennessee frequented by Ferguson, a Rebel bushwhacker and assassin. If possible, Wolford was to hunt him down.

Ferguson claimed that one of his children had been killed by a Union soldier in 1861, and he was going to make the Yankees pay for it. The best estimate of his murder roll throughout the war is upwards of a hundred — including women and children, unarmed prisoners and wounded and crippled soldiers. He was devoid of pity, as were the partisans he led. When we heard that Wolford was going against him, every single man in the First Kentucky Cavalry volunteered to go along. Those who were selected — and I was not one of them — left the next day. The remainder of the regiment rode out for Nashville a few days later.

Wolford couldn't catch him. By mid-April the regiment was reunited, and enjoying a balmy, blossomy spring in Nashville. We heard the news of bloody Shiloh, and the fact that we had missed that battle, on top of failing to catch Ferguson, combined with the lazy, lotus-eating life we were

80

leading, made us feel we had ended in a backwater as the war surged past us.

Then John Hunt Morgan raided a wagon train at Pulaski.

Morgan and his Raiders weren't famous yet. The belles of Tennessee hadn't started to dream of waltzing in his arms across mirror-smooth dance floors in colonnaded ballrooms, being spun dizzily in graceful arcs by a handsome, mustachioed man who gazed at them with tight-reined passion in his smoldering eyes. Small boys didn't yet pray the war would last long enough to give them *their* chance to ride with Morgan. And civilians weren't yet discounting the curious rumors touching upon his honor and honesty that would begin to follow him like the first faint whiff of corruption.

But we in the First Kentucky Cavalry knew him. There were few of us indeed who didn't have friends and acquaintances in his regiment. I had my brother and my worst enemy, Danford Ranew. We had heard tales of his earliest raids, and greeted them with a kind of hidden pride — a sort of "He may be a damn Rebel, but you sure can tell he's a Kentuckian, can't you?" attitude. Wolford knew many of Morgan's officers well and considered some of them good friends. Inevitably, we hoped for a chance to try ourselves against them.

Here was the chance. We were in Murfreesboro when Morgan raided the wagon train. The next day he led his regiment northeast across middle Tennessee, passing south of Nashville and heading toward the Cumberland River. Wolford received information that the raiders were planning to spend the night at Lebanon, a little college town about twenty-odd miles from our position in Murfreesboro. We started out for Lebanon in the morning, and were nearing the outskirts of the town when a courier arrived with a message ordering us to return and guard Murfreesboro. We started back, grumbling at what we considered our unnecessary forty-mile ride, but at least content that the day would end with a hot meal and an early bed.

Just outside Murfreesboro we met two full colonels, riding hell-for-leather to intercept us. They told Wolford his orders were countermanded — they had received new information that Morgan planned to spend the night in Lebanon after all, and we were to proceed there and attack him. Wolford's response drew on his choicest invective. We reversed direction and started north again — just as we had forty miles earlier.

Soon it began to rain, and the rain increased in intensity until it became a blinding curtain of water that turned the road into a slime more treacherous than ice. We tried to maintain a trot in the gathering darkness, but horses kept stumbling and falling and throwing their riders, and our pace slowed to a half-drowned crawl.

Two other cavalry outfits overtook us — a battalion of Pennsylvania cavalry and a detachment of the Fourth Kentucky Cavalry. They had been hurriedly assigned to Wolford's command and took position in column behind us, as we continued our nightmare march.

It was after 2:00 A.M. when we halted four miles south of Lebanon. We had been in the saddle since early morning, and had covered almost sixty miles, much of it in a torrential downpour. We fell on the ground like dead men, each trooper holding the reins of his horse where he lay. Most of the horses lay down too, and we pressed our bodies against their shuddering sides for whatever warmth we could get from them. We lay there trying to sleep until the half-light before dawn.

Wolford's scouts reported that Morgan had pickets posted

a mile out of town, but some were asleep and the others were drunk. Wolford decided to go directly up the road into the middle of town, scooping up the pickets as he passed. He assigned A Troop to the van, the Fourth Kentucky to the left of the road and the Pennsylvanians to the right. He planned to lead the balance of the First Kentucky right down the middle.

We coaxed our horses to their feet in the dim gray light, and mounted at a whispered command. Awkwardly we formed column of fours on the slippery road, then moved forward at a walk, then a slow trot. The horses were blowing out great clouds of steam in the wet air. The only sounds were the creaking of leather, the fat slapping of hooves in mud, hoarse coughs and whispered curses. It was barely light enough to distinguish the features of the man riding beside you.

Then from far ahead in the column I heard Wolford's voice cry "Charge!" and five hundred men drove their spurs into their horses' ribs, bent forward in their saddles, and tugged their sabers loose from their scabbards. Suddenly the column was moving forward at a dead run, the sound of the horses' hooves in the mud swelling to a thunder, the blood pounding in our heads with a rhythm of awful joy.

Shots crackled briefly; the pickets had not been surprised. Morgan had warning — but only a minute or two. We swept into the town. There were houses on both sides of the street, a church, stores, sidewalks. We were nearing the center of town when a sustained rattle of gunfire broke out in front of us.

Morgan had managed to get a line of dismounted troopers across the road where it widened into the courthouse square. A Troop charged the line, and some of them broke through, wheeled and broke through again, slashing at the Confederates as they passed. Others fell, and riderless horses milled in the square. It was a picture of disorganization, but it gave Morgan the precious moments he needed to get most of his troops established in three formidable buildings overlooking the square — the courthouse, the hotel and the livery stable.

When Wolford and the balance of the command pushed through the weak Confederate line and charged into the square, we were met by a galling fire. Morgan's men were hidden behind half a hundred windows on three sides, firing out at us in the brightening dawn and allowing us no target but the flash of their guns in the darkened rooms. We galloped around the square, firing blindly into every window we passed. More saddles emptied. A wounded horse screamed as it tried to struggle to its feet. A man in front of me pitched to the ground and his head completely disappeared in the mud. The veranda of the hotel spun past again, and I realized K Troop was beginning its second trip around. I saw something inside a darkened window and pointed my pistol at it, but the hammer clicked down on an empty cartridge.

All of us must have emptied our pistols at the same time, because all at once the firing was coming only from inside the buildings. A rider pulled out of the circling ring into the center of the square. He swung his saber in a circle over his head. It was Captain Burrus. "K Troop, follow me!" he shouted, and spurred his horse across the open mud and into the street beyond. The first platoon followed, and I led the second platoon out right behind them.

In the comparative quiet of the street I began to load my revolver. The captain rode up to me. "Miller, dismount your men and assign three troopers to stay with the horses. Form the rest in platoon front, facing the square. We'll go

back in, dismounted, and maybe we'll have a chance of hit-
ting something!"

Just then a second lieutenant I recognized as Wolford's
aide galloped up to us. "Colonel Wolford's orders, Captain.
There's a mess of them holed up in the college — you're to
take K Troop and flush them out!"

Cumberland College wasn't on the square, but it wasn't
far from it. Burrus led us through the muddy street at a
dogtrot, and in a couple of minutes we were formed in a semi-
circle around an imposing brick building from whose many
windows rifles bristled. A brisk fire fight began, from which
no losses seemed to be suffered on either side. After five minutes Burrus crawled over to where I lay behind a horse
trough.

"Sergeant, there's an outbuilding behind the main brick
building — an attached shed of some kind. A fence comes
up to within ten feet of it, and it don't look like anybody's
covering it. Take some men and see if you can get inside."

I delegated Falk as acting first sergeant, signaled the
MacCallums and Pap Watson and Thomas Junior and two
other troopers to follow me, and swung wide of the building
until I reached the fence. Then I got my detail together, and
we crawled single-file behind the fence until we reached its
end. We were within ten feet of what seemed to be an empty
storage shed. There wasn't much firing close to us, but I
could hear a steady rattle on the other side of the college
building, and there was a storm of rifle and pistol fire from
the square, farther away.

I told the others to cover me and follow when I gave the
signal. Then I scuttled across the ten feet of open ground
and reached the side of the shed. There was a small case-
ment window there. I tried it and it was unlocked. It swung

outward. I slipped over the sill and found myself in darkness. There was a heady smell of pine tar in the air, and in a moment my fingers told me there were cut logs and kindling piled around me. I was in a woodshed.

I crawled back to the window and signaled the MacCallums and Pap Watson to join me — the others were to stay put for the time being. When the four of us were together in the shed, I found the door into the main building. It was locked. "I'm going to shoot off the lock," I whispered. "You all stay right behind me, and have your pistols ready. When I go in, you go in too. Shoot anything that looks at you cross-eyed." I heard their hoarse whispers of assent. I put the muzzle of my Navy Colt against the door's lock and pulled the trigger. The gun boomed like a cannon in the dark little shed. I kicked the door open, and the four of us stumbled into the lighted hallway of the main building. An open door was directly in front of us.

Inside the room a Confederate officer was bending over a man stretched out on a table, who was being held down by an enlisted man. The officer was in his shirtsleeves, with the cuffs rolled back, and his hands and forearms were crimson. He was applying a tourniquet to the thigh of the wounded man, who was groaning and rolling his head and shoulders.

The moment we crashed through the shed door, the officer and his assistant saw us. The officer raised his hands in front of his chest, bloody palms toward us. The assistant made a grab for a holstered pistol on his belt, and Jason MacCallum shot him dead, with a wolfish smile on his purple-stained face. Before anyone could fire again, I shouted "Stop!"

"Raise your hands over your head, get over there and face the wall, and keep your mouth shut," I told the Rebel officer. He did as he was told. I ordered Pap Watson to summon his son and our other two reserves into the shed. I sent the Mac-Callums back into the shed with him, telling them I wanted all the men together and ready, while I scouted the building. K.B. looked at me queerly, but they all obeyed my instructions.

"All right, Boone, take your hands down."

"Hello, Hacey." He turned to face me and lowered his arms. "How are you?"

"I'm all right. You know you're my prisoner."

"That seems obvious."

"I'll tell you what I'll do. I'll let you go if you give me your parole — promise you'll leave the Confederate army and go home."

"I can't do that, Hacey." He gestured to the man on the table. "If you don't let me finish that tourniquet, he's going to bleed to death."

Outside, the staccato of gunfire swelled, then ebbed a little. Whatever I was going to do, I had to do it fast. "All right — finish it, but hurry!"

Instantly he was at his patient's side. "Hold him down for me," he snapped. I seized the wounded man by the shoulders and leaned my weight down on him. His eyes rolled up at me, and his face froze in an expression of terror. He screamed in a monotonous, hopeless way as Boone tightened and secured the strap around his thigh just under the crotch. "Poor devil — he'll lose the leg for sure, but he may live," he said. "The strap will have to be loosened in half an hour."

"All right, Boone — now git!" I told him, pointing to a window. There was shrubbery outside it. He might have a chance of eluding the fire of our men outside if he could get over the sill fast enough.

He didn't move. "I won't give you my parole, Hacey."

"But you're my prisoner. Why won't you?"

"I just won't."

"God damn it, Boone, do you want to go to prison? You will, you know — being a doctor won't help."

"I know. But I won't give my parole." He spoke unemotionally, and his expression was serious, but not grave. "You might just as well accept that."

The firing outside swelled again. I opened my mouth to argue with him, then closed it without speaking. In Boone's world of absolute values, there had never been room for compromise. For a second I envied him those values, and for another second I hated him for them.

"All right — no parole then. But go! Get out of here fast!"

He looked at me with his level gaze and smiled a little. "It's nice seeing you again, big brother," he said in a conversational tone. "I about despaired I ever would."

"It's nice seeing you, Boone. Now will you please —"

"Remember what your wife said the last time we talked, in your house on Short Street — that we weren't the same kind of Millers? You know, I think she was wrong about that. I think there's only one kind of Miller." He put his hand out and I took it.

"I think so too, Boone. Good luck. You'll need it if you don't get out of here fast!"

He crossed to the window and pulled it open, standing against the wall, out of sight of anyone outside. "Remember me to Mama next time you're home, and tell Robin I'm thinking of her. Don't be too hard on her, Hacey — she's been a good wife to me, for the time we had." Then he dove out of the window and disappeared, as the glass erupted in splinters and bullets thudded into the walls.

I ran back into the hall and opened the door to the shed. The six of them burst out with their pistols in their hands.

88

"What kept you? And where's that Reb officer?" whispered K.B. MacCallum.

"Don't worry about him. He was a doctor, and he gave me his parole. Now follow me, and let's give these Johnnies a surprise!" I turned my back on them and trotted down the hall toward the front of the building. I heard them following. Ten feet ahead was another doorway. There were four Confederates in the room, crouching in front of a gaping glassless window. They were all armed with carbines. "Drop your guns," I shouted. They spun around to face us, and one of them got off a shot before Pap Watson dropped him. The others let their rifles fall to the floor. "You're prisoners of the First Kentucky Cavalry. If you try to escape, you'll be shot." I turned to old Watson. "Pap, you and Thomas Junior stay here and guard them. Don't be afraid to kill them if need be." I started down the hall again, with four men behind me.

All told, our little detachment captured nine men and shot three by the time we opened the front door of the college to Captain Burrus. In another five minutes the troop had secured the building, taking fifteen more prisoners.

I hoped that no one would think too much about the one prisoner we hadn't taken.

As soon as possible, those of us who could ran back toward the square, where the firing had suddenly reached a crescendo. We found a scene of indescribable confusion. At first I couldn't credit the evidence of my eyes, for blue-clad troopers were firing furiously at other blue-clad troopers, mounted blue-clad men were sabering dismounted blue-clad men, and a mixed group of blue-clad and gray-clad riders were galloping out of the far end of the square, down the road to Carthage and the Cumberland River.

Then the explanation dawned on me. When Morgan's

men had plundered the wagon train at Pulaski, they provided themselves with a supply of new warm Union army overcoats, and many of them had exchanged their thin butternut coats for our navy blue ones. It was this fact that caused Frank Wolford a fateful moment of confusion, and resulted in the wildest cavalry chase of the war.

During the height of the melee in the square, Chaplain Honnell rode up to a group of blue-overcoated officers near the north road. He asked them if they could direct him to Colonel Wolford. They immediately put him under arrest.

"No, no, you don't understand. I'm chaplain of the First Kentucky Cavalry," he protested. "I belong to the Union army."

"Well, *we* don't," said a captain, with a wicked grin. "Hey, boys! We got us a chaplain! What's Morgan going to say to that?"

Morgan had been forming as many of his men as he could get mounted, preparatory to leaving Lebanon. He had about a hundred sabers. The rest of his regiment was pinned down in the buildings around the square, or had been captured at the college. His time had run out. But the Goddess of Chance let the Confederates pair their hole card with the last card she dealt.

Wolford had been wounded in the hip, and could hardly sit his horse. He was dizzy from pain and the loss of blood. As he reeled in the saddle, knowing that the moment of victory was at hand if he could only keep functioning long enough to seize it, he saw his friend the chaplain crossing the square with a group of other blue-coated officers. He galloped over to intercept them. "Chaplain Honnell," he called, "do you have any idea where Morgan's headquarters is?"

"We'll take you there, Colonel," said the Confederate captain. "You and the chaplain are prisoners of Colonel Morgan. Let's go!"

A few moments later, when Morgan and his hundred galloped out of town toward Carthage and the river, twenty miles away, our chaplain and our colonel were under guard, riding right behind the Rebel commander himself.

It took us a few minutes to realize what had happened and get ourselves organized for pursuit. By the time we were pounding down the slippery clay road, Morgan's band had disappeared. It was no problem to follow their tracks; a hundred cavalrymen can't gallop down a wet unpaved road without leaving a trail.

That ride was unforgettable. We rode for a half hour at a full gallop before we saw the first of their stragglers and by that time our party, which had started out in column of fours, had stretched out into a line a quarter of a mile long. Every man was riding by himself; with no rider to the left or right, it was as if each trooper were alone on the road. There were men ahead, but he never saw them, because his eyes were glued to the road in front of his horse's hoofs, trying to guide them away from potholes, ruts and puddles. After a few minutes, the rhythm of the horse became so much his own rhythm it was as if he had never known any other. His face was stiff beneath a crust of drying mud, and above his head a gray sky stretched out as cold as wet putty.

Then we began to overtake the Rebels, a solitary rider at first, then two or three, then a cluster. The men in our vanguard pulled out of the race to fight them or take them prisoner, and those of us who had been in the middle of the Union column found ourselves nearing its head. Five miles from Carthage, Reverend Honnell was overtaken. He left the pursued and joined the pursuers without breaking his stride. Morgan's command was now reduced to about twenty men, but Wolford, almost unconscious, was still riding by his captor's side.

I looked up from the road and suddenly broke free from the hypnotic trance into which I had sunk. I saw that I was the second man in the Union column; there was only one blue-coated rider between me and three butternut Confederates thirty feet ahead. I spurred Jenny Lind furiously, and the gallant little mare answered with what must have been her last remaining strength. As I began to overtake the man ahead, I shouted, "Let's get them!"

He turned to look at me over his shoulder, and, despite the mask of red clay that covered his face, I recognized Danford Ranew.

I was coming up on his right side, and was not more than five feet away from him. He whipped his saber from its scabbard with his right hand and delivered a vicious backhand swipe at my head. I ducked, instinctively, and the blade passed harmlessly over me. My pistol was holstered on my right hip, but instead of simply drawing it and shooting him dead, I tugged out my own saber, barely in time to parry his second slash. The two of us pounded down the road, almost side by side, sabers crossed and locked, as we pushed and pulled at one another for advantage.

A wild exaltation surged in my heart. This was the duel I should have fought eight years before — the duel that my brother had fought after I had refused Ranew's challenge. It didn't matter that my reasons for the refusal had been right — that dueling was a brute and imbecile code that gave bullies the license to murder, and that no man of intelligence should ever feel obliged to offer another the opportunity to assassinate him. What mattered was that Boone had felt that my refusal threatened to dishonor the family, and so had fought the duel in my place. The fact that neither combatant was injured had done nothing to wipe out my responsibility. I should have accepted Ranew's challenge and tried to kill him then — my blood told me so.

Suddenly, miraculously, I was to be offered a second chance!

Ranew was at a disadvantage. He was fighting right-handed, and I was on his right side and slightly behind him. He couldn't thrust at me without turning almost completely around in the saddle; the only stroke he could use was a backhand swipe. My position was almost as difficult, however. I was also fighting right-handed, and so had to cross my own body and left arm with the blade.

We both decided to improve our positions simultaneously. I made a sudden switch of saber and reins, and as soon as the saber was in my left hand, I thrust. This maneuver brought the point of my blade a foot closer to Ranew's body, and my thrust put five inches of steel into his right armpit.

He chose the same moment to abandon me momentarily as a target. He chopped down at Jenny Lind's head, which was even with him and only a yard away. The saber cut down at an angle, through her forehead into the brain, and he killed her instantly. In the long moment before she failed to take the next necessary step forward and began to fall, Ranew felt my blade enter his body. He threw his weight to the left in a vain effort to neutralize it. I pitched myself forward from the saddle, spreading my arms and clutching for his waist, as I kicked my feet free from the stirrups. Jenny Lind dropped out from under me, and I felt my boots dragging in the mud, but I was hanging on to Ranew like grim death, and he came out of the saddle on top of me.

We hit the mud in a welter of arms and legs. First I was face down in water and slime, then the dirty sky was above me, then something like bone hit my face, then Ranew's open mouth was inches away, and blood splattered from it and blinded me for a moment. My vision cleared, and I saw I could reach his face with my hands. I clutched at his eyes with fingers like talons, but missed. Then we were apart, and I didn't know where he was. I was conscious of lying on the edge of the road, and could feel horses' hoofs pounding the ground a foot or two from where I lay. But where was Ranew?

I rolled over, and trees and sky spun past my eyes, and there was Ranew resting on one elbow a yard or so away, with his pistol drawn and leveled at my head. Blood bubbled from his mouth and dripped down and darkened the wet red clay; his eyes were crazed; but the gun in his hand was steady.

As steady as the gun Boone had held on him, I thought with a strange, wild joy. *Fair is fair!*

There was nothing to do but lie there and wait for the shot. I could see the knuckle turn white as his finger tightened on the trigger. Round and round in my brain, with a kind of cheerful incredulity, the words repeated: *Who would have thought it would end like this?*

Then the muzzle of the pistol wobbled, just the slightest degree, but enough. At the same moment, it exploded, and a giant invisible club smashed me hard, above the heart. I slipped away into a deep, dark pool.

I was unconscious for the better part of two days. During that time a pistol ball was removed from my body, and a number of other things happened:

Morgan, with four of his men, abandoned their horses and escaped across the Cumberland River in a skiff. About half his command was killed or captured; the others escaped across country. Frank Wolford was recaptured by his own regiment only a mile from Carthage — somehow he had ridden nineteen miles in a coma. Boone Miller disappeared; there was no mention of his presence at the college, or of his escape.

The man upon whose leg he had put a tourniquet lived.

Danford Ranew — died.

Falk Padgett came to see me in the field hospital in Carthage, three days after the fight. "What's this I hear about you turning your collar and joining the enemy, Brother-in-law?" he asked.

"What are you babbling about now? Didn't they tell you I'm a sick man, and shouldn't be annoyed with silly questions?"

"I could hardly credit it when I heard it. Hasty Miller, of all people, joining up with the enemies of mankind to be an officer!"

"Oh, that. Well, Captain Burrus said we were going to try a new policy. From now on, he says we're going to have officers who are at least as smart as the men. He asked me if I would give up my purely natural prejudice and allow myself to be brevetted second lieutenant, as the first of the New Breed." I looked at my fingernails modestly. "I allowed as how, if my country demanded it, I would."

"You're an inspiration to us all," said Falk reverently.

Falk was promoted to first sergeant of 2nd Platoon, following in the footsteps of Sergeant Otis and myself — "I've really got a future to look forward to now," he predicted gloomily — but we were destined never to explore our new relationship. My wound required me to remain in bed for an extended period, and as soon as possible the surgeon sent me home to Hazelwood to recuperate.

The First Kentucky Cavalry carried on its pursuit of John

Hunt Morgan, and finally Frank Wolford received the Rebel Raider's surrender and his sword at East Liverpool, Ohio — five miles from the Pennsylvania line. But I wasn't with them.

I returned to my wife and son near the sleepy little town of Richmond, Kentucky. Nobody ever would have guessed that, for a week at the end of August, 1862, it would be the eye of the hurricane.

VII

RICHMOND

I CAME HOME to Hazelwood near the end of May, and remained in bed all during the month of June. Boone's old medical partner, Dr. Miles Renfro, fussed around me every day, worrying because the wound wasn't generating enough "laudable pus" — such was the state of the art of healing in 1862. When I wasn't having bandages put on or taken off and poultices changed, I napped and read and made the acquaintance of my son.

Young Boone was eight months old, and a fine, alert, bushy-tailed little rapscallion he was. He had an engaging way of looking at me with his head cocked over to one side, and a half-smile on his lips, as if he were thinking, "You may be my daddy — but do I have to take you seriously?" He could scoot across the floor almost as fast as Ellie could chase him, and had a special talent for digging out the contents of drawers and strewing them around.

One day he was exercising this special talent with the bottom drawer of my bureau, and before Ellie could subdue him he had pulled out two shirts, a dozen unused Irish linen handkerchiefs — and a small, hand-carved cherrywood box.

With an exclamation of annoyance, Ellie picked the objects from the floor and started to replace them in the drawer. "Ellie, let me see that box, will you?" I asked. She hesitated a moment, then handed it to me.

I studied the skillfully carved figures in bas-relief on the lid. "Papa Legba, and Maitresse Ezille — and Damballa," I said softly, quoting the odd names I could still remember after seventeen years. "It's been a long time since I thought of them."

"I'd just as lief not think of them again for a good long time. Lordy, they're ugly." She shivered. "Especially that snake that's wrapped around the man in the middle."

"That's Damballa — Damballa *loa,* the bloody one. And don't ask me who he's wrapped around."

"Hacey, why don't you throw the old thing away?" She put one hand on my arm, and reached with her other for the box. I drew it away from her.

"Because I'm scared to, Ellie, and that's the truth." I looked at the carved design again, and once more was struck with the uncanny resemblance of the central figure — the one in the toils of the snake — to the person whose face I saw in my shaving mirror each morning. "Here, put it back in one of those drawers where Boone can't get it. Then forget about it."

She put it away as I directed, handling it gingerly, with an expression of distaste. "I declare, I wish I'd never seen the thing," she said, sweeping Boone from the floor and holding him protectively.

I lay back on my pillows and closed my eyes. I remembered the strange word, *wanga,* that Star had used when he gave the box to me on my thirteenth birthday. Star was the free Negro who lived on our land, in a shack down on the river. He was a big man with a face so black it had purple highlights, and a five-pointed scar on his forehead. He was probably my best friend in those days — although I never thought of him that way, because he was colored.

What do you mean, a wanga? I had asked. What's a wanga?

It was a good luck charm, he had told me. Like a rabbit's foot? I questioned. Not exactly, he replied, because a rabbit's foot may do you a little bitty good, and sure won't do you no harm, but a wanga will either do you a *whole mess* of good, or a *whale* of a lot of harm. The spirit is inside the wanga, and all you got to do is make sure it keeps on liking you.

And how do you do that?

Just make sure you treat black folks right — *and never try to throw away the wanga*. I remembered how Star's yellowed eyes slitted as he told me that.

I never have, I said to myself. *I never will.*

As the days passed and I became more aware of the state of the household, I began to sense a kind of quiet resolution about it that seemed to strengthen me as well. It was a quality a little lighter than determination, a little less cheerful than optimism, a little more sanguine than resignation. It was as if we were snowed in, but the house was warm and we had a reasonable amount of provisions — it would be a long siege, but we would make it through, and we were satisfied.

Mother's days seemed full; managing the house and playing grandmother to young Boone occupied her hours, and only rarely did I see evidence that the hole in her life my father's death had caused was still unfilled, and was in fact unfillable. She and Ellie got along splendidly; both were happiest when they were busy, they didn't get in one another's way and they preferred comfortable silences to trivial conversation.

Early in July I began to get out of bed for short periods of time and walk around the grounds. Ellie would accompany me on these brief constitutionals. Once, as we were walking hand in hand under the great elms, she asked me if I still thought the war would be over within the year. I laughed.

"Not this year, and maybe not next year either. Not as long as we go on trying to win it in the wrong place."

"What do you mean, the wrong place?"

"I mean in the east, in Virginia."

"But that's where Jeff Davis is, isn't it?"

"It may be where Jeff Davis is, but it sure isn't where the Confederacy is. Virginia is just the eastern tip of it, like Washington is just the eastern tip of the Union. Look, Ellie, the Confederacy stretches all the way to Texas and beyond. How can you expect to conquer all that by fighting battles on Chesapeake Bay?"

"Then how come everybody is always saying the best way to kill a snake is to chop off his head?"

"All right — if you want to talk about snakes, there are three of them, and Virginia isn't the head of any one of them! The first one is the Mississippi River, and its head is New Orleans. We've got it by the head and tail already, and if we can move in from both directions, we'll cut the Confederacy in half — lop off Arkansas and Texas and most of Louisiana. Do you see?"

"Geography was never what you'd call my strong point at Berea, honey."

"Well, look." I found a pointed stick and sketched an outline map of the southeastern United States in the dirt.

"When we hold all the Mississippi, we'll have isolated the rebellion here, in this area, east of the river. Now watch. There are two other snakes — the Cumberland and Tennessee rivers. They run into the Ohio right at the western end of Kentucky. Here are their heads — Fort Henry and Fort Donelson. When we captured both of them, the Confederate line across southern Kentucky was broken, and the Tennessee River became a highway for us, all the way past Nashville to Shiloh.

"Three rivers — three snakes. The first lets us take away Texas, Arkansas and Louisiana — *here*." I rubbed out the western end of my map with my foot. "The second and third give us Kentucky and Tennessee — *here*." Two more states disappeared. "And from eastern Tennessee we're only three hundred miles from the Atlantic Ocean, don't you see? We could cut through to it, across Georgia, and chop what's left of the Confederacy in half again!"

"It'd be like slicing up a pie, wouldn't it?" she asked brightly. "Finally there'd be nothing left but this part here." She pointed to the quadrant of the map that included the Carolinas and Virginia.

"That's right! And *then* there'd be time to worry about taking Richmond!" I threw the stick away petulantly.

"Well, never you mind. You just get yourself well again, and I reckon they'll come to you and ask you to tell them how to win the war."

I glared at her for a moment, then gave her a resounding kiss. "They could do worse, Miss Smart Aleck."

I've never known for sure that my sister-in-law tried to betray me to the Confederates, but my suspicions are strong.

John Hunt Morgan came back to the Bluegrass on his first Kentucky raid in the middle of July. Probably three-quarters of the people in the region were sympathetic to him, but most of them were also realistic enough to know that a thousand cavalrymen weren't about to capture "the dark and bloody ground" for the Confederacy — not against upwards of ten thousand Union troops within a three-day march.

He moved like lightning. On his way up from Tennessee he picked up the assassin, Champe Ferguson, as a guide, then swept across the Cumberland and the south-central part of Kentucky that we call the Penny-R'yal, bursting into the Bluegrass at Harrodsburg. That was on a Sunday, and the good ladies of the city laid out a lunch of fried chicken and beaten biscuits and honey and gravy, for all the world like they were putting on a church social.

From Harrodsburg, which is southwest of Lexington, he was only about twenty-five miles from Richmond, Kentucky, which is southeast of Lexington, and forms an equilateral triangle with the other two towns. Had he elected to lead his raiders due east after they had stuffed their bellies with Mercer County chicken, he could have been at Hazelwood by late afternoon. Fortunately for me he selected another route — even though one of the slaves from the Ledyards' Redbird estate was seen delivering a message to Morgan's aide, after a hard ride over to Harrodsburg.

I think later events proved that the message informed Morgan that Lieutenant Hacey Miller of Wolford's Cavalry was recuperating from wounds at Hazelwood. Obviously it was sent by someone who had firsthand knowledge of my presence there. Slaves aside, that meant Ellie, Mother, Dr. Miles Renfro — or Robin Ledyard Miller, who had visited us two or three times during the first month of my convalescence.

But Morgan didn't head toward Richmond then. He began to swing a circle around Lexington — first to Lawrenceburg, then Versailles, to threaten the state capital at Frankfort, then Midway, then Cynthiana, where he fought a brilliant but unnecessary cavalry action at the old covered bridge over the Licking River, and where he abandoned his wounded (I wondered what Boone had thought about that) — then, as thousands of Union troops began to converge on the Bluegrass from three directions, he swung south to Paris, then Winchester — and finally, on Sunday the 20th, a week after he had received the message from Redbird, he rode into Richmond.

His men and his horses were dead tired. They were only hours ahead of the converging Northern columns. He dispatched a detachment to cross the Kentucky River at Clay's Ferry and pay us a visit at Hazelwood; they were to rejoin the main body of raiders at Richmond, and they were pressed for time.

As they galloped up the road to our house, I was stumbling down the bluff toward Star's cabin on the riverbank, with Jubal's strong black arm around my waist. I was dressed in my uniform — I had no wish to be shot as a spy if I were taken — but felt about as militarily competent as my ten month-old son.

The detachment consisted of a lieutenant, a corporal and three privates. They were all Kentuckians and were polite to the women, and even a little embarrassed (for it was still early in the war). They searched the house and then the outbuildings. From what they said, Mother and Ellie were sure they had been informed of my presence and were searching for me personally. If they had had more time, they probably would have found me, but they were impatient to rejoin Colonel Morgan, and when a quick search didn't produce results they settled for a smoked ham and three loaves of bread, and rode back the way they had come.

Mother never spoke to Robin Ledyard Miller again as long as she lived.

•

Morgan's first Kentucky raid was barren of results, but it probably started General Braxton Bragg to thinking, and so was in large part responsible for the Confederate invasion of Kentucky the following month.

By the middle of August the Union armies west of the Alleghenies consisted of better than 100,000 men — half under Grant, along the Mississippi River; the other half, under Don Carlos Buell, moving slowly toward Chattanooga in southeastern Tennessee. At Chattanooga lay Braxton Bragg with some 35,000 Rebel troops, shielded from Buell's sight by the Cumberland plateau, which ran north-south between the two armies. Further north and east, Confederate Kirby Smith commanded 10,000 more soldiers at Knoxville.

Morgan's Bluegrass raid must have caused Bragg to wonder what would happen if a full Confederate army were to be introduced into Kentucky, cutting Buell's communications with Louisville and Cincinnati, and forming a shield behind which pro-Southern Kentuckians might form their own government. The possibilities were intriguing enough to persuade Jefferson Davis to approve the plan for the campaign, and on the 14th of August the Great Invasion of 1862 began, as Kirby Smith suddenly marched out of Knoxville and headed north toward the Cumberland River.

Smith crossed into Kentucky a few miles to the west of Cumberland Gap, forcing its evacuation. He sent a message to John Hunt Morgan, whose cavalry was assigned to his command, ordering a rendezvous in Lexington on the 2nd of September. Then he moved rapidly toward the Bluegrass with his 10,000 seasoned veterans.

Bragg started his movement unaccountably late; Kirby Smith had arrived in central Kentucky before his superior had moved out of Chattanooga. But if Bragg was slow, Buell was even slower. By the time the Union army was in motion

Bragg had already flanked it and was to the north of it —
separating Buell from his base of supplies on the Ohio
River.

Pro-Union Kentuckians were panic-stricken.

And at that momentous point in the history of the Republic, Cassius M. Clay returned to the Bluegrass — now a
major general in the United States army.

Clay had left for the Court of the Tsar the spring of
1861, and had barely arrived there and started to familiarize
himself with his duties as Minister when he received a message from Secretary of State Seward asking him if he would
relinquish the post to Simon Cameron, then Secretary of
War. Clay was offered an appointment as major general in
place of his ministry. Simon Cameron's questionable ethics
had caught up with him, and Lincoln wanted him out of the
country for a few months until the publicity about his pecca-
dilloes died down. (Lincoln once said of Cameron, "He
wouldn't steal a hot stove." When Cameron's friends demanded a retraction, Lincoln obliged them with, "I'm sorry.
Simon Cameron *would* steal a hot stove.") The plan was to
let Cameron fade from view in Russia, then relieve him and
reappoint Clay, if the Kentuckian still wanted the job. If
not, Clay could continue to wear two stars on his collar and
serve with the Union army.

At the beginning of August the Lexington *Observer* reported that Clay had arrived in Washington. He slid into
the life of the capital as unobtrusively as a walrus settling
into a bathtub. In his first public speech he criticized the Administration for not immediately emancipating the slaves. He
also began conversations with leaders of the radical wing of
the Republican Party on the subject of where best in the
army his services might be employed. Some of Lincoln's most
influential supporters, including Wendell Phillips, favored

him for Commander in Chief of the West, the third highest position in the army. At that point the President prudently called Cash Clay to the White House to talk.

Lincoln was considering the announcement of the Emancipation Proclamation, and asked Clay what he believed its effect would be in Kentucky — would it turn moderates against the Union? Clay was sure it wouldn't, and gave his reasons at length, but Lincoln professed doubt. If only there were someone he could trust in Kentucky to advise him, he mused. But why not Cassius Clay?

Of course! Would Clay undertake this mission for him — go to Frankfort and investigate the attitudes of the legislators toward an Emancipation Proclamation by the President?

Clay would. A day or two later he left Washington for Kentucky. He arrived in the Bluegrass at almost the same time as Kirby Smith.

When Clay's train reached Lexington the town was humming with rumors of imminent invasion. Kirby Smith's veterans had crossed the Cumberland River, and there was nothing between them and Lexington. General Lew Wallace was the ranking Union officer in the area, and the task of defense without adequate defenders had fallen on his shoulders.

I had just entered General Wallace's headquarters and given my name to the orderly when Clay burst through the street door. His face was redder and his hair was grayer than the last time I had seen him, but his movements were as vigorous as ever. He was in uniform, with a sword but no hat. He strode toward the orderly's desk, then stopped as he recognized me.

"Why Hacey — Hacey Miller! What in the world brings you to Lexington? Are you on the staff here?"

I told him I had been recuperating at Hazelwood for almost three months. "Doctor Renfro says I'm about ready to go back to Frank Wolford. But first I thought I better see if General Wallace needs me here."

"Wolford's Cavalry? Is that your regiment?" He asked me a number of questions about Mill Springs and Lebanon. He looked at me appraisingly for a moment, then said, "Hacey, it just may be that I'm going to need an aide here in Lexington. Lew Wallace has as much as promised me command of the defense forces in the Bluegrass. If I get the appointment, will you serve with me?"

"Why, I'd be proud to, General!"

He shook my hand. "That's settled, then. You just sit down here and wait a minute, till I straighten out a few details with Wallace." He stepped over to the orderly and said, "General Clay to see General Wallace again, Corporal."

Fifteen minutes later Clay reappeared, with a grim smile on his face and the familiar flash in his eye. "Come on, Lieutenant," he said curtly, "we've got work to do." He set a pace that made me dogtrot to keep up, and we headed for the taproom of the Phoenix Hotel.

When we were seated, with cold toddies in front of us, Clay sketched out the situation. "Lew Wallace has got to go to Cincinnati and prepare its defense, in case the Rebels are headed that way. Don Carlos Buell is still down in Tennessee, and couldn't get here in two weeks with a following wind. Bull Nelson is down there somewhere too. So even though I was sent here on a political mission rather than a military one, I'm still the only senior general officer on the spot. That means I defend Lexington." He took a drink of his toddy and gave me a candid smile. "My military credentials are all Mexican War vintage, Hacey — and the troops I have to work with have never heard a shot fired in anger. In theory, there are supposed to be 15,000 effectives in the central Kentucky area, most of them at Camp Dick Robinson on the river. But Wallace says that after we separate out the octogenarian Home Guards, and the boys who like to drill, and the military bands, and the men who have been on furlough for the past three months, we'll be lucky to have half that many. God knows how many troops Kirby Smith has, but the most conservative estimate I've heard is over ten thousand. So you can see we've got our work cut out for us."

"What do you want me to do, General?"

"First, finish your drink in comfort — there won't be time for any more for a while. Then we'll go up to my room and start working. I've got about fifty letters to get out, for a starter."

The next two days we put Clay's little army together. By the following Sunday morning we had managed to collect a little over three thousand infantry and a battery of artillery. Reports came to us that Kirby Smith's van had been seen in southern Madison County, and Clay decided to move out of Lexington.

His plan was to move down the Richmond pike toward Smith, and take position on the north bank of the Kentucky River. This would give him the advantage of the high bluffs, and require Smith to ford the river under fire and attack uphill — much the same tactical problem that was to prove so disastrous for Burnside at Fredericksburg.

We got a late start Sunday, and night found us only three miles south of Lexington. But Monday we moved out smartly and had reached our chosen positions on the river by 2:00 P.M. Clay was in excellent spirits as he superintended the placement of the artillery. "If he tries to cross here, it will cost him dearly, Manson," he said to his brigadier. "And where else can he go? East or west, he'll have to detour twenty miles out of his way, and since we have the interior lines, he'll find us in position when he gets there!"

Brigadier General Manson was a silent man with a cold eye and a prissy mouth. "Then your only plan is defensive, General?" he asked with a touch of disapproval in his tone.

Clay looked at him incredulously. "For the time being, certainly! Can you see any virtue in attacking an experienced large army with a small, green army in the open fields? Come now, General!"

Manson set his lips in a stubborn line and didn't answer.

"Besides," Clay continued, "we're due to pick up another four or five thousand men within the next three days. That will bring us close to parity with the Rebels, at least in numbers. Time then to consider offensive operations."

"What about Bragg's army?" asked the Brigadier.

"What about Buell's?" countered Clay. "Let them worry about each other, and we'll worry about Kirby Smith!"

Manson saluted smartly, wheeled his horse and galloped off toward his brigade. Clay gave me an unmilitary wink that wasn't visible to the rest of the staff, and I grinned back, feeling very glad that Clay and not Manson was in charge of our little army.

Then everything went to hell on a handcar. Bull Nelson arrived on the field.

He had traveled like the wind from Tennessee, and he was hot, tired, hungry and in a filthy temper. He charged up on a horse that was bleary-eyed and caked with dry sweat, and reined in two feet from Clay. Ignoring our salutes and Clay's surprised but friendly greeting, he snarled, "What the bloody hell do you think you're doing?"

Clay straightened in the saddle in shocked surprise. "I
don't believe I understand your question, General," he answered.

"What's the matter, can't you politicians understand a soldier's plain English? God damn it, I asked you what the
bloody hell you think you're doing. Why are you deploying
the men here? Who told you to position your artillery on
that bluff?" His voice rose to a bellow, and the veins on his
forehead stood out in high relief. He looked as if he was
about to attack Clay physically.

Clay's face showed the same controlled fury I had seen
there when he faced the hired assassins of the slavery power
more than ten years before. His right hand moved around
his waist until the fingers were curled loosely around the hilt
of his saber. But his voice was low and steady as he answered, "I ordered the men to deploy and the guns to be
placed where they are, General. If you have any questions
about my reasons, I'll be glad to answer them in private — "

"Oh, you will, will you?" interrupted Nelson rudely.

" — but I'll not stand any more of this foul-mouth bully-
ragging in front of my staff, do you hear?" Then, turning his
back on Nelson, he spurred his horse into a trot and rode
toward a clump of trees fifty feet away. After a moment
Nelson followed him, and the two dismounted and faced
each other in the shade. We couldn't hear their voices, but
their expressions and movements showed they were in angry
disagreement. For several minutes we staff officers gazed
elaborately at the river, or the guns, or the sky — anywhere
but at the two generals, or at one another. Then from the
corner of my eye I saw that Clay and Nelson had mounted
again and were rejoining us.

"General Nelson has agreed to assume command of our
forces, gentlemen," Clay announced in a clear, loud voice.

"This will give us the benefit of his wide military experience and will free me to continue the private mission which brought me to Kentucky last week. I have every expectation of victory. It has been a pleasure to serve with you. If you would join me for a few minutes, Lieutenant Miller? Thank you, gentlemen, and goodbye." He rode down the road toward the river, and I followed him. We crossed at Clay's Ferry, and rode on to White Hall. We were in the library before he began to speak of the events of the past few minutes.

He stood with his back toward me, looking into the cold fireplace. When he spoke, his voice was a low rumble in the quiet room. "Nelson outranks me — his commission is dated almost three months earlier than mine," he said. "Legally, he has the right to command, if he chooses to. Besides, he's more experienced than I am. He's been on active duty for the past twenty years."

"But in the *navy*, General, not in the army," I protested. "He's only been in the army a year. What does he know about deploying infantry?"

"He thought my plans were overly careful," mused Clay, as if he hadn't heard my interruption. "Me — overly careful! In my life I've been called many things, but never overly careful!" He began to pound one fist into the other palm in a slow rhythm, gently at first, then with increasing force. "That abusive, overbearing wretch! How dared he talk to me that way? But he *ranked* me — he *ranked* me! What could I do? What in God's name could I do?"

"General, you could refuse to give up command, and go over his head to General Buell or General Halleck for support —"

He turned and gave me a half-smile. "Hacey, I'm afraid you suffer from a short memory. It's the *law* that the ranking officer should command if he chooses. It's the *law* for the junior officer to obey the senior. It's the *law* that in the army you do as you're told, and don't go over your superior's head."

"But what about defending Lexington against Kirby Smith? Isn't that more important?"

"Of course it is — and that's why the decision about how to defend it must be made by the best qualified man — the senior officer present!"

I had nothing more to say. I sat in silence and watched him struggle with his passions. He paced across the room and back for a few moments, and then became aware that his saber was striking his left boot with each step. Deliberately he unbuckled the belt and placed belt and saber on a table. His fingers stroked the hilt of the weapon for a moment, then he raised his eyes and fixed them on a framed and autographed daguerreotype on the library wall. It was a picture of the President.

An expression of pain and perplexity crossed General Clay's face. His voice, when he spoke, was thick and muffled.

"But why wasn't it I? It should have been! For twenty years I fought, while the rest of them played their dirty politics? I faced the slave trader and the slave master on their own ground. It was my knife that defied their assassins and their mobs! And when the Party finally came, I campaigned for it, wherever men could heed the voice of truth and justice! I gave my whole life to the Dream — but when the time came to choose the candidate for President — " He wrenched his eyes from the picture on the wall and turned them on me, and they were bloodshot and wild. His voice suddenly rose to a hoarse shout as he cried, *"It just isn't fair!"*

For a moment that seemed endless we stared at one another in shocked surprise: shocked by the childishness of what he had said, shocked by the events that had made him say it. I rose to my feet just as his big body collapsed into a chair. He rested his head in his hands.

"General Clay . . ." I began.

"Lieutenant Miller, I hope you'll see fit to forget the histrionics I was weak enough to indulge in just now." He lowered his hands, and his heavy, square face was composed. "It was good seeing you again. Tomorrow I'll go over to Frankfort, pursuant to my instructions from the Commander in Chief. I imagine you'll be with General Nelson's forces, in any capacity in which he sees fit to employ you."

I straightened my back. "Yes, General."

"Then it may be some time till we meet again." He put out his hand. "Good luck, my boy."

We shook hands, and I said goodbye awkwardly. He didn't see me to the door; as I left the library he was standing beside the cold fireplace again, staring unseeingly at the picture on the wall.

From White Hall I rode to Hazelwood. Our family home lay directly between Kirby Smith's army and Lexington, and I wanted to see Mother and Ellie and little Boone moved to safer surroundings. But they weren't about to leave.

"You say the enemy army's coming, Hacey," Mother said dryly. "And I expect it is, as far as you're concerned. But it seems to me I remember another member of the family who wouldn't agree with you. As far as he's concerned, Ellie and little Boone and I are the sister-in-law, the nephew, and the mother of a Confederate officer, and I hardly think folks like that have much to fear from Kirby Smith."

Ellie agreed with Mother, and after a while I got tired of

arguing with them, partly because I thought they were probably right, and partly because I wasn't sure that Lexington
would prove to be any safer than Hazelwood, in case they
were wrong.

I rode back to the bluffs overlooking the river. The army
was still deployed as Clay had left it. I found General Nelson's headquarters and reported to a major on the staff. He
didn't seem to have any idea of what to do with me.

"I'm sorry, Lieutenant, but we don't really have any cavalry to speak of, you see — "

"Well, can't you assign me to whatever cavalry you *do*
have?"

"What I mean to say is, we don't have any cavalry at all."
He picked up a penholder, turned it around and put it down,
looking as if he had accomplished something.

"Then assign me to an infantry company, Major."

This made him unhappier. "Well, I don't know if that
would work out, Lieutenant. You haven't been trained as an
infantryman, have you? How can we be sure you'll fit in
with an infantry company? What I mean is — "

"Christ's cock, Major," bellowed a voice behind me, "if
the bastard wants to fight, put him where he can fight!"
General Nelson had entered the tent. I turned to salute him,
and he gave me a fierce glare of recognition. "You —
you're Clay's shavetail, aren't you?"

"Lieutenant Hacey Miller, on leave from the First Kentucky Cavalry, General."

"Oh, Wolford's regiment. You people think you'll ever
catch John Hunt Morgan?" From his sardonic grin, I knew
he'd heard of the fracas at Lebanon.

"It's only a matter of time, sir," I replied.

"I hope you're right. But you better keep a couple of
spare colonels and chaplains handy. Major, assign this offi-

cer to one of the companies in Manson's brigade. Give him a platoon. And stop worrying — if he knows how to wipe his ass, he knows more than half the officers in the army!"

The platoon I drew was an unimpressive collection of old men and young boys from the Home Guards, who had been trying to learn how to tell their left feet from their right feet at Camp Dick Robinson when they were ordered to Lexington. My company commander could only function on massive infusions of Dutch courage, which made him a lion at noon and a lump by 3:00 P.M. The other platoon commander was completely incompetent, and he knew it almost as well as his men did. Two of the sergeants seemed to have a modicum of ability, and I leaned on them during the next three days to try to instill some eleventh-hour military competence into the company. But it was a hopeless job.

Reports indicated that Kirby Smith was delaying his advance, in hopes that Bragg's main force would catch up to him and allow the full Rebel army to move into the Bluegrass together. To General Nelson this indicated temerity on Smith's part. The four thousand additional soldiers Clay had expected had joined us by that time, and Nelson added them to Manson's brigade, and ordered his brigadier to move down from the river bluffs, cross over into Madison County, and advance to threaten the Confederates.

Then, inexplicably, he went back to Lexington.

On Friday, the 29th of August, Manson's overweight brigade moved toward Kirby Smith's two divisions. We passed through Richmond and continued south toward Berea. Five miles south of Richmond we encountered elements of Smith's cavalry. There was a brisk little fire fight, and at sundown the Confederates pulled back. That night our troops were jubilant with their first taste of blood. They believed they had all but won a major battle, and that on the

morrow they would see "the sun of Austerlitz." I kept my
own counsel, but there was the brassy taste of fear in my
mouth as I tried to close my ears to the snores of my tent
mate and fortify myself with a few hours' sleep.

The next day dawned hot and still. There wasn't a breath
of wind; we awoke to find our uniforms already sticking to
our bodies. The sky was still gray when we heard the pop-
pop-popping of rifles directly to the south. The firing was
coming from a ridge about 500 feet in front of our line. It
was lightly held by our pickets, and, as we watched, we saw
them driven back toward our main line of battle. In a matter of minutes our side of the ridge was deserted, and the
pickets were running through our line to the rear.

We wondered what was on the other side of that ridge.

Smith didn't keep us in suspense long. He had a full division back there, along with two artillery batteries, under
command of General Pat Cleburne. Smith ordered an immediate attack, and Cleburne's butternut riflemen swarmed
over the skyline and down on us, yip-yip-yips and all.

Somehow we held them the first time, against all reason.
Beardless boys lay in their shallow trenches and died beside
old men dribbling tobacco juice, who also died. The Rebel
wave crested, and broke, and ebbed away.

Then, as we counted our dead in the center, Manson coun-
terattacked on the left, and even as his men were stumbling
across the open field Kirby Smith launched a second Rebel
attack, this time on our right. It was as if two boxers simultaneously launched left-handed haymakers at one another —
but the other boxer connected, and we didn't.

The Confederates turned our right flank, then attacked
again from the side and rear, and began to roll up our line.
Instead of breaking off his abortive attack on the other

flank, General Manson chose to renew it. The Union troops that might have supported the center were thrown into another bootless charge on the left. Within twenty minutes our right was turned, broken, and in retreat; our center was under enfilading fire it couldn't withstand; and our left was thrown forward in a doomed and pointless gesture.

Everybody started to run.

We ran for two miles before we stopped and formed another line of battle. The Rebels were so close behind us they were yip-yipping in our ears before we had our clumsy muzzle-loaders pointed to receive them. They attacked on our right and center, and washed over our line like surf over a sand castle. One boy lying near me fired his piece, missed, and then just lay on his rifle and sobbed in mortification until a Confederate soldier bayoneted him through the body.

We started running again.

Bull Nelson met us two miles from Richmond. He took command of what was left, and deployed us across the crest of a commanding hill he had selected. My spirits rose as I took in the terrain; our center was sheltered behind the crest of the hill, and both our flanks were protected by woods. It was a strong position, and one we surely could have held three hours before — that we might still be able to hold, even with our reduced forces.

And our forces had been reduced to half. There couldn't have been more than four thousand of us, facing better than twice that many Confederates. We had scarcely thrown ourselves down behind the rise and reloaded our weapons when they were on us again, charging up the hill and rushing the woods on our right. I thought I could hear Bull Nelson's voice roaring above the gunfire, and also — incongruously — the bells of a Richmond church tolling. The enemy disappeared behind the swelling clouds of grayish-black smoke, and a stink of exploded gunpowder rasped in the nose and throat.

Our position *was* strong. For a moment the battle balanced on a knife edge. The Confederate attack wavered, a wild surge of hope swept through our hearts, some of us cried out in sudden exaltation.

Then their cavalry struck us from the rear.

Kirby Smith had sent his five hundred troopers around our flank, to secure Richmond before our retreat could arrive there. They had waited behind us as we improvised our last desperate line behind the hill, waited until their infantry arrived to engage us, and they could launch an unexpected thrust at our backs.

We didn't see them until they were upon us. I heard a kind of whimpering groan from the men around me, and looked over my shoulder to discover the cause. A line of charging cavalry was fifty feet away, so close I could see the long yellow teeth of one of the horses, his bloodshot eyes rolled back into his head, and the saber along his neck pointed at me.

My pistol was holstered, my rifle too clumsy to reverse quickly. All I could do was roll up into a ball, with my arms around my head and my knees pulled up in front of my belly. The saber missed me, but the horse smashed one hoof into my left shoulder as it passed. I rolled away, one side of my body suddenly numb, as the screams and cries and curses above me rose to an ear-splitting peak and then receded into vast distances.

They passed through our line and paused to reform on the slope of the hill in front of us. Then they came back. For the third time that day we stumbled to our feet and began to run, but this time there would be no halting, no new battle lines formed, no last-gasp defense. The Union army defending Lexington had ceased to exist.

Bull Nelson tried to stop the rout, but fell with two bullets through him, and was carried from the field more dead than alive, only seconds ahead of the pursuing Confederate cavalry. A few hundred of us got through Richmond and were able to find cover north of town. The rest of the army surrendered — almost 4000 men.

My left arm was broken, just below the shoulder. The wound in my chest had reopened, and sticky blood pumped out in time to the pounding of my heart. My breath burst from my mouth in sobs, and darkness hung at the edge of my vision, ready to slide across like a closing curtain.

I had to get to Hazelwood. There was no place else to go. There was no Union army to rejoin short of the Ohio River. It was every man for himself, and the only way to avoid capture was concealment. I started to walk the ten miles across country, avoiding roads, following fences and staying down when I crossed high ground. My mind was chaotic with rage and disgust and humiliation; the numbness wore off, and my left arm and chest began to ache with a throbbing, nauseous pain. Twice my route took me across roads, and I lay in tall grass listening to Kirby Smith's cavalry ride by, saddles creaking and horses blowing, as the soft Southern voices of the riders rose in songs and laughter.

I gave White Hall a wide berth, for I was sure Cassius Clay's notoriety would attract Confederate attention. It was after dark when I reached the Kentucky River. There I was checked, for with only one arm that functioned, swimming the river was impossible. Since the ferry was certainly in the hands of the Rebels, I knew I should have to find a skiff. But it was beyond me, and I lay down beneath a low-hanging willow near the water's edge and went to sleep.

I woke before dawn, burning with fever. I realized that if I were to get across the river at all, I would have to do it very soon. I struggled to my feet and started along the bank, downstream, away from the ferry. The mist on the water was thick and wet; sometimes it felt like live steam on my skin, and other times it was as clammy as the grave. The air was very still. Occasionally birds cried — not many. The clumsy sound of my own steps was the loudest noise I could hear.

I walked a mile before I found a boat. It was tied to a root and almost concealed by overhanging bushes. There was three inches of water in the bottom, but it was rainwater, not river water; the planking was sound enough. There were two oars, one more than I could use. I cast off the line that secured it and pushed out into the river just as the sun began trying to break through the mist. I crossed without incident.

The current was moderately swift, and during the twenty minutes it took me to get across I was carried downstream a half mile. That meant I had a mile and a half to cover on foot before I was on Miller property.

I did it with a thrumming in my ears, a taste like sulphur in my mouth, and my feet looking as though I were seeing them through the wrong end of a telescope.

I was at the end of my tether when Star's cabin appeared through the trees. It was all I could do to push open the groaning door and then close it. I collapsed to the floor and lay there for almost twenty-four hours, until our slave Jubal found me.

VIII

A Letter from Wentworth

My second recuperation took place on a camp cot in the old cabin on the bank of the river. I couldn't be moved into Hazelwood because the whole neighborhood was swarming with Confederates. Still, I was tolerably comfortable, once my fever broke. Ellie was my nurse, and I told her she was becoming more expert with experience; next time, I was sure, she'd put Florence Nightingale to shame.

"Next time!" she said with a sniff that reminded me of Mother. "Next time I'm not even going to bother having you fixed — I'm going to have you stuffed and mounted!"

Kirby Smith moved into Lexington after the battle, and a few days later John Hunt Morgan joined him there. All through September and early October the Confederate army occupied the Bluegrass. Bragg arrived with his 35,000 men, and staged a charade in Frankfort, inaugurating a pro-Southern "Governor" of Kentucky. John Hunt Morgan made many a feminine heart flutter as he twirled his silky mustaches and led the "Paul Jones" on the dance floors of the slavocracy.

And Boone came back to Hazelwood.

Everyone in the household agreed that my brother should

not know of my presence in Star's cabin, as it would place him in a difficult and unnecessary conflict of loyalties. Whether or not he did suspect anything, I never knew. But certainly he took no walks down beside the river.

I remember one conversation Ellie and I had during that time. Boone had just left to ride into Lexington, after having spent the night at Hazelwood. Ellie was recounting his conversation. "The only thing that really worrits him is this man Ferguson," she said.

"Ferguson? Champe Ferguson? I remember him — he's a bushwhacker in Tennessee. Frank Wolford almost caught him last spring. What's he got to do with Boone?"

"I guess he's joined up with John Hunt Morgan — not as an officer, more like a scout, or guide. Boone's had some trouble with him."

"How so?"

"Over prisoners. Boone says Ferguson doesn't believe in taking any, and if he has to take them, sometimes things happen to them afterward. Boone didn't want to talk about it much. I think he was sorry he brought it up, once your Ma started asking him questions."

"You mean this Ferguson kills prisoners? Or tortures them?"

"A little of both, to hear Boone tell it."

"Does Morgan know this?"

"Boone doesn't think so, Hacey. He says Morgan would never suffer it. He says Morgan's a gentleman, no matter what the Yankee newspapers say."

"Well, I expect he's right — but I hope he watches himself. That Ferguson has a mighty dirty reputation."

She went on to another subject, and in a few minutes the name of Champe Ferguson had slipped to the back of my mind once more.

The first week in October Don Carlos Buell maneuvered his army between Bragg and Louisville, and cautiously began to move toward the Rebels. Bragg ordered Kirby Smith to join him, and meanwhile fell back toward Harrodsburg. Before the Confederate forces were united, however, Buell hit Bragg at Perryville, and drove him from the field.

That night Bragg pulled back toward Cumberland Gap, and the invasion of Kentucky was over.

Once Bragg had left the state, all marks of Confederate occupancy faded like the snows of yesteryear. Union troops returned to garrison Lexington, and you would have been hard pressed to find anyone who was willing to admit he had attended the inauguration of the Confederate "Governor" in Frankfort.

No sooner had the word of Perryville come than I moved up to my bedroom in the big house. Old Dr. Miles Renfro took charge of my recuperation. Unfortunately the bone of my upper arm was knitting wrong, and he broke it and reset it correctly. That was an afternoon's work that doesn't bear remembering, and it set me back three weeks in my convalescence.

So October drew toward its close, and the lower leaves of the tobacco plants turned from green to gold, and the ears hung heavy on the cornstalks, and the walnuts and hedge apples fell unexpectedly from their branches and soon lay on the ground like oversized marbles. Outside my window the world turned russet and yellow, while I lay on my back most of the day. November arrived, and the weather became chilly and gray. My spirits followed the weather. I complained to Ellie, and growled at my mother, and shouted at the Negroes, and glared furiously at little Boone, who took to avoiding me whenever possible. Even Thanksgiving did little to cheer me up.

Then I received a letter that sprinkled new flavor on the bland pottage of my convalescing. It was postmarked "Beaufort, South Carolina," and signed by Colonel Thomas Wentworth Higginson, First South Carolina Volunteers.

November 28, 1862

Dear Hacey,

Lest you should begin reading this letter under the impression that your old friend Wentworth has joined the ranks of Bobbie Lee, please note that my regiment is the First South Carolina, *U.S.A.*, not *C.S.A.*!

And in case that should make you wonder how enough South Carolinians could be rallied to the Union cause to make up a regiment, let me assure you that it is not difficult, if the regiment consists of Negroes!

In a word, Hacey, most improbably I find myself in command of the first black regiment to be officially raised in this country — the first, but certainly far from the last.

The question of black troops had occupied us since the war began — more so in Massachusetts than in Kentucky, no doubt. Early this year General David Hunter took the responsibility of raising a black regiment here in occupied South Carolina. His attempt was not a success; he didn't have necessary authorization from Washington, which meant that his men weren't paid, and he became impatient with the slow enlistment rate and allowed his officers to dragoon unwilling blacks from the surrounding plantations into uniform, with predictable effect on the regiment's morale. After a few months "Hunter's Regiment" was allowed to disintegrate, and everyone connected with it hoped the experiment would be forgotten. Everyone except Brigadier General Rufus Saxton, an officer of formidable initiative. Saxton went to Washington to persuade the Secretary of War to authorize the raising of another black regiment, avoiding the mistakes that had crippled Hunter's attempt. Stanton was convinced, and signed the necessary orders.

At this point I was occupied with mustering in and training the Fifty-First Massachusetts, a new regiment which I had recruited myself. The thought of commanding black troops in South Carolina was as far from my mind as leading Brobdingnagians in the Mountains of the Moon. When Saxton offered me command of the First South Carolina, I was extremely doubtful. But a visit to the troops at their camp near Beaufort convinced me that the decision had been taken from my hands — that Providence had decreed my destiny was to be entwined with that of these staunch and simple black warriors.

The month I have been here in Beaufort has been enough to show everyone with eyes to see — including the War Department — that the experiment will succeed this time, and that black regiments will inevitably become an important and integral part of our army.

But where are their officers to come from? General Saxton has asked me for recommendations, and I have not hesitated to put your name at the top of my list.

A request to the War Department elicited the facts of your enlistment in the First Kentucky Cavalry, your engagement in the Battle of Mill Springs, your battlefield promotion to Lieutenant, and your wounding at Lebanon. Subsequent information placed you at Richmond, Kentucky, during the recent battle, and Colonel Wolford reports that you were there wounded a second time. This fine record, combined with your Southern background and long-standing abolitionist (or, as you always insisted, *emancipationist*) sympathies, convinces me you would be an asset to the Officer's Mess of any black regiment.

I would not expect you to accept or reject an appointment of this seriousness without first-hand information. If you have any interest at all in the project, I hope you will report to the War Department in Washington as soon as you are able. Consider this letter as your orders. Transportation will be arranged to Beaufort, where you can see our amazing Ethiops with your own eyes, and then make your decision. If you do not choose to join

125

us, you will return to your old regiment without prejudice, of course.

May Mother Nature speed her mending, and bring you to us soon.

I am, as always, your devoted friend,

T. W. Higginson,
Col., First S.C. Volunteers

Even though I spent many hours pressing Ellie and Mother for their opinions on this remarkable opportunity, I don't believe I had any doubts about at least visiting Wentworth's regiment — whether or not I would elect to join him was something else again. Much as I loved Wolford's Cavalry, I felt that I had already *done* that — it was time to move forward into the novel, the unknown. I couldn't begin to imagine what it would be like to command blacks. Splendid? Barbarous? Desperately dangerous? There was no helping it — I would have to find out for myself.

Old Dr. Renfro was amazed at the speed of my recovery. By the beginning of December I was able to throw a saddle on a little sorrel mare and take a canter on the Lexington pike. Then Ellie and I knew it was only a matter of days until I must leave.

One morning we lay in bed late. We had made love, and now we were lazy and warm, and the floor outside was cold. Ellie drew her finger across my chest, tracing some design known only to her. "Hacey, you really do reckon it's the right thing to do, don't you?" she asked pensively.

I shifted comfortably against her silky-smooth warm nakedness. "What's that, honey?"

"Taking charge of black men, to lead them against whites. You know."

I sighed. "You want me to answer the absolute truth, Ellie? Then I'll tell you — I don't know. I don't know if it's

right to lead black men against my own kind. I don't imagine Abe Lincoln knows. Why? Do you think it's wrong?"

"No — that is, I don't *positively* think it's wrong. But I
don't *positively* think it's right, either. It does seem pretty
extreme. Isn't there any other way, Hacey?"

"If I remember, you were the first person I ever heard
mention the possibility of blacks in the army, Ellie — back
before I even joined up in Wolford's Cavalry."

"But that didn't mean that I favored it."

"Does that mean you didn't?"

"No, it doesn't mean that, either." She hesitated, putting
her thoughts in order. "Sometimes I think that maybe white
people ought to stick together — but it's a little late for that,
isn't it? And the reason whites are fighting whites is all *on
account* of the blacks. It's unfair when you look at it that
way. Oh, Hacey, I just hate this damned war!"

For a moment I remembered a dream I'd had many years
before — of Ellie and me lying in bed just like this, and then
of a crushing weight on our legs, and Ellie crying out in horror, "Something's coiling around the bed!" as bloody Damballa, the great snake carved on my cherrywood box, took us
in his awful embrace. I shivered.

Ellie felt my movement and slid one smooth knee over my
thigh. "You're sure you don't want to just forget Colonel
Higginson's letter, and go on back to the First Kentucky? It
sure would be easier all around."

Her hair looked like woodsmoke and smelled of lilac soap.
I kissed her for a reasonably long time and then said, "Look,
Circe, just because you have me trapped in a warm bed,
don't try your wiles on me. I'm going to Washington day
after tomorrow, and then I'm going down to look at black
soldiers for a while. And then I'm going to come back here
and have my way with you again. Understand?"

"I don't know if I can wait till then. Do I have to?" She slipped her arms around my neck, and we forgot about Wentworth Higginson's Africans.

But her question didn't go away. I thought of it often during the next two days at Hazelwood, and all during the tiresome train trip to Washington. It was a profound and difficult question, but not peculiar to our age. Probably it is the oldest moral question mankind has faced, and every generation it returns, clad in new trappings which do nothing to ease its implacable options: will you follow truth at the expense of loyalties, or hold to your loyalties and turn your back on truth?

I arrived at the capital no closer to a satisfactory answer than I had been when I left Lexington.

IX

THE COURT-MARTIAL

WASHINGTON was unbelievable.

I was no stranger to great cities. I had spent four years studying in Boston, had roamed about New York, honeymooned in St. Louis and often visited Louisville and Cincinnati. But nothing I had ever experienced in any of them prepared me for the nation's capital in December, 1862.

My train entered the city from the northeast, by way of Baltimore. The dismal Anacostia Flats beside the river gave way to an even more dismal shantytown, which straightened up and took on a more permanent appearance as we neared the railroad station. By the time we arrived in the center of the city, the surroundings had become impressive, although the huge buildings seemed to have been erected in a mud wallow rather than along city streets.

Handling my own luggage, I pushed through the shouting throng of porters, travelers, hucksters, idlers, pimps and pickpockets in the great hall of the station, and, after a half hour's delay, managed to secure a shabby hack on the street outside. The air was dirty, cold and wet, and low-hanging dark clouds scudded across the sullen sky. The cabbie glowered at me as if I were imposing on his good nature when I told him I wanted to go to the National Hotel.

"It's on Pennsylvania Avenue," I said helpfully.

He glared at me in outrage. "Mother Mary damn me for a Protestant, *I* know that!" he snarled, and flicked his whip across the bony rump before him. We swung away from the curb and into the mad traffic of New Jersey Avenue.

Above the dashing horses, the cursing drivers, the creaking coaches, the groaning wagons, the civilian dandies and military gawkers and bold-eyed ladies of fashion, the unfinished dome of the Capitol was silhouetted against the sky. Only the base had been completed, and above it projected a skeleton framework and a tall thin crane, like a bony finger emerging from a full sleeve. Somehow the pretentiousness of its beginnings combined with the gaucherie of its present incompleteness made it a perfect symbol of the city over which it presided.

Our hack swung around a corner on two wheels, and Pennsylvania Avenue opened before me. It was wide enough for any three normal streets, a great sprawling river of vehicles that dashed across and around one another heedlessly, splashing their passengers with a steady patter of mud that fell like a gentle spring shower. If there had ever been cobblestones on the road they had disappeared under the muck years before. Along the north side, a brick sidewalk afforded a promenade for pedestrians as they strolled in front of the city's finest hotels and restaurants; on the south side stretched the odorous Center Market, where domestics, Negroes and the poor poked among rotting potatoes and darkening meat. Ahead lay the White House, behind lay the Capitol, and a few hundred yards to the left, to the rear of the market and the shacks that surrounded it, lay the old City Canal, stinking like an open sewer.

My driver pulled his horse to a halt at the rear of the line of hacks in front of the National Hotel. I paid him what he asked, and a dime more, but he glared at me furiously nevertheless. As I started to step to the curb the nag moved, the hack moved, and I buried my boot up to the instep in slimy black mud. I gained the sidewalk only to be elbowed off into the street again by an irascible-looking civilian in a high stock collar, who didn't even bother to glance at me as I stood in the street with both boots ankle-deep in the mud. I gained the sidewalk a second time and pushed into the hotel. My reservation had apparently been misplaced, and, after five minutes of wrangling with the desk clerk, I was allowed to share a tiny room with an artillery captain from Wisconsin, who snored.

By the time I awoke the next morning I felt as if I had been in Washington forever.

I polished my own boots, had a brief breakfast in the National's great restaurant hall and inquired my way to the War Department. It was located in the President's Park, two hundred yards or so from the White House. I was looking for the office of the Department of the South, but none of the clerks, junior officers and enlisted men who dashed frantically up and down the corridors of the crowded and rickety old building seemed ever to have heard of such a department; indeed, some of those I buttonholed looked so suspicious at the word "South" that I expected them to call the provost.

Finally luck alone directed my steps past an inconspicuous door that spelled out the words I sought. Entering, I waited before a sergeant who was copying the contents of one sheet of paper onto another. At a desk beside him, a very young lieutenant turned the pages in a folder, a lip-pursing expression of concentration on his round face. Beyond him, a clerk in shirt-sleeves and sleeve garters bit down on the edge of his tongue as he wrote slowly on a sheet of foolscap. Bustling privates and corporals formed an animated web of movement around them.

At length the sergeant raised his eyes and took notice of me, and I told him my business. "So I would appreciate your arranging transportation to Beaufort, South Carolina, as soon as possible," I concluded.

He reached out a bored hand toward me. "Orders?" he asked.

"I don't have any official orders. Here is a letter from Colonel Higginson of the First South Carolina Volunteers, which he says can be used in place of orders."

He frowned. "Give me." I placed Wentworth's letter in his hand. He unfolded it and glanced across the first page. "Very irregular. I never heard nothing about using letters for orders," he said suspiciously.

"Well, I can't help that, Sergeant. Here, look on the last page, where he says, 'Consider this letter as your orders.' " I underscored the sentence with my finger. "Isn't that enough authority?"

"Maybe for an officer, but not for me. I'll have to put this through channels. When you don't do things regulation, you mess things up, Lieutenant." He looked at me with an expression more sorrowful than angry.

"Look, Sergeant. I understand you have to do things by the book. But I'd like to see your superior officer, and explain things to him."

"I'm sorry, sir, but he's home with the influenza."

"Well, who can I see, then?"

"There ain't nobody you can see until you see him first, so you might as well wait till we go through channels, like I said. Why don't you come back day after tomorrow, and we'll see where we are then."

I sighed. "All right, Sergeant, you win. I'll enjoy your

beautiful city for two days, while you do things through channels. I'll be back Wednesday." I turned and started out the door, leaving him frowning at Higginson's letter as if it was some unclassified botanical specimen.

In the hall I was trying to get my bearings when a hand tapped me on the arm. "Excuse me, but you did say that letter was from Colonel Higginson, didn't you?" said a pleasant voice with the nasal and slightly broad accent of one of the better New England colleges.

I turned to discover the round-faced young lieutenant I had noticed before. "Yes, that's right," I answered. "Colonel Higginson, of the First South Carolina."

"Colonel *Thomas Wentworth* Higginson, formerly of Massachusetts?" he asked.

"Yes, that's his name. Why?"

"Colonel Higginson is very highly regarded in many quarters here. Many *extremely important* quarters, I might add." He squeezed both eyes shut, in what was apparently intended as a double wink. "May I ask if Colonel Higginson requested that you, *personally,* be assigned to his command?"

"Yes. We're old friends," I replied, puzzled by his interest.

"Then allow me to introduce myself. My name is Nathaniel Crocker, Harvard, Class of 'Fifty-eight. Higginson's alma mater, you know."

"Also mine." I shook his proffered hand. "My room in the Old Den was right next door to the one he used to live in. My name is Hacey Miller, Lieutenant."

"Delighted, Lieutenant. But why be so formal? Two Harvard men, after all . . . I'll call you Hacey, and you call me Nat. How's that? Champion!" He double-winked again. "Where are you staying, friend Hacey?"

"The National Hotel."

"That will never do. You may be here for weeks, even with a tycoon like Higginson asking for you. You must move to a boardinghouse. I know just the place. Capital food, the right kind of people — I stay there myself. Mrs. Cullowee's, Eleventh and G streets. I happen to know she has a room empty. Tell her I sent you, Hacey."

"That's very good of you — but are you sure I'll be here long enough to make it worthwhile? I'm anxious to leave as soon as I can."

"Of course you are! I would be too! But you can't keep staying at the National. Alpha, the food's poisonous — a few years ago people were literally *dying* from it! Beta, the tariff is prohibitive, if you have any other use for your money. Gamma, it's a political wasteland — there's not a single tycoon worthy of a second glance staying there this year!"

Before he could continue his Greek alphabet of criticism, I interrupted him. "That word — tycoon. What's it mean?"

"Ah-ha! That's the question to ask in Washington! Everything's tycoons — unless you're attached to one of the right size and persuasion, you might just as well be marching in the mud with Burnside. Mine's General Saxton — I'd call him middle-sized. Bigger than your Higginson, but nowhere near Hunter or Holt, of course. You might call Hunter the tycoon's tycoon, as a matter of fact, what with his appointment as president of the court-martial, and Mr. Lincoln's partiality to him. Personally, I'm very well satisfied with Saxton, you understand —"

"Wait a minute, Nat," I interrupted, "I can't understand a word you're saying. I still don't know what a tycoon is."

He looked at me with surprised skepticism, as though he suspected I was pulling his leg. "Tycoon — you know, a

Japanese mucketymuck. Wears a kimono and carries a big sword and chops people's heads off. Word that Perry brought back from Japan. John Hay always calls the President his tycoon. That's where we all got it."

"Oh — and so Higginson is my tycoon." I thought that over for a moment. "Well, you may be right, although I would have thought Cassius Clay was. He's a major general, for one thing."

Crocker's shiny little eyes swelled to twice their normal size. "Cassius Clay? Do you know him too?"

"Very well indeed. We're neighbors down in Kentucky, and we've worked together for ten years."

He regarded me with open admiration. *"Two* tycoons! Isn't that remarkable! There's no doubt about it — you simply *must* move into Mrs. Cullowee's boardinghouse. One moment!" He popped back through the door marked Department of the South, and almost immediately emerged with his hat and coat. Hooking his arm through mine, he led me down the hall toward the front door. "I shouldn't spare the time, Hacey, but I'm going to see to your accommodations myself. No innocent lieutenant with two tycoons should be allowed to roam loose in Washington City!"

We returned to the National Hotel to claim my belongings, then rode down Pennsylvania Avenue, circled the Capitol and continued on to G Street. We stopped in front of a comfortably sized frame house with a broad porch, a fanshaped transom, rotting front steps and a general air of past pride and present discouragement. Crocker paid the driver, grabbed the smaller of my two bags, and led the way into the gloomy and slightly odorous hall. "Mrs. Cullowee! Oh, Mrs. Cullowee!" he called, "I have a surprise for you!"

The little woman who appeared in answer to his call at first seemed to me to be about eleven years old — rosy-lipped, bright-eyed, she danced into the hall under a vibrating mass of copper curls almost too heavy for her diminutive head to carry. "Yea-uss, Lieutenant?" she trilled in a Tidewater accent, with a full beat between the first and second syllables of "Yes." "Now, tell-tell-tell, you heah? Ah cannot abide mysteries!"

Closer inspection, even in the crepuscular light of the hallway, revealed this honey-tongued child to be a woman in her seventies, with a ruin of a face entirely covered with rice powder and rouge. Her shoe-button eyes glittered from sockets that might have been holes cut through crepe paper.

Nat Crocker introduced me with a flourish, and Mrs. Cullowee responded to his enthusiasm with a kind of breathless coquettishness. She seized my arm and led me up the front stairway to a large but shabby room on the second floor.

"Call me snobbish if you like, Lieutenant, but I simply will not rent my rooms to every roughneck with two pennies to rub together. I declare, I'd rather live here all alone than share my little house with some of them. Why, I'd be afraid they'd cut my throat. *You* understand."

"Lucky for us Mrs. Cullowee feels that way," said Crocker, who was standing behind me. "Makes for a place a gentleman can be proud to live in, with the right sort of people around him."

"That's all I ask for — just the right sort of people around," said Mrs. Cullowee, squeezing my elbow against her bony breast. I detected the aroma of gin in the air.

"It looks very nice," I told her. "I'm sure I'll be very comfortable. How much is it?"

"Twelve dollars a week — and that includes your linens, hot water and two meals a day."

"Well —" I hesitated, mentally casting my eye over my balance book.

"— As I said, twelve dollars would be the *regular* price," she hastened on. "But because you're Lieutenant Crocker's friend, I won't take a penny more than ten dollars, you hear?" She regarded me with an anxious gaze, and I hastened to accept her terms before she felt obliged to cut the price again.

That night at dinner I met my fellow boarders. In addition to the vivacious Mrs. Cullowee and the animated Lieutenant Crocker, the other diners were a journalist named Richard Ewing, a big, slovenly man in his early thirties, who had apparently let his lank hair grow long in hopes it would conceal a large bald spot; a little old clerk named Hungerford, who looked as though he should have been named Hummingbird instead; Mrs. Crilly, a widow lady in rusty black, whose manner was almost impenetrably pious and subdued; and Captain Bixbee of the U.S. Army Engineers, a pop-eyed and excitable officer who tended to spray unwary listeners with frequent flecks of saliva.

Nat Crocker made a point of mentioning Wentworth Higginson and Cassius Clay when he introduced me to the table. Both Ewing the journalist and Captain Bixbee reacted to their names; Ewing by raising his sleepy lids and looking at me for the first time, and Bixbee by insisting he was absolutely delighted to meet a man of such eminent friendships.

During the course of the meal I noticed Ewing hardly took his eyes off me. Finally, during the bread pudding, he spoke for the first time. "Tell me, Miller — you wouldn't have been at Second Bull Run, would you?"

"Why no — that was the day I got involved in the Battle of Richmond. Why do you ask?"

"With the friends you have, it occurred to me your conscience might have brought you to Washington to testify at the court-martial." He spoke with an unpleasant sarcastic edge to his voice.

"What court-martial is that, Mr. Ewing?" I asked politely.

He snorted. *"The* court-martial — the court-martial of McClellan, Burnside and the entire Democratic Party. You mean you haven't heard?"

"Really, Ewing, you shouldn't talk that way," said Nat Crocker in a worried tone.

"Well, what would you call it, Crocker? The righteous punishment of traitors?"

Nat turned to me. "He's talking about the Fitz John Porter trial, Hacey," he said apologetically.

"Or lynching," said Ewing.

"Unfortunately, it's stirring up a good deal of talk around Washington. Too much, I should say. Can't do anybody any good, and may do some of us some harm."

"Not the least of whom will be Fitz John Porter," Ewing interrupted.

"You should leave these things to the army, Mr. Ewing," said Captain Bixbee. "The army knows best how to handle its own problems."

"Sure it does," answered the journalist. "That's why it's letting Ben Wade and Charles Sumner and Zach Chaffee tell it what to do!"

"Excuse me, but I haven't heard anything about this," I said. "As far as I know, Fitz John Porter is a loyal officer and an excellent general, who held off Stonewall Jackson at Mechanicsville and Gaines's Mill, during the Seven Days battles. You don't mean he's being court-martialed?"

"The trial began last Thursday," Ewing said, "so you can expect the hanging any day now."

"But *why*, for heaven's sake?"

"Let Crocker tell you." Ewing threw his napkin on the table, belched and pushed his chair back. "It depresses me to talk about it." He rose and slouched from the room.

I looked at Nat inquiringly, and, with an expression of distaste, he explained, "It's General Porter's behavior at Second Bull Run that's under investigation, not the Seven Days battles. There seems to be some question about whether he did as much as he could to help General Pope, once the fighting started. I'm not sure of the details . . ."

"The point is, civilians should keep their noses out of it," said Captain Bixbee. "It's a matter for professional military men to decide." He spoke with the martial positiveness of a militiaman who has been in the army for six months; the two ladies and Mr. Hungerford nodded respectfully.

"From what Mr. Ewing said, I gather there are political overtones," I said. "What did he mean about McClellan and Burnside and the Democratic Party being on trial?"

Crocker looked uncomfortable. "As I said before, there's entirely too much talk going around about this, Hacey. I'm sure we must be boring Mrs. Crilly and Mrs. Cullowee. Your pardon, ladies. The bread pudding was delicious today. Excuse me." He rose from his chair and followed Ewing from the dining room.

The rest of us finished the meal with little conversation, and afterward I went up to Ewing's room and knocked on the door. He admitted me with a disagreeable grunt. There was a sour smell in the air, vaguely reminiscent of foxes.

"Don't tell me," he said. "You want to talk some more about the court-martial."

"That's right. You got me curious, and Nat didn't do much to satisfy my curiosity."

"Oh, Nat. He'd be afraid to agree with you that the sun

139

would rise tomorrow, unless he heard one of his tycoons say it first." He sat down at a battered desk, and pointed to a sagging armchair beside it. "Sit down, Lieutenant, and I'll endeavor to lead you through some of the whys and where-fores — although, with friends like Clay and Higginson to guide you, I don't know why you need avail yourself of my poor powers." He glared at me shrewdly. "Are you sure nei-ther of them has written you anything about Porter?"

"I told you, I didn't even hear about the trial until today."

"Hmmmm. If you say so — but it seems strange." He was silent for a moment. "All right — like everything else in this stupid war, it all goes back to the niggers."

"How do you mean?"

"Well, why is this war being fought? To free the blacks, or to preserve the Union?"

"Both."

"No, you can't have it that way, Miller. If it's to preserve the Union, then when it's over, all the Rebs in the South will return to their homes and start voting the straight Demo-cratic ticket, just like they used to — and as long as they can keep the party from splitting again like it did in eighteen-sixty, the Republicans won't ever win another national elec-tion.

"But if the point of all this is freeing the slaves, then they'll be made citizens, with the right to vote, and of course they'll gratefully vote Republican. Assuming that consider-able Rebs are disfranchised at the same time, the Republican Party will suddenly become a national party, able to organ-ize Congress and re-elect the President year after year. Freeing the blacks, or preserving the Union — it's one or the other, Lieutenant. You've got to make a choice."

I thought over what he had said. "Yes, I see what you mean. The two ideas are almost contradictory, if you look at them like that. But I still don't see how General Porter comes into it."

He scratched an armpit and answered me in a patronizing tone. "Fitz John Porter is McClellan's man, and McClellan is a War Democrat. He's also the ablest general we have, although for the last year he's been slandered worse than anybody since Judas Iscariot. His crime is that he wouldn't be hurried. He took the time to build the Army of the Potomac into a fighting machine that was capable of stopping Bobby Lee at Antietam. Why, at the rate he was going, he might have accomplished the unthinkable — finished the war before the Republicans were ready, before the niggers had gotten their vote, and the Rebs had lost theirs!"

"Oh, come on now, Ewing — you don't really believe that, do you?"

He looked at me with the pained sympathy a busy parent shows a backward child. "Miller, right now there's a trial going on down at Fourteenth Street and Pennsylvania Avenue. The defendant is as gallant an officer as any in the whole damned Union army. He's accused of disobeying orders, of shameless cowardice or worse in the face of the enemy, of ordering an unnecessary retreat — in a word, of being the architect for the defeat at Second Bull Run. The true authors of the charges are Secretary of War Stanton, who's hand in glove with Ben Wade and his Committee on the Conduct of the War, and that paragon of military virtue, General John Pope, the biggest blowhard in Washington, which is saying a good deal. You can hardly call Pope disinterested, since he was in command at Second Bull Run.

"Now take a look at the court. The prosecutor is Judge Advocate General Holt, a creature of Stanton's. The president of the court is General David Hunter, a close friend of

Lincoln's, who was relieved of his command of the Department of the South for trying to free all the slaves there and turn them into a black army without any legal authority to do so — a radical of the wildest type.

"Two of the other judges are Generals King and Ricketts. Both of them were also commanding troops at Second Bull Run, and both were involved in the debacle up to their necks. People who know say King was dead drunk, and Ricketts pulled his troops out of line and let Longstreet through Thoroughfare Gap, which is what caused most of the trouble. Neither of them would mind too much if Porter took the blame for their mistakes.

"Then there's General Casey. Six months ago Stanton appointed him to command one of Porter's divisions, and Porter rejected him for incompetency. So you know how unbiased *he'll* be!

"That's four of the nine judges that I *know* about, Miller. God knows what Stanton may have on the other five. But I'm telling you, none of them would be on that court unless the radical Republicans were sure they would vote to convict!"

"But why Porter?" I asked. "I understand why McClellan would be a target for them, but why Porter? What's he ever done to make him the object of a political vendetta?"

"Not a single goddamned thing!" Ewing shouted, his veneer of patronizing irony wiped away. "His only crime is being a loyal lieutenant to his commander. But they can't get their hands on McClellan — and Fitz John Porter is available, because his corps was transferred away from the Army of the Potomac and assigned to Pope's army for the Bull Run battle. If they can claim that he conspired with McClellan to prevent Pope from winning the battle, then they've tarred both of them with the same brush — and, by the same token, tarred every War Democrat who believes like McClellan and Porter that this war is being fought to preserve the Union!"

"Then what you're saying is that this court-martial is purely political?"

"That's just exactly what I'm saying. If Porter had been a radical Republican like Frémont or Ben Butler, he would have been decorated and promoted. But unfortunately for him, he never claimed to believe the future of the United States would be safer in the hands of illiterate black field hands than educated Anglo-Saxon gentlemen!"

I sat in silence for a moment, thinking. Ewing pulled open a drawer that seemed to be full of dirty laundry, and dug out a small smoked-glass bottle. He opened it and raised it to his lips, took a large swallow, and shivered. Then he replaced the bottle under the clothes without offering me any. I was just as glad.

Much of what he had told me was surprising, but not completely unexpected. Every officer in the army was aware that politics motivated many events and decisions in the High Command. Barracks rumor had it that certain generals would never have achieved their rank without political influence, and that others more competent were held in subordinate positions because their voting record was suspect. I supposed that was true in all armies.

But I wasn't prepared for the fact that, if Ewing was to be believed, politics had become so important in the Union army that honor, reputation, and even victory itself might be gambled for political advantage. It was a profoundly shocking idea.

But, on the other hand, I asked myself, is this simply a *political* issue? Or isn't it rather a *moral* issue — the one great moral issue that underlies the very war itself? Isn't the freeing of the slaves and their immediate elevation to full citizenship the overriding necessity, the end that justifies any means required to achieve it? John G. Fee felt so, when he turned Berea College into a station on the Underground Railroad; Wentworth Higginson felt so when he led armed settlers into Kansas to battle the Border Ruffians; Cassius Clay felt so when he installed his cannons to sweep the stairs leading to the office of *The True American*.

Or — did they? Did they believe that the end justifies *any* means?

Wentworth did, certainly. But Fee drew the line at violence, and Clay refused to countenance the breaking of the law. So the operative word was *any*. Were *any* means justified, or only those means which were necessary and unavoidable? And who besides God could tell if the conviction of Fitz John Porter was necessary and unavoidable?

I sat and turned the question over in my mind, until I became aware of Ewing standing beside me. He was grinning sardonically. "What's the matter, Lieutenant? Did I tell you more than you bargained for?" At close quarters, the foxy smell was very strong. I felt it was time for me to leave.

"It's an interesting story, Mr. Ewing. Thank you." I rose to my feet.

"Don't just take my word for it. Ask some of your famous friends — those tycoons Nat Crocker's always talking about. If you *really* want to know, I mean," he jeered.

"I intend to." I gave him a formal little nod and left the room.

On Wednesday, when I returned to the Department of the South, I found that the sergeant's superior was still on the sick list, and nothing had been done about my orders. This left me with the choice of either getting tense and trying to hurry matters up, or relaxing and taking advantage of the opportunity of seeing the capital. I chose the latter alternative, and, after making an appointment with Nat Crocker to lunch at Willard's Hotel, I set out on foot for a sightseeing tour.

My steps led me south on 15th Street, along the east side of the President's Park, to the City Canal. I crossed it on the 16th Street Bridge, for the first time being thankful for the freezing rain, for it held the stench of the sewage close to its source. To the southwest an open field jutted out between the canal basin and the Potomac River. This field held two structures — the uncompleted Washington Monument, and a U.S. Government slaughterhouse.

The Washington Monument stood squat and flat-topped, surrounded by a haphazard collection of carved stone figures and bas-reliefs which were intended to grace it when it was finished. The subscriptions necessary to complete the heroic edifice had never been raised, and certainly would not be until the war was over.

A herd of cattle had been pastured in the field near the Monument, and for convenience a slaughtering facility was located there also. Now, in the chilly December drizzle, rotting offal was piled two or three feet high, in some places partly covering the marble statuary that celebrated the career of the Father of his Country.

It was not an inappropriate place to spend an hour on the eve of the battle of Fredericksburg.

I poked around in the debris abstractedly, a prey to doubts and premonitions. I couldn't get my thoughts away from Ewing's comments on the Porter court-martial, and those comments were enough to open the Pandora's box of unsettled questions I had carried with me for years. Phrases like "The Higher Law" and "The Peculiar Institution" and "The Irrepressible Conflict" chased each other through my brain like rats in an empty house. I felt I was as far from reconciling law and loyalty, morality and tolerance as I had ever been — and now the time for reconciling anything was running out.

Chilled and depressed, I walked back over the bridge and north to Pennsylvania Avenue. It was a little early to meet Nat Crocker at Willard's, so I idled along the sidewalk looking at my fellow citizens with a dubious eye. I was standing on the curb and waiting for the traffic to thin when I heard a woman's voice cry, "Why, Hacey — Hacey Miller!"

A carriage pulled up alongside the walk, and a pretty woman was smiling at me from the window. She wore a modish little hat with a veil, a white lace collar, and a solemn but flatteringly cut black dress. Her eyes were a merry brown under heavy lashes, her nose was impertinent and her full little mouth was as bright and moist as a candied cherry in a fruitcake.

I whipped off my hat and bowed with slightly exaggerated formality. "Still after these many years, your servant, Miss Binder," I said in my best d'Artagnan manner.

"Oh, Hacey, how *lovely* to see you!" She put out her white-gloved hand, and I pressed the small fingers warmly. "I believe you're as dashing as ever. What are you doing in Washington?"

"Waiting for orders and transportation south, and trying to while away the lonely hours. But what are *you* doing so far from Beacon Street?"

"No doubt you hadn't heard," she said, lowering her eyes demurely, "but my late husband, Representative Buckles, and I made our home here in Washington. Since he — passed over — last spring, I just haven't had the heart to close our beautiful house and say goodbye to so many memories."

"I'm sorry, Prudence. No, I hadn't heard. It must have been a terrible loss for you."

"Oh, you have no idea!" She looked at me with as resigned an expression as her impish features could contrive. "But the Lord giveth and the Lord taketh away, Hacey."

"Your father must have been a great comfort to you at a time like that. How is Reverend Binder, by the way?"

"Why, you wouldn't know he was a day older than the last time you saw him. Still writing his sermons and inviting young men to the house to meet my sisters."

"Any luck with the matchmaking?"

"Not really, I'm afraid. Charity was engaged to an entomologist for two months, back about four years ago, but it didn't take." She shook her head. "I just don't know what's the matter with those Boston men."

"When I used to attend the musical evenings at your house, it was *you* who were the trouble with those Boston men," I said. "With you in the room, nobody could spare a glance for any other girl."

"Oh, la!" she interrupted.

"But once you were out of the house, I would have thought they stood a better chance. Well, at least *you* finally entered the matrimonial estate, Prue. How long were you and your husband married?"

"Less than three years. Three fleeting little years. Out, out, brief candle." She touched her eyes carefully with a wisp of lace handkerchief. "But I must spare you my sorrow. How long do you plan to be in Washington, Hacey?"

"I'm not sure. But at least a week, I think."

"Then you must come to dinner Friday evening."

"I'd love to."

"There will only be a few people there — just a simple little evening at home, really. Come at eight. Do you know where Minnesota Row is?" When I shook my head she explained that it was on I Street west of New Jersey Avenue. "It's the house right next door to Senator Douglas's."

I promised I'd be there on the minute, and took her hand again. Her fingers squeezed mine briefly, then she called to her driver, and the carriage pulled away from the curb into the furious traffic.

I stared after her for a moment, remembering my days at Harvard, when I had argued with Frederick Douglass, and drunk sherry with Wentworth Higginson, and been sure that Prudence Binder represented the apotheosis of female loveliness. That had been before Berea, before Ellie, and before the Reb slid down my bayonet at Camp Wild Cat. It seemed a long, long time ago.

Willard's Hotel was seething with activity. The vast dining hall was shared by the late breakfasters, still gorging themselves on fried oysters, pâté de foie gras, kidneys, tripe and blanc mange, and the early luncheoners, just beginning to attend to steak and kidney pie, mutton, terrapin and a variety of game birds. Men were crowded three-deep around the bar, shouting at the top of their lungs to reach the ears of listeners six inches away. There were generals and admirals, senators and congressmen, financiers and journalists, diplomats and jurists and all kinds of unidentifiable *personages* — but, as far as I could see, only one lieutenant. Nat Crocker stood on the outer fringe, holding a glass of Fish House Punch in both hands, protectively, his round face frozen in an expression of unconvincing self-sufficiency.

He looked glad to see me, when I got close enough to let him hear my shout. In the few minutes it took me to get myself a toddy we made an effort to converse, but gave it up

148

as a hopeless job and stood silently together until we could carry our glasses to a table. Then he burst into an animated monologue, as he pointed out famous and infamous personalities around us. There was very little malice in his recitation; he seemed to feel that notoriety in itself was a kind of success, and successful people were beyond the criticism of the likes of us. It was really very innocent.

I listened with half an ear while I sipped my whiskey and watched the movers and shakers. By the time I was nearly through with my second drink, the scene had begun to pall. I interrupted Nat in mid-sentence. "How much do you know about the facts in the Fitz John Porter case?" I asked.

His mouth hung open for the moment it took him to change his conversational direction, then he replied, "No more than is absolutely unavoidable, Hacey."

"Well, tell me something. What is he *specifically* charged with? An error of judgment? Less than enthusiastic obedience to orders? Cowardice? Or deliberate treason?"

"Hacey, of all the subjects for discussion I know, that one is the least rewarding for young officers with their way to make in the world. Alpha, General Porter was involved in a military disaster that demands a scapegoat. Beta, of all the senior generals present at that fiasco, he is the only one who has close personal ties with a certain military person now out of favor with the Administration. Gamma, he apparently was unwise enough to express his lack of enthusiasm for his commander, in no uncertain terms, on the eve of the battle. Delta —"

"But all that's not what he's charged with, Nat. What about the specific charges against him? What are they?"

He sighed and frowned, indicating the whole subject was distasteful to him. "To tell you the truth, I don't know enough strategy and tactics to understand it all, but the main charge seems to boil down to this." He moved the salt and pepper shakers and the sugar bowl from the center of the table and picked up our two knives and forks. "Imagine this is the battlefield. This knife is Pope's army and this knife is Stonewall Jackson." He set the knives down parallel to each other. "They're facing one another. Jackson's men are protected by an old railway cut, which gives their position added strength. Pope wants to destroy Jackson before Longstreet — this fork here — can arrive with the balance of the Confederate army. Pope is sure that Longstreet is two days' march away, so we won't worry about him." He set the Longstreet fork by the sugar bowl.

"This other fork is Fitz John Porter. His corps is on Pope's left, but how close to Pope is a matter of conjecture." He set the fork down so its tines were two inches from Pope's knife, and its handle slanted slightly backward, away from Jackson. The angle between Porter and Pope might have been 150 degrees.

"Pope believed he could put Jackson in the jaws of a nutcracker. If Porter could pivot his corps on his own right flank, he could hit Jackson's flank and roll it up, while Pope held Jackson pinned from the front. Like this." He rotated the Porter fork to the right, keeping the tines in place but moving the handle in an arc until it touched one end of the Jackson knife and formed a right angle with the Pope knife. "He ordered Porter to attack at once, because he believed that between the two of them, they could polish off old Stonewall before Longstreet could reach the field."

He picked up the second fork — Longstreet — and juggled it idly. "But Porter says Longstreet was *already on the field*, facing Porter's position, and deployed for battle, cannons and all." He placed the Longstreet fork so that it paralleled the Porter fork and touched the end of the Jackson knife. "He claims Longstreet had already made contact with Jackson, and had twenty-five thousand men concealed in the underbrush facing his own ten thousand."

"If that's so, Porter couldn't possibly have obeyed Pope's order," I said. "He would have had to cross directly in front of Longstreet and present his flank to an army more than twice his size! He would have been wiped out!"

"That's certainly true — if you believe Porter. But Pope doesn't. He swears Longstreet didn't arrive until evening, and Porter had all the time in the world to make his attack. Furthermore, he claims that Porter was intentionally slow in moving his troops up to support Pope later, and so forced Pope to fight both Jackson and Longstreet single-handed. If that's true, then Porter is obviously responsible for the defeat."

"Can't Porter establish the time Longstreet arrived?"

"How?" An ironical smile flitted across his face. "By asking Longstreet to come to Washington to testify?"

"What about his own witnesses?"

"He has some, of course. But Pope has just as many, or more. They cancel each other out — and it finally boils down to a question of attitude. If Pope and the prosecution can establish the fact that Porter — and his friend, the certain military person I mentioned before — wanted to see Pope fail, then there's a presupposition of guilt."

"And that means treason?"

"That's right. But if they can't establish it, then — just possibly — a certain Caesar may find himself in position to cross a Rubicon and march back to a triumph in Rome."

"Proving that the war was only fought to preserve the Union, after all," I said, half-audibly.

151

"What's that?"

"Nothing." A waiter passed, and I stopped him and ordered two more drinks.

"It's a sticky thing, isn't it, Nat?" I asked.

"Isn't that what I tried to tell you when you brought the whole thing up? Alpha —"

"Please, no alphas. Or even omegas." Neither of us spoke for a minute or two. Then our drinks arrived. I raised my glass to Nat. "To Harvard — and to the clear and simple ethics they taught us there," I toasted.

"To Harvard," he said, with a pleased smile. We both drank, and suddenly I didn't want to talk about Fitz John Porter anymore. I wanted to talk about a pretty woman.

"Tell me, Nat, did you ever hear of a Congressman Buckles?"

"Certainly. A rather foolish old gentleman from Boston. He's dead, though — why do you ask?"

"Oh, no reason. He was married, wasn't he?"

"I should say he was! Not to stretch a point, to one of the loveliest creatures ever seen in Washington! May and December — almost a classic example. Every time I ever saw them together, I became very conscious of the fact that I, too, am still May!"

"Their home was on a new street called Minnesota Row, I believe?"

"Indeed it was! With Stephen A. Douglas's house on one side, and John C. Breckinridge's on the other. An architectural gem — presided over by a nymph. Oh, you're talking about the best that Washington society can offer, Hacey!"

I took a pull on my drink. "I'm glad, because I'm going there to dinner with Mrs. Buckles Friday," I said casually.

He searched my face for any signs of levity, and finding

none, drained his glass. Then he looked at me with an expression close to reverence, and said, "May the ghost of Cotton Mather close my upstaring eyes! Two tycoons — and Mrs. Congressman Buckles to boot!"

X

Results of a Midnight Melee

Few people can handle large quantities of French champagne laced with peach brandy. Chase Cottrell wasn't one of them.

He was far from sober when I was introduced to him in the opulent drawing room of Prudence Buckles's home on Minnesota Row. His tunic was unbuttoned at the throat, and his long yellow hair hung down over his eyes. There were flushed patches in his pale cheeks, and his manner was overbrisk.

"Captain Cottrell, allow me to introduce a specially dear old friend of mine, Lieutenant Miller," said Prudence, one arm linked through mine, the other hand resting as lightly as a butterfly on his shoulder. She was a confection in pale blue watered silk and much décolletage.

He shifted his drink and shook hands. "How dear is 'specially dear,' dear?" he asked brightly. "Too dear? Glad to know you, Lieutenant. Sometimes I think we need to declare open season on dears — know what I mean?" He laughed more than the witticism deserved.

"How do you do, Captain. Prudence just likes to be provocative. I was a friend of the family, back in Boston before the war."

"Well, I like that!" Prudence said archly. "I was under the impression you entertained feelings toward me that would have been inappropriate toward my mother or father."

"It's true that I never felt a hopeless desire to beat your mother or father at lawn tennis. Are you attached to the War Department, Captain?"

"On temporary assignment, Lieutenant. My regular billet is Headquarters, Fifth Corps, Army of the Potomac." He swished the spiced peach around in his glass and smiled.

"Isn't that General Porter's corps?" I asked.

"*Was*, Lieutenant, *was*. General Butterfield is commanding now, and it's assigned to General Hooker's Grand Division of Burnside's army. *Sic transit gloria mundi,* Tuesday and Wednesday. Gives a man pause, doesn't it?"

"I can see how it would, yes."

He emptied his glass. Prudence squeezed my arm and said, "Hacey just told me he's waiting to go down to South Carolina to see Wentworth Higginson, who's another old friend of the family."

Cottrell looked at me shrewdly. "Oh, going to make soldiers out of our African brethren, are you? A worthy cause, my friend. Glad to see you're on the side of the angels."

"Thank you — although I can't remember seeing many halos around lately."

"Oh, they're here. Every Republican has one under his hat. And the damn Democrats have long red tails under their pants, agreed? Or at least we'll make everybody think so before we're through with them." He laughed again, and turned away from me to say something to Prudence in a voice I couldn't hear. I couldn't hear her reply either, but she smiled coquettishly and tapped his lips with her finger. Then he went off to the punch bowl to refill his glass, and Prudence introduced me to more of her guests.

Most of the men I met were civilians, attached to one or another government department. There were two Congressmen, and a few businessmen who were contractors to the army. The only other military man besides Chase Cottrell and myself was a doddering old naval commodore. All the males ogled Prudence, and there was a good deal of heavyhanded gallantry which didn't seem to please their wives much.

One man stood alone in a corner of the hall, surveying the other guests with a sardonic eye. He was a short man in a well-cut black suit and snowy linen, with his hair brushed in a pompadour to reveal a surprisingly narrow strip of forehead, not more than an inch and a half from eyebrow to hairline. The brows were heavy, his cheekbones high and his chin receding, so that his features combined to give him a simian appearance. He looked like an intelligent and malicious ape.

Prudence introduced him as Charles Hanslow, who was employed in the War Department "in some mysterious capacity."

"Nonsense, Mrs. Buckles. There's nothing mysterious about it. Soldiers have a word for it, don't they, Lieutenant? Dog robber. I'm Stanton's dog robber." His voice was surprisingly deep and melodious.

"Goodness, what kind of a profession is that for a Christian gentleman?"

"It's not as lawless as it sounds, Prue," I said. "Actually, all it means is personal assistant. In the army, it's a term for an aide-de-camp."

"Well, I don't see why you don't say aide-de-camp, then. It's ever so much more genteel."

"True — and in times like these we must hang on to our gentility with a grip of iron. I beg your pardon, madame." His rich voice, as he made his apology, was tinged with mockery. It seemed to me that Prudence's color heightened by the faintest added blush.

"Tell me, Mr. Hanslow, is there any news from Burnside?" I asked. There were rumors that General Burnside had ordered the Army of the Potomac to cross the Rappahannock at Fredericksburg two days before. At least some, possibly all, of Lee's army was known to be near the city, and a battle seemed imminent.

"I can tell you that the army's across, occupying Fredericksburg, and safely protected by artillery on the heights behind them," he answered negligently, his eyes still on Prudence.

"What about Lee? Is he going to fight, or pull back?"

"I really couldn't say, Lieutenant. Now, I wonder if you'd excuse Mrs. Buckles and me for a moment. I'd suggest you try a glass of punch — it really is delicious."

Before I could answer, Prudence quickly added, "Oh, Hacey — would you be a lamb and bring me a glass too?" So I had no choice but to accept Hanslow's rudeness, bow, and leave them together.

When I returned with the two drinks, Prudence had finished her conversation with him, and was talking to the ancient naval commodore. Hanslow had his back to me and was studying the guests at the other end of the room. I made no comment on his behavior to my hostess, and neither did she.

Dinner was served buffet style, and was excellent. After coffee, brandy, and cigars, I realized that the hour was late.

157

Guests began to leave, and I joined them, waiting to say good night to Prudence.

My turn came, and I thanked her for the evening. Her eyes sparkled mischievously. "Are you going to tell your wife you came visiting another woman?" she asked.

"I'm going to brag about it to everybody else, so I might as well," I answered.

"You're sweet. I'm so glad you could come, Hacey. I hope we'll have a chance to talk again before you leave Washington."

"So do I. Good night, Prudence." I left, feeling that it was highly doubtful that I would see her, or any of her friends, again.

The first news of the battle of Fredericksburg reached the capital that Sunday, but the full extent of the disaster wasn't known until the wounded began to arrive two days later. We had lost over 12,000 men in the suicidal attacks on Marye's Heights, and those of them who were still alive were brought back to Washington by train, wagon, and steamship — first a trickle, then a stream, and finally a flood. There was no end to them. Hundreds were unloaded at the docks, and lay there under somber drizzling skies until hospital space could be found. Hotels were emptied of guests and pressed into service. Wagon after wagon creaked through the muddy streets carrying men too damaged to walk — and more wagons carried away amputated arms and legs, and carted bodies to the graveyards. Shock and fear and pain combined in a grim miasma that was almost palpable.

I walked the streets futilely looking for something to do to help. Doctors and nurses were desperately needed, but everyone else was a supernumerary. Government departments were half staffed, or less; the War Department had almost ceased to function; stores and offices were deserted. Only the bars were busy.

I arrived back at Mrs. Cullowee's boardinghouse to find my landlady drinking tea with Mrs. Crilly and Mr. Hungerford in the drawing room. Richard Ewing was standing by the window and staring out into the street. He hadn't shaved in two or three days, and his face was blotched and puffy.

Mrs. Cullowee seized upon me as soon as I arrived. "Oh, Lieutenant, is it true that General Burnside is a drug fiend? The man at the meat market swears he heard it from a very important personage."

"Understand they're talking about moving the government to Philadelphia, and just leaving us here," said Mr. Hungerford, in an anxious chirp.

"Is there really a cholera epidemic?" asked Mrs. Crilly.

"Please, ladies — Mr. Hungerford — I don't know any more than you do. But I'm sure the government has everything under control." I refused a cup of tea and walked over to Ewing. "It's terrible. Have you heard any more news?"

He answered heavily. "Burnside wanted to continue the attack. His generals unanimously opposed him. Thank God for that — he would have pissed away another ten thousand men. But the army's safe now, anyway."

"Is Burnside still in command?"

"Did you think they were going to give it back to McClellan? Yes, Burnside's still in command — but he may not be after today. The Republican caucus is meeting."

"What does that mean?" We were speaking in low voices, so my face was close to his. His breath smelled of poor whiskey and poor teeth.

"Nobody seems to be sure — or at least nobody's telling. But there are rumors that Ben Wade is going to demand that Lincoln fire Secretary Seward from the cabinet, and appoint a radical Republican general as dictator of the army. The meeting's still going on, so nothing is resolved yet."

"What's your best guess as to what will happen, Ewing?"

"That they've got the blood bath they needed to take over the army," he said savagely. "They can blame Fredericksburg on the Democrats, and they will. Burnside is a close friend of Fitz John Porter, and they're both loyal to McClellan. That's all the evidence they'll need."

"What general would they want to make dictator?"

He glared at me from bloodshot eyes. "Well, not your friend Cassius Clay, I'm afraid. Too bad he decided to go back to Russia — he might have had a shot at it. And I'm afraid your friend Higginson is a little too junior. Hard luck, old man!"

"I'm not Nat Crocker, Ewing," I said coldly.

He grunted. "There're enough radical generals around, God knows. Besides Frémont and Butler, there's Banks, Howard, Sickles — they'd even settle for Hooker, I think. But the point is, it's going to be war to the knife now. Whatever general's in command, his mission will be to destroy the South, root and branch. So much for restoring the Union."

We stood in silence a few moments, watching the wagons carrying their grisly freight. Then I turned away and started out of the room. I wanted to go lie down, but Mrs. Cullowee halted me.

"Oh, Lieutenant, are you sure you won't join us for a cup of tea? It always makes everything seem a little more bearable, I think." Whatever she had in her cup, it wasn't tea. The liquid in Mrs. Crilly's and Mr. Hungerford's cups was brown; that in Mrs. Cullowee's was clear and colorless.

"I think not, ma'am. I'd like to go to my room for a while."

"Well, you know best." She regarded me brightly from under her copper curls. "It's so reassuring having military men in the house at a time like this, Lieutenant. We poor women feel so helpless and inadequate in the face of adversity, don't we, dear?" she said, suddenly switching her attention to Mrs. Crilly, who nodded dumbly. "We think of you young men as our shield and our buckler, you know," she continued, addressing me again. "I haven't asked you if you will be remaining with us through the coming week."

"As far as I know, I will. At any rate, I'll pay for the full week, whether I stay that long or not."

Her eyes sparkled brilliantly, even though she dismissed my words with a flick of her wrist. "Poo! As though I cared anything about money, at a time like this!" I bowed to her and went up to my room, where I lay on my bed and stared at the ceiling.

Inevitably, the feeling of emergency began to wear off after two or three days. Washington was safe; the Army of the Potomac still stood between Lee and the capital. By the end of the week the War Department was functioning again. The officer who was in charge of transportation for the Department of the South had returned to work, and was able to tell me that I would have a place on the first available transport sailing south — but that weather conditions were so bad off Cape Hatteras that no ships were departing for the next few days.

I learned the outcome of the Republican caucus: a group of senators, including Sumner, Grimes and Fessenden, called at the White House and met with the President. All of the cabinet except Secretary of State Seward were present. The senators urged the removal of Seward from the cabinet, and went so far as to suggest that the President institute a kind of collective leadership, and allow himself to be outvoted by a majority of his cabinet, and, presumably, also by a majority of the Republican Party's senatorial caucus.

The President proceeded with great tact. He agreed to consider the demands of the senators, then quietly arranged to get letters of resignation from both Seward and Secretary of the Treasury Chase, who was a favorite of the radicals in Congress. He then announced to the press that he had asked both Seward and Chase to withdraw their resignations. The implication to the senators was clear — if they wanted to push, they could remove Seward — but it would cost them Chase if they did. They decided the price was too high.

"So we're spared the dictatorship — at least for now," said Ewing to me.

"Maybe it wasn't really so close, after all."

He looked at me pityingly. "You poor fool. Don't you know we're going to pay a high price to free those niggers of yours?"

"Nobody ever said it was going to be cheap," I replied.

One evening I felt restless, and walked to Willard's Hotel for a drink. One glass suggested a second, and the second a third, and it was after eleven o'clock when I started back to the boardinghouse. I stayed on Pennsylvania Avenue, as did most of the other few law-abiding pedestrians who were abroad at that hour. The city was guarded at night by a police force of only fifty officers, who were paid by the federal government, and conceived their duty as limited to the protection of government buildings. They tended to cluster in warm, well-lighted places, leaving the outside shadows to the brawlers and footpads from Swampoodle, English Hill and Marble Alley.

I had covered most of the distance to Mrs. Cullowee's before I had to leave the comparative brightness of Pennsylvania Avenue for the dark side streets. I increased my pace, and looked closely into shadows. For two blocks, the only living thing I saw was a stray mongrel who snarled at me.

Then I heard a cry for help. It came from my left, apparently from the mouth of an alley fifty yards away. There was the fear of death in it, and it turned my body to ice.

It took me a second or two to overcome my paralysis. I sprinted down the side street and into the alley. Very dimly I could see three figures twisted together. Two men were grappling with the third, who was thrashing his arms and legs in an effort to free himself. The third man cried out again, and the other two grunted and swore.

"Help, murder!" I shouted, and threw myself on top of the tangled bodies. One of the attackers turned to meet me, and I saw a glint of metal in his hand. He struck at me with the knife, but the blade passed under my arm. I hit him a jarring blow on the side of the head, and he went down to his knees. He put his hands on the ground to push himself up again, and I stamped on his knife-hand. The hand opened by reflex, and I caught the knife with my toe and sent it flying into the darkness.

A moment later the man was on his feet again, and his powerful arms were wrapped around my chest. He smelled like something dead. I drove my knee into his crotch, thrust my fingers at his eyes, and continued to shout for help at the top of my lungs. One of his hands moved up to my neck, then the other. I pulled my head into my shoulders as he tried for a strangler's grip. I got two fingers into his nostrils, and he jerked his head away. I struck his jaw with the other hand, and suddenly I was free again.

I was aware of more light in the alley. It was coming from the window of a house a few feet from us, and revealed the brutish face of my antagonist, as well as the other two men who were rolling on the muddy ground. A window in the house opened, and a voice called out, "You there! Stop it!" A second later there was the crack of a pistol shot. A man in a nightshirt stood at the window, holding a smoking pistol pointed toward the sky.

My antagonist froze, staring at the lighted window with his mouth agape. Then he shouted, "Crikey! Let's go, Colley!" He spun around and dashed away down the alley, to be followed a moment later by his partner.

Only then did I recognize the victim of their attack. He was struggling to his feet and shaking his head as though he was dazed. It was Captain Chase Cottrell.

"What's happening out there?" called the man in the window. "I can't see a blessed thing!"

"It's all right now, sir. There were two of them, but they skedaddled when you fired your pistol." I stepped directly into the light-spill from the window, so my uniform could be identified. "They attacked this other officer, but I don't think he's injured." I turned to Cottrell. "Are you all right, Captain?"

"I — I think so," he answered shakily. "Yes, I think I am. No broken bones." He came close to me and peered into my face. "Don't I know you?"

"We met at Mrs. Buckles's dinner last week. My name's Hacey Miller."

"That's right. Well, I'm certainly grateful we met again tonight, Miller. I believe those scoundrels were going to cut my throat."

"We can both be grateful to this gentleman. If it wasn't for his pistol, we'd probably be dead." Cottrell and I introduced ourselves to the man in the nightshirt, and shook hands through the open window. We exchanged two or three remarks about the dangers of Washington after dark, but when he invited us into his house, Cottrell refused for both of us, pleading the lateness of the hour as an excuse.

"I've got to have a drink after that. Maybe two," he said, as we walked down the side street toward the lights of Pennsylvania Avenue. "And so do you, Miller. Don't give me any nonsense about going home, damn it. After all, you saved my bloody life, didn't you? So you owe me something!"

We caught a hack on the Avenue, and he directed the driver to take us to Willard's. When we had cleaned the mud off our uniforms, and were seated in the taproom, he with a brandy flip in his hand, and I with a cold toddy, he studied my face carefully. "Now I remember," he said, brushing the lank yellow hair back on his forehead. "You're the one who knows Higginson. You're going down to Carolina to train blacks."

"That's right."

"That's good. That makes you one of the clique." He raised his glass. "Cheers, and confusion to Little Mac." He downed the punch in one gulp, and ordered another.

"You said you were on staff in the Fifth Corps, Captain. Porter's old corps. Does your being in Washington have anything to do with his court-martial?"

"What do you think?" He grinned a slack-lipped grin, and I realized that again he was drunk; even the brawl in the alley couldn't have done much to sober him up. "Certainly it has something to do with the court-martial. I'm a key man."

"Oh? Are you going to testify?"

He saw his second drink coming, and waited for it, then drank half of it before answering. He waggled a finger at me teasingly. "You ask a lot of questions for a lieutenant,

Lieutenant — even one on our side." He giggled. "What a piece of goods she is, damn it! I mean, a man could ride a mount like that all night!"

"Who's that?"

"As if you didn't know, you sly dog! Ah, Miller, I like you. You saved my bloody life. You can tell me — have you ever had her?"

"You're not talking about Mrs. Buckles, are you?" I asked in a chilly tone that was lost on him.

"None other. Our Circe — our Helen of Troy. Mark my words, Miller, I mean to have her, and have her so good she'll never want to wrap her legs around another man's ass!"

I pushed back my chair. "I'm not going to fight you, Captain. But if I stayed here and listened to any more of that, I'd have to. So I'll say good night."

He stared at me with a look of consternation on his foolish face. "But what's the matter? Surely you've been there, haven't you?"

"It's none of your business, but no, I haven't — and as far as I know, neither has anybody else, except her husband, and from his age, I'm not even sure about him. Now, if you'll excuse me —"

He half-rose from his chair and grabbed my arm. "But you can't go, Miller — you saved my bloody life! Here, sit down — have a drink. I take it all back. She's a lovely lady — I respect her. Like my mother! It's the truth. I respect her like my own damn mother!"

I remained standing, resisting his entreaties. "You can't go, Miller," he went on. "We're on the same side. You know what I mean. The court-martial. The blacks. You know. Sit down now. Have a drink. I'll tell you how we're going to do the bastards in." He tugged sharply at my arm. "God damn it, Lieutenant, sit down!"

Partly to avoid a scene, and partly because he had caught my attention with his last offer, I allowed myself to sink back into my chair. He sighed and sat down too. A waiter passed, and Cottrell stopped him to order us two more drinks. When they came, I let mine sit undisturbed.

Cottrell began to talk, but not about the Porter trial, or Republican politics, or the course of the war. He talked about the women in his life. There were quite a number of them, and he remembered them all vividly. I listened for five or ten minutes. When he started repeating details, I stopped him.

"That's not what I stayed here to talk about," I said.

He stared at me blankly, his mind in a limbo halfway between a divan in the parlor of a grand home on 16th Street, and the noisy taproom at Willard's.

"The court-martial. You were going to tell me how we're going to do the bastards in. Remember?"

He squinted his eyes warily. "What bastards?" he asked with drunken cunning.

"Oh, come off it. You know what bastards. Remember me? I'm the man that saved your life. You said you'd tell me all about it."

Comprehension flooded his face. "You saved my bloody life! We're on the same side — going to fix old ramrod Porter and Little Mac besides! Wait till I tell them how Porter said he was going to make sure John Pope lost the battle! Tell them I heard him say so myself! That'll take care of Mister damn-your-eyes Fitz John Porter!"

"Tell who? The court-martial board?"

"Of course! Who do you think?"

167

"You're going to tell them you heard Porter say he was going to make sure Pope lost the battle? When?"

"Twenty-ninth of August. In his tent, five-thirty, six o'clock in the afternoon. Talking to somebody, never found out who. Heard Porter's voice clear as a bell. 'Let John Pope fight his own battle' he said. 'We're not going to move an inch to help him. Let Jackson eat him up. *Then* maybe those fools in Washington will realize they better put Mac back in command!'" He looked at me proudly but anxiously, like a well-trained retriever who has done his job and hopes for his master's approval.

"He really said that? And you heard him say it?"

He grinned. "He *could* have said it. I *could* have heard him." He ordered two more drinks, even though I hadn't touched the one in front of me. "Beautiful!" he whispered hoarsely after the waiter had left. "Proves it was treason — not just incompetence or cowardice. Hangs McClellan right beside Porter, higher than Haman. And every other damn Democrat in the army besides. Clean sweep. *We'll* run things from now on!"

I spoke very carefully. "Beautiful is right. And you say you *could* have heard him say it? I bet you really did hear him say it! Didn't you?"

"Hmmm?"

"I said, I bet you really did hear Porter say that about Pope. I bet you couldn't make up a story like that."

"Who says so? I could make up any kind of story I wanted to."

"I bet somebody helped you make up the story. Didn't they?" I pressed.

He straightened in his chair in offended dignity. "All my own idea. Nobody helped me make it up. Didn't need any help." He glared at me for a moment, then smirked. "I can tell which way the wind is blowing. Holt was as pleased as Punch when I told him."

"You told Judge Advocate General Holt you heard Porter say that? And he believed you?"

"Who cares whether he believes me or not? He wants me to testify."

"And are you?"

"Certainly. Next week. Holt plans to rest the prosecution Tuesday or Wednesday. Going to call me as last witness. Pow! Bastards won't know what hit them. Porter'll be lucky to get off with less than ten years. They might even hang the son of a bitch. Bye-bye, General Porter. Bye-bye, General McClellan. Hello, Captain Chase Cottrell, you child of fortune!"

"I can see you deserve congratulations," I said evenly.

He nodded condescendingly. "Thank you, Miller. Wouldn't have told anybody else in the world, but you saved my bloody life, after all. And we're on the same side. Can see that you've got an eye for the main chance, too. Right?"

"Oh, yes, Captain. I'm sure we're birds of a feather. And as you say, we're on the same side."

A few minutes later we left the taproom. I put him into a hack and hailed another for myself, for I didn't fancy a second walk through the night streets to Mrs. Cullowee's.

XI

———•·•———

Two Kinds of Persuasion

COTTRELL must have awakened the next morning with that gnawing uneasiness all drinking men experience sooner or later: *I'm not sure exactly what I said, but I know I shouldn't have said it.*

He appeared at the boardinghouse just after breakfast, and insisted we both go up to my room. There, he sat down on my bed and wiped a hand across his pasty face. "How are you fixed in the hair-of-the-dog department?" he asked.

"Not a drop," I replied unsympathetically, although as a matter of fact I had a pint bottle of bourbon in my dresser drawer.

"Oh." He realized he was going to have to get through the conversation the hard way, and grimaced. "I have a vague recollection I talked a good deal last night. Carried away by gratitude and feelings of common cause, and all that." He paused, but I didn't say anything. "Lord knows what kind of foolishness I was babbling. I mean, you know, I wouldn't take anything I said too seriously."

"*In vino veritas,*" I said coolly.

"Yes, well I don't know about that. In any case, I seem to

remember juggling a few famous names. Now of course I realize what your position is — I mean a friend of Higginson, going to train the blacks, and all — I know it's foolish for me even to bring it up, isn't it?"

"Isn't what?"

"Isn't it foolish to remind you that what I told you last night was confidential? I mean, of course you know that."

"As I remember, you didn't say so when you told me."

"Oh, didn't I? Well, I should have. Anyway, I don't want to insult you by suggesting that you might betray a confidence."

"I'm not insulted."

"Politics aside, it's something no gentleman would do."

"Politics aside? I thought politics was the reason for the whole thing."

"Well, that's right, of course." Tiny beads of sweat stood out on his brow. "And I know you're a man who can understand the situation. There are important people involved in this, and it could be a disaster for anybody who botched things up. I mean, I'd hate to have a friend of mine get hurt, Miller."

"Thank you." I watched him in silence, wondering how long he could endure my ambiguous remarks. He rose from the bed and walked across the room to the washstand and splashed water on his face, then wiped himself dry. "Jesus, it's a vile day," he said. I didn't answer.

"It's not as if you really *knew* anything, you know. I mean, a little conversation in a saloon. What's that amount to? Not enough to jeopardize a man's career over, certainly. Rumors. Everybody in Washington hears rumors. But nobody repeats them in court. Not if he knows what's good for him."

"I suppose not."

"Particularly since it would be absolutely futile anyway. Any man who makes trouble will be squashed like a bug, without gaining a thing for it."

"It doesn't sound like a very smart idea, does it?"

"Of course not. Absolutely insane, for a fact." He studied my face for a moment. "All right, Miller. I want your word you won't mention anything about our conversation last night to a living soul."

"I'm afraid I can't give you my word on that, Captain."

Fear and anger combined in his expression to make him look nauseated. "What do you think you're going to do?" he asked, almost inaudibly.

"I have no idea. Maybe nothing at all." Abandoning my equivocation, I spoke to him directly. "Look, Cottrell. What you told me last night shocked the hell out of me. I'd be a liar if I said it didn't. But I have absolutely no idea of what, if anything, I can do about it. Or even if I *want* to do anything about it. I mean that. I'm sure what you say is true — that anybody who tries to make trouble will be squashed like a bug, and that it would be futile anyway. I'm not very anxious to be squashed like a bug for something futile, I can tell you."

"If you'd feel better about it, I can order you to keep quiet."

"You don't have the authority, Captain."

"I could get someone to do it who *does* have the authority."

"I'm not sure that would work, either. Listen — I'm not being dramatic, and I'm not trying to threaten anybody. I honestly don't know how I feel about this. I've got a lot of thinking to do. That's all I can say."

"Miller, you'll be making the biggest mistake of your life —"

"And that's all I *will* say. I think that concludes our conversation, Captain."

He glared at me for a second from bloodshot eyes, then he picked up his hat and walked to the door. He turned as if he wanted to say something more, thought better of it, and left, closing the door quietly behind him.

That night at dinner I felt the need of advice. When I tried to talk to Nat Crocker, he was as skittish as a filly flirting with her first stud. He pleaded an engagement, and left the house immediately after dessert. I concluded that, in some supernatural manner, he was receiving vibrations from his tycoons, telling him I was no longer a person to cultivate.

I stopped Ewing on his way to his room. Without preamble, I said, "Let me ask you a hypothetical question."

"Don't tell me. You've got this friend who's picked up a loathsome disease, and it hurts when you piss."

"You're not even warm. Look, let's say a person came into some information that proved that part of the testimony in a certain court-martial was perjured."

Ewing's little eyes glittered from the puffy folds around them. "Might that certain court-martial be the one we've discussed before?" It might, I said. "Whose testimony is it?" he asked eagerly.

"I can't tell you that. Just assume that it's very important — that it would be the single piece of testimony that sends Port — that sends the defendant to prison."

"And your friend can testify that it's perjured?"

"That's right."

"Does your friend know he's shaving himself with a ripsaw? If he goes on the stand to testify, he'll make personal enemies of the meanest and most powerful sons of bitches in Washington. There won't be enough of him left for cat meat."

"He knows that."

"Then what's the question?"

"Who should he take his information to? Is there any way to get the facts out and still avoid appearing in open court?"

One side of his mouth twisted up in a grin. "Your friend isn't actually lusting for martyrdom, I take it."

"Not so as you could notice it."

"That's sensible." His brow creased as he stood in thought for a moment. "All right. There are two things your friend could do. He could try to get to the President, or he could go to the defendant's lawyer. If he got to the President, he'd have a good chance of keeping his own involvement quiet — if he went to the lawyer, he might find himself called on to testify in court."

"Then you think — *he* ought to try to see the President?"

"I didn't say that." He was silent again, his face twisted into a lumpy mask of concentration. Then he spoke swiftly. "No. His chances of seeing the President are too slim. He'd have to go through Montgomery Blair, or possibly old Gideon Welles, but even with their help, he might not be able to get the facts across. Stanton has the President's ear — they play general together at the War Department every day — and has probably already got him convinced that Porter's guilty of treason. So even if your friend did get to Lincoln, I doubt if it would do any good.

"No — his best bet is Porter's lawyer. Tell him to see Reverdy Johnson. Johnson will listen to him and put his testimony to the best use. Maybe he'll make him take the stand, maybe not. But whichever, it will be the best thing for Porter. And for Justice. That's what you care about, isn't it, Miller?"

"Yes, that's what I care about." I said it again, to convince myself. "Yes, that's what I care about. Whatever's best for Justice."

The next day was Sunday — the last Sunday before Christmas. There was a fine, crisp tingle in the air, and I decided to spend my morning walking. As I let myself out the front door, a man was coming toward me, up the porch stairs. The small amount of face that showed between fur cap and muffler was recognizably simian; the caller was Hanslow, who had referred to himself as Secretary of War Stanton's dog robber.

He recognized me at the same moment. "Lieutenant Miller! Well met! I was just coming to see you!" His deep voice was friendly, and he put out his hand to shake mine. Remembering his rudeness at Prudence Buckles's dinner party I hesitated a moment before taking it.

"Good morning, Mr. Hanslow," I said in a neutral tone.

"Ah, you remember me. I'm flattered. Do I deduce correctly that you're about to embark on a constitutional? You are? Then you must allow me to accompany you. Exercise — that's the ticket! None of us Washington paper-shufflers ever gets enough of it. Fill the lungs with fresh air! It keeps the heart strong and the blood clear!"

He walked beside me, chattering inconsequentially, as I directed my steps toward the Potomac. The streets were full of handsome carriages, carrying the ladies and gentlemen of Washington society to church.

I waited for him to run out of small talk, and after we had walked a block he did. "I happened to see Captain Cottrell last evening, and your name came up, Miller."

"I thought it might have."

"After our conversation, I decided to look you up and congratulate you on your good fortune."

"My good fortune?"

"Your double good fortune, actually. It isn't often that a man has the opportunity to help the cause he believes in and further his career at the same time."

"I'm not sure I understand you, Mr. Hanslow."

"Let's be frank, Lieutenant. There's no reason for any misunderstanding between us. You happen to be privy to some information of considerable importance. If that information were to fall into irresponsible hands, the cause we believe in could be harmed. I don't have to tell you how cynically, how unscrupulously, the Copperheads of the Democratic Party would flaunt such knowledge.

"On the other hand, if that information stays where it is now — locked in the brain of a loyal and realistic officer — a truly heroic blow can be struck for the cause of freedom. The defeatists who have led our armies into disaster after disaster can be convicted and turned out — the caste-ridden officer corps can be purged of its treasonous sympathizers with slavery — and the Union can finally move forward to victory." His melodious voice was almost hypnotic.

"You believe all that is riding on this one court-martial?"

"It's very possible. That's why there is such a great opportunity for the aforesaid officer to further his career. Powerful people would be extremely grateful to him. I could almost guarantee him swift promotion and a choice of assignments. And that would just be the beginning."

His eyes studied me shrewdly. When I didn't say anything, he simplified his language. "Miller, we want to get Porter, and through him, we want to get McClellan. We know we can do it if you cooperate. It's your duty, and also it's the best chance to better yourself you'll ever have. Do you understand me?"

"Yes, I understand you." We walked in silence for a few moments. The wind whipped my face, bringing with it the chill promise of snow. "I also understand that the success of your plan depends on perjury."

"How do you know it's perjury? Just because Cottrell didn't actually hear what he says he heard doesn't mean that Porter never said it. On the contrary. Everything we know about the man proves that Porter was disloyal. The letters he wrote to his friend Burnside practically spell it out. He hoped Pope would lose the battle. He wanted McClellan back in command, and was willing to do his part to bring it about. If we could have listened to his private conversations, we would have heard a hundred things more damaging than what Cottrell will testify to."

"But just the same, the one thing that Cottrell *will* testify to, never happened."

"What's the difference, as long as the real truth comes out?"

We walked along beside the river for fifteen or twenty minutes. Hanslow did most of the talking, developing an argument that weaved between my duty as a Republican, the opportunities in store for me if I cooperated, and the dangers in store if I didn't. He managed to suggest a great deal without saying very much that was specific. After a while I stopped giving him my full attention, and in a minute or two he noticed it. "I'd like an answer, Miller," he said sharply.

"I'll give you the same answer I gave Cottrell. I'm not sure what I'm going to do. I don't like slavery, and I don't like perjury. That's all I can say."

"Can? Or will?"

"Can. I'm sorry, Mr. Hanslow. I'd like to be able to tell you more, but I don't see how I can."

We had stopped walking, and he stood in front of me, looking into my face. His lipless mouth stretched in a smile, but his eyes were bright with malice.

"Think things over very carefully, Lieutenant. It wouldn't pay you to make a mistake. It really wouldn't." I didn't reply. "Well, there's no point in talking it to death, is there? I enjoyed our walk. There's nothing like exercise, and that's a fact. Good day, Lieutenant Miller." He touched a finger to his fur cap in a parody of a salute, then turned and walked away down the embankment.

At that moment the first flurries of the promised snow began to swirl around me.

I must have walked for two hours, and when I got back to Mrs. Cullowee's I found I had missed my Sunday dinner. Chilled, hungry, and still unsettled in mind, I went to my room and tried to forget myself in the well-worn pages of Thoreau's *Walden,* the only book I had packed in my portmanteau when I left Hazelwood.

I had read fifty pages or so when there was a knock on my door. It was the landlady, with a note. "Oh, Lieutenant, this was just delivered, and the man's waiting downstairs for an answer. I'm sure it's as important as it can be!" she said, coquettishly awed.

The note, on lavender paper scented with sandalwood, was from Prudence Buckles. "Hacey, it's too cruel of you not to come see me again," it read. "We have so much to talk over. Can you come to supper tonight, *à deux?* Please say you can. The driver will come for you at eight. Yours, Prudence."

Mrs. Cullowee waited for my answer, her head cocked to one side and her mouth a brightly painted little O. I found a pen and ink and wrote the word "Delighted!" below the signature, and refolded the note and handed it back to her, together with a half dollar. "Please give these to the man, if it's not too much trouble, Mrs. Cullowee. And thank you."

"You're more than welcome, I'm sure." She went down the stairs like an aged ingenue in a touring company, tossing her copper curls.

Precisely at eight o'clock the coach arrived in front of the house. The temperature had fallen, and I was grateful for the fur robe on the seat. The streets were almost empty as we drove to Minnesota Row. Occasionally the chiming of church bells rose above the clatter of the horses and the creak of the carriage.

Prudence met me at the door. Her dress was of soft, lustrous black velvet, and her round shoulders were creamy in contrast. She gave me her hand. "It was sweet of you to come, Hacey. I do so want to talk to you."

"I couldn't have kept myself away," I answered.

We had a glass of champagne in the drawing room while we chatted about her family in Boston, and mine in Kentucky. She asked about Ellie. When I had described her, she touched my hand with her fingers. "Oh, Hacey, I can see how much you love her. I'm so happy for you, my dear. I hope I'll have the opportunity to meet her some day." I thought how nice it was of her to feel that way, and felt guilty over the tingle her touch caused.

The supper was excellent — cherrystone clams, pheasant, a salad, and Stilton cheese, with a heady Beaujolais and an authoritative Port. We didn't talk much at the table; she ate with as good appetite as I did. But her dark eyes sparkled at me in the candlelight.

We took our coffee in the library. She sat on a wide couch in front of the fireplace, with her little feet tucked under her, smiling into the crackling flames. I walked around the book-lined walls, peering at the gleaming leather bindings in the semi-darkness.

"This was my husband's favorite room. He loved it here," she said quietly.

"I can understand that."

"Often I spend my evenings here. It makes him seem closer, somehow — makes me feel a little less lonely." She smiled at me. "Does that sound foolish?"

"Not at all. You must have felt a terrible sense of loss."

"During the first few weeks, I wondered if I would survive it." She patted the cushion beside her. "Here, sit down, Hacey. Let me tell you about my husband. He was a man you would have liked."

I sat beside her on the couch and put my coffee cup on the little end table. We looked into the flames together for a moment. "You must have heard that Congressman Buckles was a good deal older than I," she said. "It's true — he was almost old enough to be my father. And yet — how utterly unimportant that was! How trivial — how meaningless — compared with the really valuable things!"

"You mean — his work?"

"Oh, Hacey, he was a believer, like you are! He believed in freedom — and he knew that no price was too high to pay for it! Every day when he went down to the House of Representatives, it was like a knight of old embarking on a Crusade. He was fearless. After Charles Sumner was attacked by Preston Brooks in the Senate, he used to say, 'If they want to stop me, they'll have to club me down like they did Charles.' And he meant every word of it."

"He sounds like a wonderful man."

"Oh, if you could only have known him. He was *your* kind of man — the kind of man who follows his ideal wherever it may lead him. That's the only kind of man I could ever love, you know." She sat in silence, and the flames cast dancing shadows across her face. I thought I saw a tiny gleam of moisture in her eye.

"Don't talk about it anymore if it upsets you, Prue," I said awkwardly.

"No, I want to talk about it, Hacey. I want you to understand. You see, I've often remembered the evenings you and I spent together in Boston — probably more often than I should have." She paused and glanced down modestly, then went on. "I've been so proud of the way you worked in the antislavery movement all these years, at that little college in the mountains. It meant we were really still together, in a way, even though we were many miles apart.

"And now that my husband's work is so close to completion — now that we are so near to driving out the traitors and cowards and Copperheads from our army, I wanted you to know how he felt about things, Hacey." She turned to face me, and her body moved a little toward me. "And how *I* feel," she added softly. "Most of all, how *I* feel."

She closed her eyes and tilted her face upward. The firelight swam across her smooth cheek. Her lips were slightly parted. I was driven as inexorably toward her as a man falling downstairs is driven toward the ground. I hung back for one agonizing, pounding second, and then kissed her. Her lips were sweet as honey, and then, so was her tongue.

"Oh, Hacey," she whispered as she curled up in my arms, "we shouldn't — but I want you so much." Her softly rounded body pressed against mine, her velvet thigh between my legs and her full breasts against my chest. The smell of her was sandalwood with a wild hint of female musk concealed in it. Her eyes were half closed, and as her lips clung to mine, she gave a moan deep in her throat.

And even as I returned her kiss, my mind flashed back to another woman's body I had held in my arms, in a sun-filled bedroom, with a cow lowing in the field outside. I remembered the drum-tight smoothness of my wife's belly under my hand as I felt the stirring of my son within — the small hardness of her nipples as she pressed my face against her milk-swollen breasts.

"Ellie!" my mind's voice called, and Prudence must have sensed the intrusion of another woman's presence, for she pulled her head away and opened her eyes wide to look into mine. "Hacey?" she breathed questioningly.

I shifted my body back into a sitting position, regardless of the throbbing blood that pounded in my veins. "Forgive me, Prudence," I said hoarsely.

She smiled, and her eyelids drooped languidly over her bright eyes. She leaned toward me again.

I moved away from her and grabbed my coffee cup from the end table. The coffee was as cold as virtuous memories. "Prudence, I always said you were the prettiest girl I ever knew. Anybody that pretty has a responsibility not to turn men's heads," I said banteringly.

She searched my face for a moment, and then the slightest smile flitted across her lips. She smoothed her dress down over her bosom as she arched her back, and two inches more of rosy-white skin appeared over her bodice. "I'll try to bear that in mind from now on," she said.

My emotions were seething, and I felt so uncomfortable all I could think of was getting away. Prudence pressed me to join her in a brandy, but I pleaded an early appointment the next day. In a few minutes we were standing together in the hall, waiting for her driver to bring her carriage to the door.

"Hacey, I meant what I said about my husband's work. I believe the most important thing any man could do for his country today would be to help clean the army of traitors." She put her hand on my arm. "I know you'll do what's right — just as you always have."

"I hope I will." I covered her hand with my own. "Good night, pretty lady. It was an evening I'll remember."

The sound of the carriage came from outside. "Give my regards to your wife," said Prudence as she opened the door. "Good night, Hacey Miller — you irritating man."

XII

RESOLUTION

WELL BEFORE EIGHT O'CLOCK the next morning I was waiting outside the front door of the building on Fourteenth Street where the Fitz John Porter court-martial was being held.

Every so often, through gaps in the surging current of army wagons, carriages, hacks, horsemen and pedestrians that thrust along the street, I could see the two men who lounged against a low stone fence across the way. They had taken up their position a minute or two after I had arrived, the tall one with the mustache pulling a folded newspaper from his hip pocket and opening it wide, the heavyset one squatting down with his back against the wall and starting to peel an apple with a jackknife. Neither showed any apparent interest in me.

Just at eight the principals of the court-martial began to arrive. I recognized some of the officers of the court by descriptions I had heard from Ewing and Nat Crocker. First came a burly brigadier general with a full black beard, an aquiline nose and an imperious eye — James A. Garfield of Ohio, who had first attracted attention with a small campaign in the Big Sandy country of eastern Kentucky, then had served with distinction at Shiloh. As commanding a figure as he was, there was something of the politician about the way he smiled at his aide, and I remembered he had been a radical Republican in Columbus before the war.

Two more brigadiers arrived together in a coach — I identified them as Generals Ricketts and King, both of whom had much to answer for in their behavior at Second Bull Run. Then, by himself, General Prentiss arrived, still with the marks of his confinement at Libby Prison written on his drawn face.

Next to appear was the President of the Court-Martial, Major General David Hunter. He was either wearing a wig or his hair was dyed — it was jet black, although the deeply lined face beneath it was that of an old man. He walked with a stoop, and there were angry grooves around his downturned mouth. This was Lincoln's friend, the first to try to recruit blacks into the Union army, who had raised such a storm of protest by his highhanded methods that the President had been forced to repudiate him. Hunter, together with Banks, Butler, and Carl Schurz, represented the extreme radical position among the many political generals in the army. Alone of the four, he was presently unassigned in any military capacity.

Looking into his embittered face, I felt that, regardless of the charges against me, I would hate to be judged by him.

Hunter had no sooner entered the building than another carriage drew up, and two men stepped from it to the sidewalk, one an officer, the other a civilian. I felt a tingle of excitement run through my body as I recognized them from their descriptions. The officer was one of the finest looking men I have ever seen. He was dressed in the uniform of a major general, complete with gold-handled ceremonial saber and ostrich-plumed hat. It became him handsomely. He was of slightly above middle height, slender and athletic of figure, in his early forties, but carrying himself as if he were

ten years younger. He had a full beard and mustache, a pro-
file as cleanly chiseled as a cameo, and snapping eyes. Un-
questionably, he was Fitz John Porter.

The man with him was, in many ways, even more striking.
Since the death of Daniel Webster, Reverdy Johnson had
come to be considered the outstanding lawyer in the United
States. He had appeared against Stanton and Lincoln in the
famous McCormick reaper case, and had won the Dred Scott
case, *Scott* vs. *Sanford,* for his client, against the eloquence
of the ex-slave's attorney, Montgomery Blair. A staunch
War Democrat, he had been elected senator from Maryland
in the fall of 1862, but had yet to take his seat.

He was a massive man, not especially tall, but heroically
proportioned, as though each major part of him had been
oversized to begin with, but the connecting sections were
merely normal. His shoulders were wide, his chest deep, and
his head huge. Under his white, short-cropped hair his skull
swelled upwards in a dome, and sideways and backwards like
a barrel, as if it were full to bursting. He was clean-shaven,
and carried his head slightly cocked to one side, to compen-
sate for the blindness of his left eye.

The two men crossed the sidewalk toward where I was
standing. Johnson was talking in a low voice, and General
Porter listened intently. As they started around me, I
stepped forward to block their way.

"Pardon me, General Porter, Senator Johnson — I must
speak to you. It's a matter of the utmost importance."

They both stopped and stared at me, Johnson quizzical,
Porter forbidding. Porter spoke first. "You must forgive us,
Lieutenant, but we have a matter of some priority inside,"
he said coldly.

"Please, General — believe me when I say I wouldn't
dream of bothering you unless it was about your own trial."

186

"Excuse me, Fitz," said Johnson, in a deep, pleasant voice. "Lieutenant, as General Porter's lawyer, it's my job to act as a sort of gatekeeper, to make sure nobody bothers the General without he has a mighty good reason. You can understand that. So if you have something to tell us, you just come around to my law office this afternoon, sometime after three o'clock —"

"Senator, I don't know if I'll be alive at three o'clock this afternoon."

Porter puckered his mouth in distaste at such melodrama, but Johnson raised his eyebrows in interest. "Well, I declare. What reason would you have for wondering about a thing like that?"

"Those two men on the other side of the street. They've been covering me ever since I started waiting for you here."

"And what makes you think they mean you any harm, Lieutenant?"

"It's because of the information I have — what I want to tell you about. The perjured testimony that's going to be introduced in the court-martial this week."

"Perjured testimony?" Johnson's head cocked sharply to one side, and his good eye narrowed penetratingly. Porter straightened his back, and the look of annoyance on his face deepened into disgust. "Fitz, why don't you go on into the courtroom? I'll see what's biting this young man and join you directly," Johnson said, in his soft Tidewater drawl. Porter nodded curtly, as if glad to get away from something as degrading as perjury, and went into the building.

The big lawyer put a hand on my arm. "Now what is all this, boy?"

I quickly told him the essentials of what I knew — Cottrell's story of overhearing Porter's remarks on August 29, his subsequent panicky visit to Mrs. Cullowee's, then Hanslow's call, with his promises and threats, and finally an edited version of Mrs. Congressman Buckles's entrance into the affair. Johnson watched me expressionlessly as I finished my story. Then he said, "A bounteously endowed woman — and one with an affectionate disposition, I would expect." His eye was as steady and unblinking as an old turtle's.

"No doubt, Senator Johnson."

"Hmmm." He rubbed his chin reflectively. "Well, if what you say about those two men across the street is true, I'd just as soon not have you walking the streets until I get your John Hancock on an affidavit. Tell you what: the trial is due to start any minute — you come in with me, and get a seat in the visitors' section. Stay until we adjourn. Then I'll take you back to my office, and we'll dictate your whole story, and you can sign it."

"Will I be allowed in court?"

He smiled ironically. "Oh, Lordy, this is a public court-martial. Visitors are welcome — it's just that not very many people in Washington are anxious to take an undue interest in these proceedings. Somehow they have the idea it wouldn't do their careers much good."

"I see."

"As a matter of fact, what you're doing doesn't promise to do your career much good either, Lieutenant. But you must know that."

"Yes, sir, I know that."

He looked at me shrewdly for a second. "I guess you do. Well, let's go on in."

Inside the courtroom he went to join General Porter at the defense table, and I found a seat in the spectators' section. It was almost empty, and the six or eight other onlookers were all civilians.

In a minute or two the nine generals who constituted the

board entered the room and took their seats. There were two major generals and seven brigadiers — enough gold leaf, I thought, to gild a dozen picture frames. The long table behind which they sat faced two other smaller tables — one occupied by Porter and Johnson, the other by the Judge Advocate General, Joseph Holt.

Holt was a small man with a smooth-shaven face, cold pale eyes, and a cruel mouth. He was a Kentuckian, but, when he began to talk, there was very little of the mellow warmth of the Bluegrass in his speech. As he called his first witness of the day, he seemed as impatient as a hound waiting for the hunt to begin.

The first witness was Lieutenant Colonel Thomas Smith, who had been aide-de-camp to General Pope at Second Bull Run. At Holt's prompting, he told of meeting Porter on the day before the battle, and of conversing with him for ten minutes about some ammunition, which had apparently been transported to Alexandria. Smith quoted Porter as saying, "That's where we're all going anyway." Since Alexandria is just outside Washington, the implication was that Porter expected the Union army to retreat back to the capital.

"How did General Porter deliver himself of these sentiments?" Holt asked.

Reverdy Johnson's objection was overruled, and Smith answered, "In a *sneering* manner, and it appeared to me to express a great indifference."

"You felt it indicated a lack of enthusiasm for the coming battle?" Holt pressed.

"That's right — and I reported as much to General Pope."

"Will you tell the court about that?"

"When I returned, I said to General Pope, 'General, Porter will fail you.' 'Fail me? What do you mean? What did he say?' Said I, 'It is not so much what he said, though he said enough; he is going to fail you, that's all.' Said General Pope, 'How can he fail me? He will fight where I put him!' General Pope said this in an impetuous and possibly overbearing manner. I replied in the same way, saying I was certain Fitz John Porter was a traitor, and that I would shoot him that night if the law would allow me to do it!"

Of course Johnson was on his feet objecting to this immediately, but General Hunter overruled him again, and Holt continued his questioning.

"Colonel Smith, had you entertained feelings of prejudice against General Porter before this time?"

"No, sir; my presuppositions of him were favorable."

"Then how do you explain your sudden change of heart?"

"I had one of those clear convictions that a man has a few times in his life as to the character and purposes of another, when he sees him for the first time."

I waited in vain for the court to order this preposterous testimony stricken from the record. Instead, Holt led his witness into even more imaginative flight. "Without ever having seen the defendant before, how were you able to be sure that what you took for treasonable sentiments was not merely General Porter's usual manner of expressing himself?"

Smith uncrossed his legs and recrossed them the other way. He answered, with a look of deep sincerity on his rodentlike face, "His expression, combined with his look and manner, seemed to me like those of a man with a crime on his mind."

"If the witness intends to testify as a mind reader," Reverdy Johnson interposed, "perhaps we should be informed of his credentials."

General Hunter frowned at the defense counsel. "Senator

Johnson, if I were you, I would consider whether the use of levity in this courtroom is in the best interests of your client. Colonel Holt, you may continue your examination of the witness." Johnson sat down, and Holt resumed his questions.

Smith was on the stand for most of the morning. On cross-examination, Johnson tried to shake his evidence with sarcasm, but was unable to hack his way through the thicket of objections that Holt proposed and Hunter sustained. Porter sat stiffly at the table, rigid with outrage, but Johnson somehow preserved his temper through it all. I don't know how he did it.

The clairvoyant Colonel Smith finally was excused, to be succeeded by General Samuel Heintzelman, who appeared to be a fair-minded man. His testimony mainly concerned the condition of the roads around Manassas at the time of the battle, and it seemed unremarkable to me. I found my mind wandering — first to the two men across the street, then to Prudence, curled up on the couch in the library, then — in guilty haste, as if to make amends for the sudden excitement that memory evoked — to Ellie and little Boone at Hazelwood. Then my thoughts broadened, and I was once again in the old familiar debate with myself over the Means and the End.

In eastern Kentucky the children of the mountain folk believe in hoop snakes. These fearful reptiles are thought to form themselves into hoops by taking their tails in their mouths, after which they roll down the hills, attaining such meteoric speeds that no unwary youngster has a chance of escaping them. The only difference between a hoop snake going downhill and me debating Means and Ends with myself is that the hoop snake is getting somewhere.

I was pulled back to reality as the spectators around me

rose to their feet, and the court-martial board began to file from the room. Tardily I scrambled out of my chair, realizing with chagrin that all the formalities of adjournment had been completed while I engaged myself in futile argument.

Porter and Johnson exchanged a few words, and Porter put on his ostrich-plumed hat and left. Johnson waved me over. "Well, how did you enjoy the raree show, Lieutenant?" he asked with a half-smile.

"That Colonel Smith — I couldn't believe they'd let him say the things he said in a court of law!"

"Yes, he's a bird, all right. Of course, this isn't exactly what *I'd* call a court of law . . ." He let his voice trail off, so the silence made his comment for him. He picked up his pencils and the few sheets of paper his notes were scribbled on, and stuffed them untidily into his pockets. "Well, lets us get away from this bloodstained arena. We'll go to my office and restore the inner man."

The two men across the street were still leaning against the low stone wall. Johnson studied them with his good eye. "The only way those faces will ever look presentable is when there's a rope around the necks under them," he said. We walked down the street for half a block before we were able to signal a hack. Through the confusion of traffic, I wasn't able to tell whether the two men followed us or not.

At his office the senator poured us each a stout peg of bourbon, and then turned me over to one of his clerks. "I want you to get that affidavit done as soon as possible, Lieutenant. We'll have time for a chat afterward." I dictated a reasonably complete reconstruction of my conversation with Cottrell, and swore to its veracity. The clerk went off to make a fair copy for my signature, and I accepted Johnson's offer of another drink.

I asked him how he planned to use my statement. "Well, I'll tell you," he replied, leaning back in his chair with one large foot on his desk. "Tomorrow morning, before court begins, I'll show Holt your little billet-doux, and tell him that if he puts Captain Cottrell on the stand, I'm prepared to call you to swear to the truth of the facts contained herein. And even if the War Department might order you out of Washington immediately — 'for the good of the service' — which has happened to more than one defense witness in this trial, by the way — I still have your affidavit, which I shall introduce into the record.

"Unless I'm very much mistaken, Holt will decide not to put his thumb into that particular pie. I wouldn't, if I were in his shoes."

"Then he won't call Cottrell, and I won't have to testify at all. You won't even have to use my affidavit," I said hopefully.

"I'd guess not. But don't get any foolish idea that your friends in the War Department are going to forgive and forget, just because you don't have to testify. Edwin Stanton isn't famous for his forgiving nature."

"Senator Johnson, how much help to General Porter do you think it will be, keeping Cottrell's testimony out of court?"

"Some. I don't think they can convict Fitz of treason now. Probably they couldn't have anyway, but now it's surer. As far as the lesser charges go, I don't reckon it changes much."

"What would you say the odds were for conviction on at least some of the charges?"

He grimaced and took a swallow of whiskey. "Boy, I've made a career out of not predicting the outcome of court cases. If I could foresee the results of my own actions, do you think I would have fathered fifteen children?"

"No, honestly, Senator. What do you think?" I insisted.

"Oh, well," he sighed. "I'd guess we'll win, knock wood. There are too many holes in their case — too many of their witnesses are like that peerless prophet, Colonel Smith. They lack all credibility. But on the other hand, I've never played with such a stacked deck in my life."

"It must be mighty discouraging, going up against that kind of thing every day."

"Oh, a man gets used to it." He dismissed the subject with a gesture. "But tell me about yourself, Lieutenant. Hearing you talk, I'd guess you were a Kentuckian." I told him I came from just outside Lexington. "I imagine you're a War Democrat, then."

"No, sir, I'm a Republican. I campaigned for Lincoln in the election." This surprised him, and under his prodding I told him a fair amount about where I was in my life, and how I had got there, and where I hoped to go. He was particularly interested that I was joining Wentworth Higginson in South Carolina.

"So you're going down there to help him enlist darkies, are you?" He fixed me with his right eye, which was pale and luminously blue. "You know you are going to be laboring in the tactical center of the radical Republican vineyard? Training black soldiers is just about the dearest wish in Stanton's generous heart. Do you believe in it too?"

"Yes sir — I'm pretty sure I do."

"And training black Union soldiers is one side of the coin. Turn it over and the other side is disfranchising white Confederate soldiers. Put them together, and what you buy is a Republican dictatorship of the South. Do you want to see that?"

"I think the slaves have a right to help fight for their own freedom."

He was silent for a moment, studying me. Then he said, "I must admit I'm puzzled. Feeling the way you do, what in the name of Henry Ward Beecher caused you to come to General Porter's assistance the way you did?"

"The evidence was perjured."

"The evidence was perjured," he repeated musingly. "Glory hallelujah — have I finally met an honest man? It's enough to cast doubts on the experience of a lifetime!"

We both drank our bourbon. In a minute or two the clerk came in with my affidavit ready for signing. I read it over, then scrawled my signature on the bottom, and Johnson and the clerk added their names as witnesses. Then I rose to leave. Reverdy Johnson also rose, and reached out a huge hand to shake mine.

"I'll say goodbye now, Lieutenant, because I have a hunch you'll be leaving Washington before I have another chance to see you."

"I've been waiting three weeks for transportation, Senator," I said wryly.

"Nevertheless, I venture you're on the very brink of a precipitate departure. Thank you for coming to us, both for General Porter's sake, and my own." His hand was as strong and hard as a farmer's. "Godspeed, Lieutenant Miller."

"Goodbye, Senator. Tell General Porter I hope he wins."

I left the office. Outside, there was no sign of the two men who had followed me earlier.

Reverdy Johnson scored very high as a prophet. One out of two of his predictions came true.

I returned to Mrs. Cullowee's about five-thirty, and went to my room to await dinner. A few minutes later Nat

Crocker knocked at my door. When he came in, I saw he was carrying a sheaf of papers, and also that he looked near tears.

"Hacey, these are your orders. They came in this afternoon. You're to leave by transport at eleven tomorrow morning."

A slight chill went up my spine, but I also felt a wave of relief at the prospect of leaving Washington. "Why, that's splendid news, Nat! I'm delighted! But I didn't know there were any ships sailing."

"There's one, anyway," he said glumly.

"Why, what's the matter, Nat? Why the long face? I'm tickled to death to be leaving!"

Nat's expression became even more doleful. "Well, I'm not," he said.

"You're not tickled I'm leaving?"

"No — I'm not tickled *I'm* leaving!"

"You're leaving?" I could hardly believe my ears. "Why would you be leaving? You've got your work at the War Department!"

"Don't ask me, Lieutenant Miller — ask your tycoons," he said with a brave attempt at dignity. "Apparently you set certain forces in motion. I want to congratulate you on your influence."

"But why you, Nat? There are reasons why some people might want *me* out of town, but why you?"

Nat began counting on his fingers. "Alpha, because I brought you home to my lodgings with me, and offered you the hand of friendship in a strange city. Beta—" He paused on the second finger, then said helplessly, "I can't think of anything but alpha."

The next day Nat Crocker and I embarked for Beaufort,

South Carolina, and the day after that, Christmas Eve, Reverdy Johnson began to call witnesses for the defense. Captain Cottrell was never called to give his perjured testimony for the prosecution.

Reverdy Johnson's prediction about the outcome of the trial miscarried. Fitz John Porter was found guilty of four of the six charges against him. He was ordered cashiered from the army, and forever disqualified from holding any office of trust under the government of the United States.

Many months later I received a letter from General Porter. It had followed me from one post to another.

26 December 1863

Dear Lieutenant Miller,

Senator Johnson has informed me of your efforts in my behalf. I cannot begin to tell you how grateful I am. I know that what you did cannot have been easy for you. No doubt its effects will follow you throughout your military career.

When I met you, I fear my own feeling of persecution, combined with the informality of your approach, created in me a stiffness and reserve that may have seemed to one not well acquainted with me, to indicate hostility. If such was the case, I apologize most sincerely.

As you were generous enough to believe, I can declare that I have never done anything my country has reason to regret. God willing, the day will come when all my fellow citizens will admit the truth of that statement. Until then, I am

Your thankful debtor,
Fitz John Porter,
Major General

66 Union Place,
New York, N.Y.

197

XIII

———•◦•———

BEAUFORT

THE MONITOR, victor in the most important sea battle of modern times, sank like a stone off Cape Hatteras that week, drowning sixteen men. At about the same time, and not too many miles away, I was wishing for a similar fate.

I had never been to sea before, and Hatteras in winter is not the place to begin one's nautical education. I didn't eat for seventy-two hours, and the only taste in my mouth was my own bile. All passengers were confined to their quarters below decks, where hammocks were slung so close together that when a man descended to the deck to vomit into a bucket, it was almost impossible for him to struggle back through the wall of bodies into his berth again. The lamps burned kerosene, smoked, and stank foully. Hour after hour my ears were filled with the moans of the passengers, the uncontrollable retching of some sufferer at the bucket below me, the booming of the water on the hull a few feet away, and the hair-raising screech of protesting metal. There was no way to tell night from day, and there seemed no end to the misery.

Nat Crocker had been raised close to the sea, and had sailed since he was a boy, but that didn't prevent him from sharing the universal seasickness. Indeed, I believe Neptune himself would have spewed up his belly after one sniff of the air below decks. But at least the experience wasn't unprecedented for Nat; he knew that, unlikely as it seemed, we might expect to emerge from this vale of vomit relatively unscathed. He tried to infuse me with his own cautious optimism, and I believe it helped me a bit.

Finally we could tell the seas were subsiding, and then the hatches were opened to admit pale cold light and glorious fresh air. One by one we staggered up the ladder to the main deck, to hang on the rail and stare at the mountainous piles of sullen gray water that swept up as high as our crow's-nest, then suddenly fell away and became wet valleys beneath us. Salt spray stung our faces, sharp wind whipped our hair and our clothes, and, tentatively at first, we began to address one another in conversational shouts.

"Nothing like a sea voyage, eh, Nat?" I bellowed, with a fair part of my normal vigor. "Why didn't you tell me it was so refreshing?"

"I wanted it to come as a pleasant surprise," Nat shouted back. "I thought you deserved it!"

It was just before the first of the year when we arrived at Headquarters, First South Carolina Volunteers, Colonel Thomas Wentworth Higginson commanding. The regiment, seven hundred strong, was encamped around a ruined mansion; some of the tents were pitched underneath great live oaks, from which soft gray swathes of moss hung down, half shielding them from sight; the remainder were set out on the sand beach a few feet lower, surrounded by a waist-high jungle of palmetto. The soldiers we saw were in Zouave uniform, with baggy bright red trousers and white gaiters, which, combined with their glossy black skins and flashing eyes and teeth, gave them a startling and barbaric appearance. Upon inquiry, one of them directed us to Regimental H.Q. "Colonel Higgie, him live in two tent together, up'm the bluff," he told me in the almost indecipherable accent of the Sea Islands of Georgia and South Carolina, which I later heard referred to as "Gullah."

It had been ten years since I had seen Wentworth Higginson, but aside from the graying of his hair, he didn't seem to have aged at all. He greeted Nat and me with the same warmth and boyish ardor I remembered. His slender, high-shouldered body moved with brisk grace, and the sensitive features of his long face communicated an expression of permanent half-amusement. It was as hard as ever to realize that this man was Boston's most reckless antislavery crusader, who had tried to free the fugitive slave, Anthony Burns, from Boston jail at pistol point, who had led armed settlers from Massachusetts to Kansas during the border wars, and who had conspired to kidnap the governor of Virginia as a hostage against John Brown's execution.

Nat Crocker stared at him with the worshipful gaze he reserved for tycoons. Wentworth put him at his ease immediately, and then turned to me. "Hacey Miller! Bless my tarnished buttons but I'm glad to see you! This sea air will turn your brass green in twenty-four hours. I expected to see ennobling lines of pain and wisdom on your stern warrior's visage, but you look like the beardless innocent I last saw a decade ago! How do you explain that? Don't bother — come sit down, both of you, and have a glass of our official regimental beverage, known hereabouts as 'Fust Souf Cahlina Flip,' or 'Fust Souf' for short." He waved to a hugely grinning orderly, who poured us each a glassful of unwholesome-looking liquid from an earthenware pitcher. "Drink up, bretheren," Wentworth cried, "and defy the foul fiend!"

The Negro handed me a glass and I took a swallow. It was horrible. I shuddered. "What *is* this?" I managed to ask after a few moments of desperate swallowing.

"Molasses-water, with fresh ginger and vinegar." He smiled proudly. "The men love it, and it's totally nonalcoholic. Isn't it good?"

I replied truthfully that I had never tasted anything like it, and Nat echoed me fervently. Higginson clapped his hands in delight. "We had ten barrels of it for Christmas, along with ten roast oxen! What a feast! You would have had to see it to believe it! Gentlemen, these troops are affectionate, enthusiastic, grotesque, and dramatic beyond any other peoples of the world! Serving with them is a nineteenth-century *Thousand and One Nights,* told by a dusky Scheherazade with a fantastic imagination! It's worth a week's pay to walk around the camp at night and stop beside their campfires and listen to their songs and stories. Every one of them is a natural entertainer, and their sense of rhythm is beyond belief!"

He went on in this rapturous way a good while longer. I found myself becoming doubtful as I listened to his panegyric. After all, I had been raised among slaves, and was no stranger to their ways. Wentworth's enthusiasm began to sound like the first flush of puppy love, rather than the abiding affection of maturity. I would have expected the blacks to clown and sing splendidly for their uncritical New England officers — but how did they behave in the face of the enemy? I managed to interrupt Wentworth long enough to ask the question, and he became suddenly serious.

"Hacey, last month I led the regiment on a short expedition up the Saint Mary's River. We've been suffering from a shortage of lumber and brick here at Beaufort, and we heard there were supplies of both available for the taking a few

miles inland in Florida. We embarked three steamboats and
450 officers and men.

"This was to be the regiment's first taste of action, so we
viewed it with a good deal of concern. We knew they were as
good or better than any white troops in the army on the drill
field, but this proved nothing about their fighting qualities,
since automatic obedience and docility are considerably
more valuable on the parade ground than on the battlefield.
We didn't know what to expect, and every officer in the regiment spent a sleepless night or two, I can tell you."

He took a long swallow of his Fust Souf and smiled with
satisfaction. "Ahhh! Well, we needn't have worried about
them. They behaved magnificently. Our first engagement
took place at night, in a pine grove about two miles from the
river. We were surrounded by Confederate cavalry, and it
was so dark under the trees the men couldn't see what they
were shooting at. Our attackers were ghostly — pale gray
shapes on horseback that appeared and disappeared like
phantoms between the trunks, as they rode around our little
stand of trees. That's frightening enough for a starter — but
no sooner had the firing begun than a soldier fell right beside
me, and the rumor immediately spread through the whole
regiment that 'Cunnel Higgie, he dead.' It must have
seemed to them they were in the last extremity — leader-
less, trapped in a midnight forest in the heart of the Confederacy, surrounded by spectral horsemen sworn to take no
Negro prisoners — and yet not a man faltered, not a single
one that didn't load and fire with the coolness of a British
Grenadier!"

He paused and took another swallow from his glass. "Remarkable — the men apparently have no more desire for
ardent spirits at all! Apparently molasses-water suits them
as nectar suits the gods — they tell me they've even forgot-

ten the taste of whiskey! I wouldn't have thought it possible, if I hadn't heard it with my own ears!"

"Colonel," I suggested tactfully, "about the Saint Mary's expedition — were you able to extricate the regiment without undue losses?"

"The Rebel cavalry retired after a half hour or so — we later found we had killed their commanding officer, and it took the heart out of them. We pulled back to the boats, and for the next few days we loaded bricks and lumber. There was no more trouble until we started downstream with our cargo. Then we found Confederate troops on every bluff along the river. We had to run the gauntlet, and were under heavy fire for most of the day. The captain of the flagship was killed, and things took on a decidedly gloomy aspect. Once again, it was a situation to try the fortitude of battle-hardened veterans, and once again our raw recruits showed their mettle. They accepted the enemy fire stoically, returning it as best they could, and only complained that I wouldn't pull into shore and let them attack the 'Sesesh' on dry land.

"Oh, I'm proud of them, gentlemen — and so would you have been. Give them another month's training in the field, and I wouldn't hesitate to lead them against Stonewall Jackson himself!"

He was a true enthusiast, and the First South Carolina Volunteers was his hobbyhorse. He told us story after story illustrating the picturesqueness and devotion of his blacks, and it was a half hour before we could take our leave, and return to the tent we were sharing.

Nat Crocker looked thoughtful as he unpacked his portmanteau. "Well, Nat, what's the verdict? What do you think of the Colonel?" I asked him.

He raised his fingers as if to enumerate a number of Higginson's characteristics, then realized the gesture was super-fluous. "He's a tycoon, Hacey," he said simply. "And all tycoons are crazy."

During the next two or three days I became acquainted with the officers and many of the noncoms of the regiment. As exotic as the whole experience of living with the First South Carolina Volunteers was, I felt constrained; something was holding me back from making the mental commitment a good officer must make to his men. Higginson noticed it, and asked me to come to his tent for a private conversation.

"Something's bothering you, Hacey," he said abruptly. "Maybe I can guess what it is. It's the question of you as a Southern white — a Southron, as Lee's men like to call themselves — leading black troops against other Southern whites. Isn't that it?"

"I expect it is, Colonel."

"Yes, I guess that would be a wide river to cross. I can't advise you on what you should do — but I can tell you how important I think the black troops are in this war, and how important they will be to the future of the country."

He rose from his camp chair and began to pace the floor of the tent, his lean athlete's body as erect and lithe as it had been in Cambridge. "When we began to enlist blacks in the Union army, we crossed the Rubicon. Before, it was possible to believe the war was about secession, and that we'd either end with two countries or one, and that in either case we'd shake hands, and fight by the rules, and accept the outcome philosophically, as Anglo-Saxon gentlemen should do.

"But once we armed the first black soldier, the war wasn't about secession anymore. It was about slavery, and nothing but slavery. You see, we had broken the rules, put the rifle and the torch into Nat Turner's hands, turned the slave against the master to burn his house, shoot his son, rape his daughter. That's what the Southerner thought, and he could never forgive us now. It would be war to the knife, and its legacy would be a century of hatred."

(Who had I recently heard use that same expression, *war to the knife?* Of course — Ewing, the journalist, telling me about the results of the Battle of Fredericksburg. What else had he said? "Whatever general's in command, his mission will be to destroy the South, root and branch.")

"Then why do we do it?" asked Wentworth. "Why do we sow the wind with black infantrymen, knowing that our children and our children's children will reap the whirlwind we created?"

"That's what I'm asking you, Colonel," I said softly.

"For the extra troops? Of course not — we outnumber the Confederacy three to one already. There aren't enough Negroes in the North, or in the parts of the South we control, to influence the outcome of the war materially. From a purely military point of view, the blacks are superfluous.

"Did we do it for the effect on the South's morale?" he continued rhetorically. "If so, then we're the stupidest blunderers in history, for the result of our action has been to strengthen the will of the whole Confederacy, and make any easy solution of the conflict impossible.

"No, there's only one reason why we did it — *because we had no moral choice in the matter!* If the Negro is to be free, he must deserve his freedom, and to show that he deserves it, he must be allowed to fight for it. Unless Garrison and Phillips and John Brown and all of us were liars or worse, the freed slaves must be able to stand as tall as the white man, and struggle as bravely against his enslavement."

My mouth was dry as I asked, "And must we lead him against other white men while he does this?"

205

"Certainly! Not because he prefers white officers, but because he has to take what he can get! We've denied him the opportunity to produce officers of his own kind — now that he's ready and willing to fight, it's up to us to fill the need. Don't worry — the time will come when he will create his own generals. But until then, we must fill the gap."

I sat silent for a moment, staring at my hands. Then I said, "Isn't it asking a lot of a man, to go against the loyalties of a lifetime?"

"Oh, Hacey, why do you have all this trouble with words that start with 'L'? If it isn't Law it's Loyalty. But I suppose Loyalty is a kind of Law anyway, a Law to insure the conservative approach to personal relationships. You like to think you always stand for the Law, just like your friend Cassius Clay — and you like to think you stand for Loyalty, too. But where was the law when we drove those two slave-catchers out of Boston? Where was the law when you joined the Underground Railroad back in Berea? And, face up to it, Hacey — where was what you call Loyalty, when you hitched your wagon to Cash Clay's star, and spent seven years of your life trying to build a college in the mountains to help free the slaves?"

"That's hardly fair!" I answered angrily. "I've always been loyal to what I believed in."

He pulled down on his long upper lip with his fingers, and his eyes were both affectionate and mocking. "You mean you've always followed your beliefs, and you have believed strongly. That's not the same thing at all. Being loyal to something means standing up for it even when it doesn't excite your idealism, even when it may be *opposed* to your idealism. A worthy virtue, certainly, but more valuable with people than with ideas. In fact, *worthless* with ideas! Why in the world should a person be loyal to an idea just because

he's had it for a long time? Could anything be more illogi-
cal?"

Another brief silence descended on us. I tried to think
back over my feelings about Fitz John Porter and the court-
martial, and found that I had a headache. I wanted to argue
some more, but couldn't think of anything to say. Wentworth saved me the trouble. He began to speak quietly, but
with total conviction. "Hacey, remember — this war isn't
about state's rights, or nullification, or protective tariffs, or
even really about property. It's about *freedom*. Life, liberty,
and the pursuit of happiness. It has taken us eighty years to
realize that freedom is an indivisible thing. If it's to exist for
anyone, it must exist for everyone. If it's to exist for us
whites, it must also exist, just as openly, for the blacks. And
if it is to exist for them, they must win it for themselves —
it's no good us presenting it to them like an indulgent daddy
giving a doll to his baby. If it could be given to them by one
set of hands, it could be taken away by another. No, if they
are to be free, they must stand up and take their freedom
themselves."

He leaned toward me, and his eyes glittered brightly in the
lamplight against the pallor of his fine-drawn face. "Here in
Beaufort we have touched the pivot of this war. Until we
armed the blacks, there could be no guarantee of their freedom. But now, if we do our job, Lieutenant Miller, their
behavior under arms will shame the nation into recognizing
them as men — now, and through all the years this republic
endures!"

Higginson and I agreed that for the time being I would be
assigned to temporary duty with Headquarters, First South
Carolina Volunteers. Rather than being given a platoon of
my own, I was to act as aide to the colonel. Then, as soon as

a black regiment was formed in Kentucky or Tennessee, I would be transferred to it, to serve in a line, rather than a staff, capacity. A similar arrangement was made for Nat Crocker, with the difference that he would be transferred to the first black regiment formed in New England.

This suited me perfectly, since it allowed me to feel that the door was not completely closed; I could still escape from this bizarre life and return to the no-nonsense First Kentucky Cavalry if things got too much for me.

Imperceptibly but steadily over the next six months, my original feeling of strangeness changed to a comfortable familiarity. As Higginson had promised, the Negroes were good soldiers. They were also loyal, honest, and enthusiastic. If I couldn't accept their often childlike behavior as revealing the whole truth of their characters, as my colonel could, still I found nothing sinister concealed under their surface simplicity. One day I discovered myself using the phrase "my regiment" to designate black infantrymen instead of white cavalrymen, and I realized that I had, indeed, "joined up."

The change in Nat Crocker's attitude toward his assignment was even more marked. After the initial shock of exposure to troops in the field had worn off, he became more enthusiastic about the blacks than Higginson was, and the men gave him loyalty and affection in return. He devoted himself to his duties twelve hours a day, and often would spend his off-duty hours on the drill field or beside a campfire. "I don't think you appreciate these men, Hacey," he told me once, his round face squeezed into a frown. "An officer could really make himself a reputation with troops like these, you know."

A few days after we arrived in Beaufort the regiment was ordered on an expedition up the St. John's River, to occupy

Jacksonville, Florida. We stayed in that city for almost a month, with the intention of defending it against any Confederate troops who might try to expel us from it. Then, for reasons known only to the staff of the Department of the South, we were ordered to evacuate and return to Beaufort. This we did, leaving behind us many Union sympathizers who had publicly declared their allegiance when we entered the city, and now feared for their lives if we should leave. They had good reason for their fears, we later learned.

Then we received orders for picket duty at Port Royal Ferry on the Coosaw River. The ferry hadn't been operated since our forces landed on the Sea Islands, so picket duty meant sitting on one side of the wide, marshy river and looking at the Rebels on the other side. There were oysters in abundance, and large, sweet blackberries, and a comfortable plantation home for the Officers' Mess. The air was heavy with the smell of jasmine and early magnolia, but the salt smell of the tidal marshes kept it from cloying. The days were hot and dry and the nights were cool and damp. It was a good time.

In July we saw two days of action, as Colonel Higginson sailed up the Edisto River with five companies to burn the railroad bridge on the line connecting Charleston and Savannah. We never got the bridge — the upper river was navigable only at flood tide, and not for long enough for us to complete our mission — but we brought back two hundred slaves — "contraband," as we called them.

After that there was more picket duty, and then, just when the regiment was preparing to go into winter quarters on Port Royal Island, I received orders transferring me to the Second U.S. Light Artillery (Negro). I was to report to Major L. F. Booth, at Fort Pillow, Tennessee.

No notification of any promotion accompanied the orders

— but, since my decision in Washington the winter before, I had given up any hope of advancement, and was not disappointed.

"But, Colonel," I said, when Higginson congratulated me on the assignment, "it's an artillery outfit! I've never had any experience with artillery!"

"I shouldn't worry about it, if I were you," he replied blithely. "Cannons are like small arms, only bigger. You load them, point them, and go *Boom*. Put your trust in Providence and your gunners, not necessarily in that order." He cocked his head on one side, as if he were listening to his own words. "Goodness gracious, this war is making a heathen of me," he said in a surprised voice. "Next thing you know, I'll be spiking my Fust Souf Flip. Which reminds me, Hacey, we must drink a toast to your new appointment." He poured two glasses of the stuff from his earthenware pitcher and handed me one. "To the Second U.S. Light Artillery," he proposed.

"To the First South Carolina Volunteers," I responded, and we both drank.

He set his glass down on the table empty. "Tell me, Hacey, do you suppose it would be possible to take out a government patent on that delightful drink?" he asked musingly.

I said goodbye to Nat Crocker with real regret. During the time we had shared quarters I had seen him grow from a paper-shuffler into a soldier, and I counted him a friend. "Nat, I hope you'll forgive me for the trouble I caused you," I said as I shook his hand.

"Hacey, the mysterious ways of this world never fail to perplex me," he answered, with a worried look on his apple-cheeked face. "Somehow I seem to have emerged from disaster in as good shape as I entered it, and in spite of everything, I'm actually enjoying myself. It seems very unlikely that anyone would enjoy himself while preparing to lead troops on a battlefield, wouldn't you say?"

"Some men are just natural-born soldiers, Nat. I wouldn't be surprised if you were one of them. It took you a while to find yourself, that's all."

"I'm not sure I would have chosen to be a natural-born soldier if anyone had asked me. There are a good many other careers that offer more secure futures." He brooded solemnly for a moment, then smiled. "Ah, well, who are we to question our destiny? Onward and upward, Lieutenant Miller. Forward the Ethiops!"

"Forward the Ethiops, Nat! I've had my last glass of Fust Souf Flip. Don't you wish you could say the same?"

I left him with much the same expression on his face that it had worn during the days off Cape Hatteras.

My orders gave me time to stop over at Hazelwood for a few days on my way to Fort Pillow. Ellie was on the porch when I rode up. I knew from her expression that something was wrong. I kissed her quickly, then asked her what had happened.

"Is it Mama, Ellie?"

"No, your ma's all right. She's up to her room, lying down. No, it's Boone, Hacey."

"Boone!" I cried. "Little Boone? What happened to him?"

"Not little Boone. Your brother Boone. He's dead — killed."

"My brother Boone? But how? Why? He was a doctor — why would anyone kill him?"

Ellie took my hand and drew me toward the steps. "Come on and let's take a walk while we talk about it. I don't want your ma hearing us. There's some parts of it I'd rather she didn't know about."

We walked along the path under the elms. It was a chill and blustery day, and the sky was leaden.

"You remember how after the battle at Richmond, I told you about Boone having trouble with a man named Ferguson?" Ellie began quietly.

"Champe Ferguson, the bushwhacker? Yes, I remember. Something about him not wanting to take any prisoners."

"Well, it was Ferguson who did it. Boone's friend Pritch came out last month to give your ma the news, but he only told her that Boone was killed trying to save a wounded soldier. He didn't tell her the wounded soldier was a Yankee, and the man that killed Boone was a Confederate, right from his own regiment."

I couldn't make head or tail out of her explanation. "Wait a minute, Ellie. I don't understand you. You say Boone was trying to save a Yankee soldier? And Ferguson killed him? Killed the Yankee soldier, or killed Boone?"

"Hacey, honey, this is what Pritch said happened. He didn't want to tell me, but I wormed it out of him, so you'd know." She stopped walking and turned to face me, her thin body touching mine. She brushed the fine, soft hair back from her forehead, and looked at me steadily. "It was after a fight down in Tennessee. There were some Rebs wounded in the field, and some Yankees too. The rest of the Yankees had skedaddled. Boone was out there with some stretcher bearers, getting in the ones that couldn't walk. He went down into a little hollow all full of brush, and there was Champe Ferguson and two wounded Yankee soldiers. Champe had a bayonet in his hand, and Boone saw he was sticking it into the belly of one of the Yankees — more than once. The man was hollering, and Pritch says Champe was so tickled he was laughing out loud."

"Christ!"

"So Boone yells at him to stop it, but Ferguson just pulls out the bayonet and goes over to the other wounded man to finish him off too. He doesn't pay any attention to Boone at all. It was like he couldn't hear anything in the world except those Yankees.

"Boone jumped down into the hollow and grabbed hold of Champe, and tried to pull the bayonet out of his hand. For a second or two they wrestled over it, before anybody else could get there. And Champe was a lot stouter than Boone.

"By the time the stretcher bearers got to Champe to pull him off, he'd stuck that bayonet right straight through Boone's chest. Pritch said it was real quick and merciful, Hacey — Boone never even opened his eyes afterward."

We walked in silence as I strove to accept the brutal facts. Then I said, in a voice I didn't recognize, "What about Ferguson? Did Morgan give him a medal?"

"He had him put under arrest. He said he was going to try him for murder and hang him. But that night a couple of Ferguson's bushwhacker friends helped him escape. He got clean away."

"Very convenient for Morgan!"

"Pritch says Morgan felt bad about it," Ellie said gently. "Like it was his fault, in a way, for not getting rid of Ferguson earlier. And Pritch says Morgan really liked Boone. He says Morgan will get Ferguson sooner or later, and hang him for what he did."

"That's a comfort." We walked on. Memories of my brother crowded in on me; Boone and I arguing about slavery on the banks of the Kentucky River, the summer Cassius Clay's newspaper, *The True American,* was born; his disbelief and sadness at what he could only think of as my disloyalty to our family's beliefs; the duel he fought for me — and now I'd never be able to tell him that I had settled my own affair with Danford Ranew. I remembered his clean, fierce anger with Bryan Ledyard, and his gentle loyalty to Bryan's sister Robin. I remembered his grave attempt to persuade me to do what he believed was right and necessary, and join Morgan's Raiders with him. I remembered his level gaze, always open, always unafraid.

"God damn slavery — God damn the Confederate States of America!" I cried in futile rage. Ellie didn't speak. Sensing my need to be alone, she touched me on the cheek, then left me and returned to the house.

I walked for an hour or so, under the naked trees beside the gunmetal river. My thoughts followed no orderly or logical pattern, but later, when I came back indoors and ascended the stairs to my mother's room, I knew something I hadn't known before.

I knew that, as I loved my brother, it was my duty to lead black men against the institution that was responsible for his death. Any doubts I had brought with me from Beaufort were dead and buried as deep as Boone Miller, First Lieutenant, C.S.A.

XIV

―――•—•――

The Blacks

Fort Pillow was on the Tennessee side of the Mississippi River, about forty miles north of Memphis. A long sandbar extends into the river from the Arkansas side at that point, forcing all river traffic to come close under the high bluffs of the eastern shore. The Rebel general, Gideon Pillow, saw the strategic importance of the spot in 1861, and caused a fort to be built there and named after him. In June of 1862, when Memphis was captured, Fort Pillow was abandoned to the Union, and since that time had been garrisoned by our troops.

When I first saw it in the winter of 1863, it was an ugly but impressive installation. The bluff upon which the fort was built was just to the south of a marshy little tributary called Coal Creek, which flowed into the Mississippi at right angles. Between the creek and the fort the ground began to rise precipitously, then suddenly dipped into a ravine about seventy-five yards from the earthwork walls. This was called Coal Creek Ravine, and it curled around the north and northeast sides of Fort Pillow, reaching almost to the steamboat landing on the river.

South of the fort was another ravine running down to the riverbank. A double row of barracks and other frame buildings built along the bottom gave it its name of Town Ravine.

Between these two ravines the bluff reared a hundred feet into the sky, with a six-foot earthwork on the top, and six pieces of artillery glaring out of their embrasures at the river. Fort Pillow was very near to being impregnable from the water side.

From the land side — from the east — it was nearly as formidable. The outer line of fortifications curved between Coal Creek and the river south of the fort, a half mile from the actual works. It consisted of a number of rifle pits. Halfway between this line and the water was a second line of defense, constructed on the crest of a commanding hill. The third and final line was the fort itself, crowded into the corner of the bluff, its horseshoe-shaped walls overlooked only by the sky.

All the trees that had once shaded the ground around Fort Pillow had been chopped down two years earlier. A thousand stumps scarred the red clay glacis that sloped upward to the earthworks, and dense undergrowth choked the ravines on either side.

The fort was very small — its total diameter was less than seventy-five yards. The walls were six feet high, and circling them was a ditch eight feet deep and twelve feet wide. The black troops of the garrison, some 250-odd, had their tents pitched within the walls, while the nearly 300 white troops were quartered in the barracks along Town Ravine, with the officers' tents and battalion headquarters.

Fort Pillow was commanded by Major L. F. Booth, who also commanded the black troops of the Sixth Heavy Artillery. Second in rank was Major W. F. Bradford, commanding the Thirteenth Tennessee Cavalry (white). Quartered together with the Sixth Heavy Artillery were forty troopers of the Second Light Artillery (black). This was my command.

I reported to Major Booth immediately on disembarking from the Memphis-bound steamer that had brought me. I found him to be an unimpressive-looking man with metal-rimmed spectacles and the dryly precise manner of a New England schoolteacher. He seemed capable enough, however, which was more than my first impression of Major Bradford led me to believe of him.

Bradford was a burly man with a florid face and a thick mustache that drooped down both sides of his mouth. His eyes were such a pale blue they looked watery. The pores on his face were overlarge. He had the cavalryman's habit of carrying a quirt with him, and slapping it often against his boot, but somehow he seemed self-conscious when he did it.

"Delighted you have arrived, Lieutenant Miller," said Major Booth crisply. "You rate a tent of your own, and you'll find a very nice one waiting for you in Town Ravine — just ask any of the men to show you to Captain Fellowe's old tent. Your men are quartered with the other blacks in the fort. You have one officer assigned to your command — Lieutenant Halley. He's about four months junior to you. He shares a tent with one of Major Bradford's Tennessee officers."

"I think I'll find him and have him take me around the fort, Major, if that's all right."

"Certainly. I'll see you at the mess tent at dinner, and introduce you to the other officers then." He returned to the papers on his desk, Bradford waved his quirt at me in what was intended as a horseman's casual farewell, and I left the headquarters tent. I stopped the first passing trooper and had him move my luggage to my new quarters. Then I found Lieutenant Halley.

He was a big, open-faced Ohio farm boy, whose interest in Negroes had been kindled at Oberlin College, whence so many of my old colleagues at Berea had come. In the weeks that followed we were to explore the friends and acquaintances we had in common, but during our first day together our conversation was confined to military matters.

"Tell me about the men, Lieutenant," I said, as we walked up the bald clay hill toward the entrance gate of the fort. "How good are they at their jobs? How's their morale?"

"They're good soldiers, sir, and good artillerymen. We have only one gun to service, so they have been given considerable infantry training as well. I figured that if anybody ever attacked us here, most of the men would be aiming rifles, not cannons."

"What type of gun do we have?"

"A ten-pound Parrott, sir. A very accurate weapon."

"What's the rest of the battery here?"

"Another Parrott, two six-pound field pieces, and two twelve-pound howitzers."

"Why, that's not enough firepower to close the river!" I said in surprise.

"Of course not, sir," he said, with a little of the hurt truculence of a small boy. "I don't think anybody expects any need to close the river. After all, it's in our hands all the way down to New Orleans."

"Then why are we garrisoning Fort Pillow?"

"I suppose so some Reb guerrillas don't climb up on the bluff and practice target shooting on the troopships when they steam by," he said, with a trace of disgust in his voice.

218

I glanced at him sharply. "And that brings us to the second part of my question, Lieutenant Halley. How's the morale? And that includes yours, as well as the men's."

He grinned ruefully. "I guess I sounded a bit edgy just then. To tell you the truth, I think this inactivity bothers me more than it does the men. The war's gotten so far away now — sometimes it seems like we're just sitting in some stagnant backwater, with the current rushing past, carrying everybody else down to where the action is."

"I gather you haven't been in battle yet, Lieutenant."

"No, sir."

"Well, a lot of men who have would be happy to swap you their assignments for this stagnant backwater, and throw in a horse and cow to boot. What about the men — do they share your impatience?"

"No, sir — your namesake works them so hard they don't have any time for it."

"My namesake?"

"Sergeant Miller, sir, our first sergeant. The men call him Star, because of an odd-shaped scar on his forehead. He's a wonder — I don't know what we'd do without him."

Star! The shock of finding him at Fort Pillow was severe enough to put all other thoughts out of my mind. When he was presented to me by Lieutenant Hunter, I concentrated on keeping any trace of recognition from my face. Star's expression was respectful and impassive — for a second I imagined he had forgotten me. After all, it was nineteen years since I had seen him, just after *The True American* was suppressed, during that nightmare of blood and savagery that Lexingtonians remembered as "The Night of the Black Indians" — when we could force ourselves to remember it at all. But then I saw the calculating glint in his yellowed eye, and knew he was reviewing every detail of our relationship in his mind.

Hunter had Star form the men, and I said a few words to them, and then inspected them briefly. I visited some of their tents, watched them serve the Parrott gun with dummy rounds, and took a quiet look at their sanitary arrangements, which were cleaner than those of most of the rest of the army.

On my way out of the fort and back to my quarters, I said to Star, in what I hoped was a casual tone, "Oh, Sergeant, I'd like to talk to you at greater length about the men. Would you come by my tent this evening, say, around seven o'clock?"

He nodded his head gravely. "I surely will, Lieutenant Miller, sir," he replied.

At dinner in the mess tent I was introduced to my fellow officers, and found them a mixed crew. They naturally fell into two groups; the cavalry officers of the Thirteenth Tennessee were all natives of that state, commanding white troops, with no special regard for Negroes, and even a certain resentment of them, as if they were the authors of this fratricidal war. The artillery officers commanded blacks, and their common denominator was a zealous and philanthropic regard for the freedmen and fugitives who served under them. Most of them were New Englanders, and they had learned their abolitionism at Harvard and Yale and Dartmouth.

From the way I was greeted by both factions, I sensed I might have entrée into either one I chose. As a Kentuckian and an alumnus of Wolford's Cavalry, my credentials were acceptable to the Tennesseans, and as a Harvard graduate and aide to Colonel T. W. Higginson, I would be welcomed by the abolitionists. But I decided to remain independent of both groups and make my friendships on an individual basis.

After dinner I went back to my tent and unpacked a few belongings. Then I sat on my cot and waited for Star. In a few minutes I heard him scratch on the tent flap and cough apologetically.

"Come in, Sergeant," I said.

He pushed the flap aside and stepped into the light of the coal-oil lamp. We looked at each other with the frank curiosity we hadn't been able to show that morning in the fort. He had changed very little in the years since he had left Hazelwood. His hair was gray, and the old lines on his face were cut more deeply into the flesh, and had been joined by others around his eyes. He was thinner than he had been, and the cords of his neck stood out like tarred ropes. But the livid scar on the forehead was the same, and the murky whites of his eyes.

"You haven't changed much," I said. "I would have recognized you anywhere — but not from your name. Your taking the name Miller — should I be flattered by that?"

"All buckra names are the same. They don't signify. I needed one, so I took one." His deep voice was flat, and almost without accent.

"I see. I thought maybe you had a special feeling for the Millers. You lived on our land a long time."

"I worked my rent out. No, Lieutenant, if you're hoping to hear me say that deep down in my poor old black heart I've always had a warm spot for those nice folks who let me live in that tumble-down shack back in Kentucky, I'm afraid you're going to be disappointed. White's white to me — I just can't hardly tell you people apart."

I gestured to the camp chair beside the table. "Sit down,

Star. I've got some catching up to do." He made no move to comply, and I said irritably, "Sit down, I said — tonight the army stops at the door of this tent, and the police and the slave-catchers are a hell of a lot farther away than that. Sit down!" He pulled out the chair and sat on it stiffly. His expressionless gaze never left me.

"'Well, the last time I saw you you were cutting a throat, for which I couldn't blame you too much," I said in a conversational tone. "We heard about you once, though, after you moved out of your cabin. It *was* you, wasn't it, that helped organize those slaves to escape on the Paris pike back in 'Forty-eight? Wasn't it, Star?"

He hesitated a moment, stiff and wary, then expelled the breath from his lungs and relaxed in the chair. "I seem to recollect something like that, for a fact," he answered easily.

"We never heard any more about you after that. What did you do then, and where did you go?"

"Oh, one place and another. For a while there was a camp in the swamp down in Carolina — better than five hundred black folks, and we had guns. We killed us a few buckra there. Then for a change I worked on the Railroad in Ohio." He meant the Underground Railroad. "Crossed a couple hundred slaves over the river, and carved myself up some slave-catchers in between times. I was east for a spell, and I almost went to Harper's Ferry with old John Brown, but at the last minute I had to go to Canada instead. I don't know what-all else."

"Star, what did you join the army for — to free your people, or to kill 'buckra'?"

"I expect you got to do one if you want to do the other, and to tell you the truth, Lieutenant, I like it that way."

I looked at him silently for a moment, remembering that

there had been a time during my boyhood when this man had been my closest friend. "Do you hate all of us that much?" I asked.

"All of you."

"Even the white soldiers fighting beside you. Even — me?"

"Don't never tempt me, Lieutenant — I got no memory for white friends."

"There must be a good reason why you feel that way, I guess."

"Good enough for me," he replied softly.

"I'd like to hear about it."

He hesitated a second, then began to speak in a low monotone. "My mammy and my papa lived in Kentucky, in the Bluegrass. Their master was a famous rich man, owned two hundred slaves or better. Lived in a great big house, everybody looked up to him. Mammy and Papa had three children — my little sister Violet, my brother Jesse, and me. It was a happy time, till the master decided to sell some black folks down the river to raise him some extra money. Mammy and Papa, they cry and pray and plead with the man, but he sell us all anyway. He sell us to a trader going down to New Orleans."

"The man who sold you," I said with sudden intuitive certainty, "the man who sold you was General Green Clay, Cash Clay's father!"

His eyes slitted, but he didn't raise his voice from that deadly monotone. "The stinking buckra bastard who sold us was General Green Clay," he confirmed. "When we got to New Orleans, the trader sold Papa off to a plantation on the Gulf — we never saw him again. Mammy was bought by a sporting man — she was still a handsome woman — and put

223

into a cathouse to work. I seen her once years later; she was blind from some disease she got there, and she had big sores all over her face.

"We three young ones, we were bought by a society lady, a Creole, who dressed us up in velvet clothes and had us wait on her and ride around on the back of her carriage. We didn't have to work so hard, but the lady had an awful bad temper. She'd get mad and then whip us. Sometimes she'd use a riding crop, and sometimes a hickory cane. Once Jesse dropped a little cup, and she beat him so bad she broke his back. He was a cripple ever afterwards. She tried to cover it up, but a doctor found out about it, and there was a trial, and the judge made the society lady sell us off.

"Of course nobody wanted Jesse, on account of him being paralyzed, so they put him in a home for nigger cripples. Last I heard, he was still there. A Cajun from the bayous bought Violet; I expect he had her broke in before he even got her home. I was lucky — a carpenter bought me and taught me his trade, so I could make money for him. He was generous —" Star's mouth twisted sardonically — "whenever I did work on my own for anybody, he only took three-quarters of what I made, let me keep the other fourth.

"By the time I was full-grown, I had saved enough money to buy my freedom."

He paused and stared ahead in silence, his eyes focused on something a long way away. Then he said gruffly, "Why you want to hear all this trash?"

"I don't know, but I do. Go on — what happened after you bought your freedom?"

"You ever hear of Marie Leveau, Lieutenant?"

"No — should I have?"

"Only if you was interested in Hoodoo. Marie Leveau was the Hoodoo Queen of New Orleans. She took a liking to me

— moved me into her house out on Bayou St. John, on Lake Pontchartrain. She looked like she was eighteen years old when I moved in. When I moved out eight years later, she still looked eighteen. When the big snake come for her ten years after that, she *still* looked eighteen."

"Was she a witch, Star?"

He grinned at me mirthlessly. "A witch? Why, no, sir! She was a doctor! She could doctor a rat into a woman's belly in place of a baby. She could take a handful of goofer dust and doctor old Ogoun Badagris, the bloody one, right into bed with you. She could doctor herself to walk on water, with a communion candle on her head and two others in her hands."

Remembering a courtroom and a trial long before, I asked, "And could she have doctored the tongues of two witnesses, to make them contradict each other?"

"That too, Lieutenant, that too."

"Could she have taught you to doctor that way, Star?"

He didn't answer. More to myself than him, I said, "That Emily — that slave girl that poisoned Cash Clay's little baby, back in 'Forty-five. You got her off, didn't you, by hocusing the witnesses? Why? Just because the baby's last name was Clay? Just because he was old Green Clay's grandchild?"

The two of us shared the silence in the tent. Memories and fears chased through my mind, as the big Negro regarded me impassively, his body slumped comfortably in his chair. I weighed his value as an excellent first sergeant, leading black troops, against the grim facts I knew about him but could never prove. The balance could only go one way.

"Sergeant," I said, "when you leave this tent tonight, there will never be anything more said on this subject. As far as I'm concerned, I've never met you before today. From what I've seen, you're a well-qualified noncommissioned officer, and I'm glad to have you with me. Is that clear?"

His voice slipped into a heavy Negro dialect as he replied, "Yassuh, Lieutenant, it sho am!"

"I guess that's all, then." He rose from the chair and flashed me a brilliant white smile, saluted, and turned to leave the tent. As he was pulling the flap back, I asked him one last question — one I had never dared to ask when I was a child. "Oh, Sergeant — that scar on your forehead. How did you come by it?"

"That carpenter I tole you about — well, wonst he raised his self a few head of cattle, and he had this ol' branding iron left over when he bought me. He got drunk one night and decide to make certain-sure nobody else could ever claim I was theirs. So he heat up that branding iron a while, then he give me this little ol' scar on my head." He laughed artificially, like the end man in a minstrel show. "Hee, hee, hee — that ol' branding iron, it sho 'nuff make this nigger sit up and take notice."

"Good night, Sergeant," I said.

"Good night, Lieutenant," he replied without a trace of dialect, and disappeared into the night.

The winter months at Fort Pillow passed quickly and for the most part uneventfully. As I came to know my black soldiers well, I found I liked them even better than Wentworth's First South Carolina Volunteers. For one thing, they had mostly been raised in the Border South rather than the Deep South. That meant they had been subjected to the milder form of servitude that slavery assumed in Kentucky and Tennessee, rather than the crushing oppression of the Delta and the Gulf. The result was a personality that included a leavening of irony and impudence. The Sea Island

Negroes had a great capacity for enjoyment, but it was like the skylarking of children — there was no wit about it. Our Border blacks had wit to spare.

Then of course I spoke the same language they did — or at least a language closer to theirs than it could ever be to the Gullah dialect of Beaufort. There were none of the amusing but potentially dangerous failures of communication that often bedeviled me in South Carolina.

We worked well together, the men, and Star, and Lieutenant Halley and I. As the dreary damp chill of winter settled in on us, I began to feel an easy confidence about our ability to handle any task we were called upon to perform.

Unfortunately, I couldn't feel the same confidence about Major Bradford's command. The Tennessee troopers seemed able enough, but I had a sense of a loose hand on the reins. Their exercises on the drill field were not *quite* precise, their horses were not *quite* well-groomed, their appearance was not *quite* military, and their behavior toward their officers was not *quite* respectful. In each case the shortcoming was a little thing, almost imperceptible until you became aware of the pattern, and still easily correctable by an experienced commanding officer with determination and energy. But Bradford didn't seem to be experienced, determined, or energetic. In fact, he didn't seem to be aware of the problem.

There was one unavoidable cause for friction between the white and black troops: the blacks went into battle with figurative ropes around their necks, and the whites knew they might share the same fate if captured, for a number of Confederate generals had made statements to the effect that both Negro soldiers and whites who fought with them were outside the rules of civilized warfare, and should expect no quarter from Southern troops.

227

Major Booth and the other officers serving with the blacks accepted the risk readily. Bradford and his Tennesseeans were less comfortable about it. Still, the friction was only potential; in day-to-day activities, we all got along together tolerably well.

Of all those day-to-day activities, the one I enjoyed most was my company's evening entertainment. Every night after supper a large bonfire was kindled outside the mess tent, and the men formed a circle around it for an evening of singing, dancing, and storytelling. Lieutenant Halley and I generally managed to be on hand for a few minutes each night, but we kept well in the background and never intruded.

The group singing was uniformly excellent, and some of the individual performers were superb. Star's vibrant bass formed a foundation for others to build their harmonies on, as he reminded them of the runaway's exhortation, "Follow the drinkin' gourd." A gray-haired corporal named Cato kept the company in stitches, night after night, with a serialized account of his comic escape from "Old Massa," and his subsequent adventures with slave-catchers and the Underground Railroad. Two brothers named Flowers were often called upon to dance, sometimes by themselves, sometimes with Cecily, our fat laundress. We had a lay preacher who gave the men vivid accounts of the trials of Moses and David, and a court jester who told jokes in a dialect so thick I always missed the key word. But I liked Bubba the best.

Bubba's real name was Christopher Gist Tolliver — no doubt spelled Taliaferro back on the plantation — but not even his officers could remember to call him by it. He was the worst soldier in the company, and the best singer. It was as if his stocky little body and cannonball head had only room for the one talent, which was so big it squeezed everything else out. He would stand in front of the fire in a half-crouch, keeping time by twisting his body, eyes closed, face turned upward and mottled by the flickering firelight, singing the songs the soldiers loved. Early in the evening it might be the John Brown song, or the song of the Black Fifty-fourth Massachusetts, who had fought so well in Charleston harbor:

> McClellan went to Richmond with two hundred thousand
> brave,
> He said, "Keep back the niggers, and the Union I will save."
> Little Mac he got his way, still the Union is in tears,
> So they have to call for help from the colored volunteers!

Then the whole company would join in:

> Oh, give us a flag, all free without a slave,
> We'll fight to defend it as our fathers did so brave;
> Our gallant Company "A" will make the Rebels dance,
> And we'll stand by the Union if we only have the chance!

There was another verse I remember well:

> Old Jeff says he'll hang us if we dare to meet him armed,
> He'd surely like to scare us, but we are not alarmed.
> For he first has got to catch us before the way is clear,
> And that's his biggest problem with the colored volunteer!

Later in the evening, when the bonfire was burning low, the music changed, and Bubba's songs lost their martial ardor and white man's rhymes, and harked back to the sadness of the old life, and the beauty of the Heavenly Dream:

> I know moon-rise, I know star-rise,

he would cry in his soft, pulsing tenor, and the others would reply,

Lay this body down.

— and the haunting song would continue,

I walk in the moonlight, I walk in the starlight,
Lay this body down.
I'll walk in the graveyard, I'll walk through the graveyard,
Lay this body down.
I'll lie in the grave and stretch out my arms,
Lay this body down.
I'll go to the judgment in the evening of the day,
Lay this body down.
And my soul and your soul will meet on that day
When I lay this body down.

As 1864 came in, Fort Pillow seemed more of a backwater than ever. During January there was almost no fighting anywhere in the country, least of all in western Tennessee. Aside from an occasional Rebel bushwhacker, there didn't seem to be an armed secessionist north of Meridian, Mississippi. In February the torpid tempo of the war picked up a bit, but it was mostly a matter of raids and counterraids; the news that General Nathan Bedford Forrest had won a brilliant small victory at Okolona caused no conversation that I remember. We heard that Joseph E. Johnston had replaced the unfortunate Braxton Bragg as Confederate Commander of the West, but this also went largely uncommented upon.

Then, in mid-March, Johnston gave Forrest permission to raid western Tennessee and Kentucky for guns and horses.

The first we heard of it, Forrest was already north of us, up near the Kentucky line, attacking Union City. He gave the garrison a "No Quarter" ultimatum, and they surrendered after the loss of only one man. On the 25th of March he attacked Paducah, Kentucky, with a similar "No Quarter" ultimatum, but there were gunboats in the river to protect the garrison, and Forrest satisfied himself by looting the town of military stores and horses.

For two weeks there was no news of him. We reasoned that he was probably returning south. Would he bypass us again, or would he delay a day or two to pluck us from the branch and add us to his basket?

It was the fourth anniversary of the firing on Fort Sumter when we found out. Just before sunrise on Tuesday, the 12th of April, Forrest's troopers attacked our outer defense line and drove our pickets in.

XV

HELL AT FORT PILLOW

WE WOKE to the rattle of rifle fire. I dressed hurriedly and trotted up to the fort to find that Star had the men on their feet and was assembling them in squads. The breakfast cookfire in the mess-tent area had just been kindled; aside from that there was no warmth in the company area, only wet fog and quiet cursing and a sense of fear.

When the men had fallen in and were standing easy, I reported to Major Booth. While we were talking a messenger brought the news that the rifle pits of the pickets had been overrun, and the Confederates were advancing toward the second line. At the same time word came from Bradford in Town Ravine that he was moving the Tennesseeans out to occupy the second line before the Confederates could reach it. It was a foot race, with both sides equidistant from the goal.

While we awaited the result, I positioned my men along the fifty-foot section of wall we were charged with defending. There was a platform five feet below the top of the earthwork, and the men were stationed along it at intervals of a yard or so. Our Parrott gun stood before one embrasure, pointing northeast, with the glacis sloping down gently be-

fore it, and the ground falling precipitously off to Coal Creek
Ravine on the left. The men brought up powder and shells
as I supervised a hurried exercise in training and elevating
the cannon. We had a perfect field of fire across and down
the glacis, but, as I had discovered before, the gun could not
be sufficiently depressed to bear on Coal Creek Ravine,
barely 75 yards from the walls.

About seven o'clock the sound of heightened firing told us
that Bradford's cavalrymen were engaging the Rebels. The
second line was veiled in black powder smoke and stubborn
fog, and it was impossible to see the results of the fighting
from the fort. After twenty minutes of uncertainty, Major
Booth decided to join the Tennesseeans.

"Lieutenant Miller, I'm going forward to see what's happening out there. I've given orders for the five batteries of
the Sixth Heavy Artillery to stand at their guns until further
notice. I expect your men to do the same. In case you
haven't observed it, there's a Union gunboat lying out in the
river just off the landing — the *New Era,* Captain Marshall
commanding. It represents a powerful addition to our firepower. Should I be unable to continue in command for any
reason, Major Bradford will take over. Is that clear?" He
peered at me anxiously, a small, serious man who looked
more like a clerk than a soldier.

"Yes, sir." I saluted. "Good luck, Major. They'll wish
they never started this before they're through."

He returned my salute correctly. "Yes, I'm sure they
will." He turned away and headed briskly for the gate of the
fort, followed by an aide and two noncoms.

The minutes dragged by as we waited on the gun platform
for news. It was almost eight o'clock when the Tennesseeans
suddenly appeared through the rising haze and began to retreat up the glacis, firing behind them as they came. Realiz-

ing that the second line had fallen, I shouted to Halley to open fire on it, over the heads of the approaching troopers. Our Parrott gun was immediately joined by the other batteries, and our brief view of the action was blotted out by smoke.

We kept up the cannonade until all the Tennesseeans were inside the gate, then slacked off. Major Bradford appeared on the platform, "Lieutenant Miller, I'm sorry to say Major Booth is dead. He was picked off by a sniper. I'm assuming command."

My heart sank, but I replied evenly, "Yes, sir. What are your orders, Major?"

"Keep up the firing, but at a reduced rate. We may be here for a long time, and I'd hate to run out of ammunition."

"Shall I continue firing canister, sir?"

"Right. And Miller — in case your niggers are spooked, you can tell them they're in no real danger. Major Booth and I made an arrangement with Captain Marshall of the *New Era* — if the Rebels manage to get inside the fort, we'll just move down to the boat landing. We'll be safe there under the *New Era*'s guns until they can take us aboard."

"Do you think the one gunboat can hold off Forrest's whole force, Major?"

Bradford didn't like to be questioned by his subordinates. "I just said so, didn't I?" he replied in an irritated tone. "I can see you have no idea of the effectiveness of gunboats, Lieutenant."

"That's true, sir."

"Well, for your information, the *New Era*'s armament consists of six twenty-four-pound howitzers. That's double the size of anything we have in the fort. Does that make you feel any better?" he asked sarcastically.

For answer, I saluted. He opened his mouth to say something else, then decided against it, returned my salute with a perfunctory gesture, and walked down the platform. I called Halley and Star and told them what Bradford had said. "Sergeant, you tell the men the gunboat's here to protect them," I finished.

"Gunboat'll have to protect its own self first," he replied.

"Never mind about that. Just tell them."

"Yes, sir."

Halley and I stood together, looking toward the second line. The Confederates were active little gray ants. "How do you like our stagnant backwater this morning, Bill?" I asked lightly.

His nostrils were white, but his eyes sparkled with excitement. "I think there's quite a current, all of a sudden," he said.

The news that the *New Era* was prepared to evacuate them in case the fort fell had an immediate and cheering effect on the men. They broke out in smiles, Bubba began to sing, and the Flower brothers executed a few dance steps. I adopted an outward attitude indicating more confidence than I felt, and concentrated on directing the fire of my Parrott gun.

Until eleven o'clock the Confederates seemed content to keep their distance from the fort, and harass us with sniper fire. Then General Forrest arrived on the field in person and ordered an immediate attack on the buildings in Town Ravine, which if taken would afford his marksmen excellent cover less than 100 yards south of the walls of Fort Pillow. Bradford belatedly realized the importance of these buildings and ordered a party to burn them, but it was too late. They were already infested with Rebel riflemen, and our men were driven back with considerable losses.

Town Ravine, like Coal Creek Ravine on the north side of

the walls, was below the maximum level of depression of our cannons. The Confederate troops in the sheds and barracks buildings were safe to pick off our men through the embrasures in the walls, and there was nothing we could do about it.

The sun rose to the noon apex and began to slide down the burnished sky. In spite of the crisp April weather beyond the walls, it had gotten hot inside Fort Pillow, without enough breeze to dissipate the acrid smoke that hung around us. Many of the men had stripped to the waist, and both black and white bodies glistened with sweat. It was strangely quiet — the only sounds were the regular *boom*s of the *New Era*'s guns, which sounded small and remote as they carried across the water, and the occasional *crack* of a Rebel sniper's rifle. I began to think we might survive the day, even against "No Quarter" Forrest.

About 2:00 P.M. the Confederates started to work their way into Coal Creek Ravine. They had to cross 200 yards of open ground to reach the protection of the ravine, and we killed forty or fifty of them before they got there. But once they had two or three companies in position, their firepower made us keep our heads down while they brought up additional troops. By three o'clock, more than 600 of Forrest's men were concealed in Coal Creek Ravine — as safe as if they were in church, and only 75 yards from our walls.

Now that he had his troops placed within easy storming distance both north and south of the fort, Forrest sent us a flag of truce and an ultimatum. Major Bradford read the message aloud to the officers:

"Major Booth, Commanding United States Forces, Fort Pillow: Major — The conduct of the officers and men garrisoning Fort Pillow has been such as to entitle them to being

treated as prisoners of war. I demand the unconditional surrender of this garrison, promising you that you shall be
treated as prisoners of war. My men have received a fresh
supply of ammunition, and from their present position can
easily assault and capture the fort. Should my demand be
refused, I cannot be responsible for the fate of your command. Respectfully, N. B. Forrest, Major General Commanding."

"He doesn't know Major Booth is dead," said a Tennessee
lieutenant.

"That's right," answered Bradford. "And I'm the last one
that's going to tell him! I'll sign Booth's name when I
reply."

"What do you aim to reply, Major?" asked Halley.

"That we have to consult with Captain Marshall on the
New Era, and therefore need at least an hour's truce. We
have to stall for all the time we can get, gentlemen — reinforcements are certainly on their way, and it's our job to
hold the fort until they get here."

Bradford wrote a note to that effect, and in a few minutes
it was delivered to General Forrest. His answer came back
swiftly: "Sir — I have the honor to acknowledge the receipt
of your note. Your request cannot be granted. I will allow
you twenty minutes from the receipt of this note for consideration; if at the expiration of that time the fort is not surrendered, I shall assault it. I do not demand the surrender of
the gunboat. Very respectfully, N. B. Forrest."

Then two things happened:

First, a steamship appeared from around the bend in the
Mississippi, south of the fort. It was the *Olive Branch,* a
troop transport en route from New Orleans to St. Louis, with
two full batteries of artillery aboard. It altered course and

began to approach our boat landing. Some of the men
started to cheer, but I quieted them quickly. This was no
occasion for rejoicing. By indicating its intention to land,
the *Olive Branch* was violating the truce, even if unknow-
ingly. And by not signaling her off as soon as he saw her
approach, Major Bradford was *knowingly* violating it.

Forrest reacted instantly. A hundred or more sharpshooters rushed from each ravine down to the riverbank, where
they took up positions to the north and south of the boat
landing. As they were taking cover and preparing to dispute
the *Olive Branch*'s landing, the *New Era* lowered a small
boat, which rowed over to the transport. It must have carried an order to the larger vessel to resume its original
course, for the *Olive Branch* suddenly veered away from
the riverbank and headed north. Ten minutes later it was
gone.

The grace period Forrest had allowed us was over. Bradford scrawled his answer to the Rebel general's ultimatum —
"I will not surrender" — and sent it out by messenger. A
working party on the river side of the fort lowered five cases
of rifle ammunition down the bluff to the bank below, in case
the garrison had to abandon the fort and take shelter under
the guns of the *New Era*.

And then the other thing happened, and froze my blood.

One of the blacks in my battery, a private named McGee,
scooped up a dipperful of liquid from a cook-pot near the
cannon. There were always a number of pots on the platform,
filled with drinking water, and I wouldn't have noticed Mc-
Gee's action at all if it hadn't been performed with a certain
exaggeration of gesture. He swung the dipper above his
head, tilted his face upward, and poured the liquid into his
open mouth. His eyes were closed. Then, as I watched, he
stumbled across the platform to the parapet, leaned over it,

and began screaming down at the Confederates in Coal Creek Ravine.

"Hey, you buckra bastards, you hear me? You mess with us, we cut your balls off. How you going to fuck your women then? Don't worry your mind, white man — we fuck them for you!"

I started for the man as soon as I grasped the meaning of the scene, but Star reached him first and laid him senseless with one blow of his great fist. "You fool, you! You goddamn blackass fool, you!" he panted as he stood straddling the unconscious body.

"Star, that man was drunk! He was drinking out of this cook-pot!" I picked it up, and the smell of raw whiskey made my gorge rise. I emptied it on the hard-packed dirt floor of the fort. "Check the other pots on the platform — hurry!"

Star started one direction and I went the other, checking each cook-pot I passed as I looked for Major Bradford. I looked into three pots, and two of them contained whiskey. I emptied them, ignoring the sullen looks and muttered curses of many of the men. Then I saw Bradford and ran up to him.

"Major —"

"Yes, Lieutenant Miller? Please get yourself under better control — it has a damaging effect on enlisted men."

"Major, somehow whiskey has gotten into the water pots! Half the men on the platform are drunk as a fiddler's bitch!"

"Oh?" He raised his eyebrows as though I had made an uninteresting remark about the weather. "No doubt from the barrel my troopers had in their stores in Town Ravine. I had it brought up into the fort this morning. No sense in making the Rebels a gift of it."

"But the black troops have gotten into it, too! They're not used to whiskey — there's no telling what it will do to them!"

Bradford smiled in a patronizing way. "Maybe even make them fight like white men, eh, Lieutenant? I suggest you return to your command. The Confederates may be coming any minute." He turned away, dismissing me. I walked back to my battery. Some of the men wouldn't meet my eye, and some glared back defiantly. I leaned against the Parrott gun and stared down into the ravine. There wasn't any point in saying anything. The air was dead still and the sun was merciless.

Then Forrest attacked.

His men came at us in two waves of five hundred or six hundred each — the first wave scrambling up from the two ravines and into the ditch under the walls, while the second wave remained behind cover, firing at every Union head that appeared over the parapet; when the first wave was safe, the second swept up to join it. In hardly a minute over a thousand of them were in the ditch, separated from us in the fort by less than a yard of sunbaked mud wall.

The firing stopped. Nobody had anything to shoot at. We could hear the sound of panting breaths, grunts, oaths, and the scrape of boots on clay. Without seeing them, we could tell what they were doing: half of them were boosting the other half up the inner wall of the ditch, to the narrow ledge formed by the joining of the ditch and earthwork. Then the men on the ledge were pulling the others up to join them.

The silence was broken only by our own harsh breathing, and that of the Confederates three feet away. "Steady, boys," I said softly. "They'll be coming over in a minute. You can't miss them, and you'll get the first shot. There's nothing to worry about, everything's going to work out fine.

Just stay steady — they can't hurt you if you stay steady."
I kept talking in a soft, even voice, as though I were gen-
tling a horse. Bubba, who was standing directly in front of
me, facing the parapet, looked over his shoulder, his round
little face pleading for reassurance. I put my hand on his
shoulder. "They can't hurt you," I repeated. "It's going to
be all right." For a second his eyes held mine in hope and
disbelief, then he turned to face the parapet again.

At that moment, with a great shout, the Rebels leaped to
the top of the wall. They were met with an ear-splitting blast
of musketry, as every Union soldier pulled the trigger of his
weapon. Sudden gaps appeared in the gray line, but were
filled instantly. The Confederates stood shoulder against
shoulder, so close together it was as if the walls had suddenly
grown six feet higher, and blotted out half the sky.

They began to fire down on us. Nothing could have stood
against those thousand massed rifles at pointblank range. I
emptied my navy Colt as I began to back away from the wall,
and then I was overrun by the retreating men in front of me.
Bubba's shoulder hit my chest and sent me staggering off
the platform to the dirt floor below. He fell on top of me.
When I tried to push him off, he wrapped his arms around
me and whimpered. His blood ran into my eyes; half his
face was shot away.

I struggled free as the men in my battery passed over and
around me. Here and there one would turn and fire, and
then resume his withdrawal. But most of the garrison was
panic-stricken, the white cavalrymen no less than the black
artillerymen. The Confederates on top of the horseshoe-
shaped wall were firing down from three directions, forcing
us back into the tent area that faced the bluff and the riverbank. The men jammed the narrow paths between the tents,
screaming, cursing, praying — ropes and canvas ripped,

tents fell — while the gray riflemen on the wall fired volley after volley into the defenseless mass. It became a problem to climb over the bodies, suddenly piled up three and four high between the wreckage of the tents. The wounded wriggled and tried to crawl away, which made them harder to climb over than if they had been dead. I saw my subordinate, young Halley from Oberlin, crying from a belly wound, but he didn't recognize me as I crawled across him.

When we reached the low wall that overlooked the bluff, half the garrison of Fort Pillow had fallen, and as we flung ourselves over the wall and down the steep slopes to the riverbank below, we could still hear the crashing volleys the Confederate riflemen were pouring into the dead and wounded behind us.

The plan Booth and Bradford had made with Captain Marshall of the *New Era* called for the garrison of the fort to take up a position along the riverbank at the boat landing, near the head of Town Ravine. When I reached the foot of the bluff Major Bradford was already there, waving a pistol and shouting to the men to follow him to the landing. I joined him, and in a few moments more than 200 disheveled and frightened men had fallen in around us. We started up the bank toward Town Ravine. I could see the *New Era* clearly, for it lay less than a hundred yards offshore. The bluff was clear of Union soldiers; we were down by the river and the Confederates were above us; it was the time for the big howitzers on the gunboat to open fire on our attackers with anti-personnel canister. But not a single porthole was open. The *New Era* might have been in Memphis for the good she could do us.

Forrest's sharpshooters — more than a hundred in each ravine — had concentrated their fire on the gunboat at the beginning of the attack, with such murderous effect that

Captain Marshall had been forced to order the gunports closed. For the remainder of the battle, the *New Era* only served as a silent witness to the slaughter.

As Bradford led us running down the riverbank toward the landing, I looked over my shoulder at the fort looming above and behind me. The flagpole was visible against the darkening sky, and the flag drooped limply from the halyards. "As long as the flag hasn't been struck, the fort hasn't surrendered," I said to myself. "There's nobody to lower the flag now, so even if we want to give up, there's no way to do it. They can kill us all, and say it was our fault for resisting."

We were barely halfway to the boat landing when the snipers in Town Ravine fired a volley directly into us. At least a quarter of our number went down. The rest reversed direction instinctively, milling wildly for a moment, then began to run upriver, under the bluff, toward Coal Creek Ravine.

But the Confederates inside Fort Pillow had reached the river wall and were able to fire down on us as we passed below them, and there were a hundred more sharpshooters concealed in Coal Creek Ravine to give us a volley when we approached.

The narrow riverbank had become a killing ground. There was no way out. As the men realized the hopelessness of the situation, some ran toward the sharpshooters, waving their hands in the air; some waded in to the river; some began loading their rifles for a final shot.

It didn't make any difference. Blacks and whites, by twos and threes and fives and tens, they fell. The sharpshooters shot the ones who tried to surrender and the ones who tried to reload, impartially. The men who waded into the river stained it red for fifty yards.

I made an instant decision that Town Ravine offered the best chance of a breakthrough. With a dozen blacks behind me I sprinted down the bank a second time, so close against the bluff I was protected by its overhang. When I emerged into the open, it was only fifty yards to the barracks buildings in the ravine. I had reloaded my Colt, and, selecting a patch of underbrush between two sheds, I cried, "Let's go through here!" and began firing blindly into the undergrowth. The men were close behind me, shouting and sobbing. As we neared the bushes I saw there were many Rebel riflemen concealed there. I had a second to take aim at one and pull the trigger, then a massive blow struck my left arm, and at the same instant something crashed into my head. Everything disappeared in sudden darkness.

The real horror of Fort Pillow began after the sun went down.

All fighting ended fifteen minutes after the Confederates crossed the walls. General Forrest paused only long enough to order our captured arms and ammunition loaded into wagons, and left the field before 5:00 P.M. A little after six the rest of his command followed him, taking with them every Union soldier who could walk. Three hundred dead and seriously wounded men were left at Fort Pillow — the majority of them blacks.

It was dark when I regained consciousness. I was lying on my back. My left arm had no sensation but a dull throb, nor could I move the fingers of my left hand. Something heavy lay across my legs, but when I tried to shift my body to ease the pressure, I sank back into unconsciousness again.

Gradually the surflike pounding of my pulse quieted enough to let in the sounds of the world outside my body. I could hear men around me in the underbrush. Someone close was coughing regularly — a wet, bubbling cough that was half a cry. Someone else was telling himself a story in a little-boy voice — enough words were audible to identify it as a memory of Christmas. Some man or large animal was thrashing about in the bushes. Every once in a while a voice called out, "Oh, Sweet Jesus — come for this sinner, Lord!" and another voice sobbed in hopeless despair.

Then I made out another sound, farther away than the others, but steady and clear — a man cursing. I recognized Star's voice. He was calling on his gods to punish the White Man.

"I beg that this shall come to pass — that the South Wind shall scorch their bodies and make them wither; that the North Wind shall freeze their blood and numb their muscles; that the West Wind shall blow away their life's breath, and will not leave their hair grow, and their finger-nails shall fall off and their bones crumble; that the East Wind shall make their minds grow dark, their sight shall fail and their seed dry up so they shall not multiply."

"Star!" I tried to call out, but my voice was no more than a hoarse whisper, and the effort shook my hold on consciousness.

The deep, clear voice went on, as remorseless as a hangman's noose. "May the wombs of their women not bear fruit except for strangers, may the children who are born be weak in mind and paralyzed of limb, so that they curse their white fathers for ever blowing the breath of life into the bodies. I pray that disease and death shall be with them forever. In your daughter Marie's name I pray it, Damballa *loa!* Grant my prayer for your daughter's sake, Damballa!"

"Star!" I whispered again. "Star! Can you hear me? It's Hacey!"

At that moment I heard a new sound. A group of men was

moving through the darkness, talking quietly as they came. An intermittent flash of light showed they were carrying a lantern. As the noise of their approach increased, the sounds of the wounded around me decreased proportionally. Nobody in his right mind wanted the newcomers to hear him.

"Looky here! This nigger's got a watch! Now where you reckon a black booger like him would get a watch like that?"

"Steal it off'n a white man, where else? Thieving son of a bitch — is he dead?"

"Don't think so — look at them eyeballs roll! Naw, he ain't dead yet."

There was a thudding sound, followed by a gasp and a shuddering exhalation.

"He is now. Has he got any gold in his mouth?"

"Let's see." The lantern was unmasked, and threw its light on the face of a Negro lying on the ground. A white man was visible leaning over the body, and the boots of three other men showed dimly at the edge of the light-spill. The bending man pulled the dead Negro's mouth open. "Hey, boy! Hand me them pliers, Taney! They's four beauties in here!" I turned my eyes away, but I couldn't close my ears to the sound of the teeth being ripped from the gums.

God help me, I thought in sick horror, these are bushwhackers — the filth that calls itself Irregulars or Partisans — murderers like Champe Ferguson, who killed my brother Boone. When Forrest pulled out and left the Union casualties unguarded, they moved in like hyenas in the darkness, to torture the living and rob the dead.

The little party of ghouls moved toward me, the light bobbing up and down as other bodies were inspected, dispatched, and stripped of valuables. They finished off the poor wretch with the liquid cough, and then suddenly the bull's-eye lantern was over *my* head. My eyes were closed, but the light stabbed through my eyelids and burned in my brain like fire. I held my breath.

"There's two of 'em here — one a-laying on top of t'other."

"Yeah, but that one on top — you ain't going to get no gold out of *him!* Look at that head!"

"Sheee-it!"

"I'll be dogged — this one underneath — he's a white man!"

"Don't know how you can tell under all that blood."

"He's an officer, for one thing. You ever hear tell of any nigger officers? And look at that ear — can't you see the skin's white? And the hair ain't kinky, neither. Naw, he's a white man, for a fact."

"Is he dead?"

"Ain't nobody going to lose that kind of blood and live to tell about it. Reckon his brains is spread over the ground an inch thick under there."

"Let's see what's in his pockets." I felt quick hands running over my body. "Here's a purse. Hey, it's got twenty dollars in it, and some silver."

"Give it here. Now look in his mouth. Hurry up, God damn it, I don't want to spend all night out here."

Fingers pushed into my mouth, and my jaw was pried open. The fingers tasted of dirt and blood and corruption. I almost gagged, but forced myself to lie motionless as the lantern was lowered close to my face.

"Not a single damn goldie," said a voice above me regretfully.

"Come on, then. Here's another one over here." The fierce glow receded, together with he sound of the men's movements, and after a few moments I opened my eyelids to see the group inspecting another body fifteen feet away.

The shock of my narrow escape, combined with the nausea that swept over me as the corpse-robber's filthy fingers thrust into my mouth in a kind of perverse rape, tilted me over into unconsciousness again. When I awoke, the bull's-eye lantern was fifty feet farther away. The ghouls were entering one of the wooden sheds. The light disappeared, and then a moment later reappeared, framed by a window. A voice cried out, "There's one in here, sure enough! God, ain't he a big sucker!"

"Ugly bastard, ain't he? Look at that scar on his forehead. Well, get his mouth open."

A moment later the sound of a pistol shot shattered the night, followed almost instantly by two more. The light that showed through the shed window swung wildly and then went out. A voice screamed, other voices cursed, and boots thumped on wooden boards.

"He's got a gun! He shot Huger! Christ, where's the light?"

More thuds, cries, oaths, and after a few seconds the light came on again. "You got him, boys? You got him pinned? Hold him good, you hear? Let me see that gun . . ."

"It's all right, he only had three bullets, and Huger got 'em all. Poor Huger — they ain't much of his face left for burying. We'll have to close the casket up for services. You all got that nigger pinned so he can't move? You sure?" Reassured, his tone changed from agitation to cold malevolence. "You black bastard, now you going to find out what happens to a nigger that kills a white man!"

There was a moment of silence, and then all at once Star's voice bellowed in pain and rage, another voice shrieked out in fear, bodies crashed against the boards, and the light went out again. As the sound of the struggle continued, I knew the time had come for me to try to help my friend. I managed to achieve a sitting position, as waves of nausea swept over me. I put out my right hand and felt the body lying across my legs. No wonder the ghouls hadn't wasted any time on it; almost all of its head was gone. I pushed as hard as I could, but it didn't move. I grabbed a handful of jacket and tugged, and felt the dead weight shift slightly. Ignoring the throbbing pain in my left arm, I tried to bring my left hand into use as well, at the same time bunching the muscles in my legs and preparing to push upward. I couldn't close my fingers, so I thrust the numb hand under the corpse's chest and heaved, tugging at the cloth and beginning to straighten my legs at the same instant. The body rolled clumsily to one side, and I rose to a bent-kneed crouch, but that was as far as I could get. I swayed there for a moment, with the sounds of the struggle in the shed swelling and receding in my ears, and then spinning red flashes exploded behind my eyes, and I fell back to the ground unconscious.

When I opened my eyes next, it was dawn, and a wet gray fog hung over the river. There were no sounds. Directly ahead of me was the shed in which Star had hidden. It was burned to ashes. From where I lay I could see nothing but the charred embers, sodden by the morning dew — but later I learned that Star's body was inside, half consumed by fire.

He had been nailed to the wooden floor, blinded, and then mutilated. The shed had been splashed with coal oil and fired while he was still alive.

Some of Forrest's men returned to the fort to arrange a truce with the two gunboats which now lay off shore — the *New Era* had been joined by the *Silver Cloud* during the night — and about 8:00 A.M. the boats tied up at the landing to begin embarking the wounded. At the same time those of the garrison who could handle a spade were put to work burying their dead companions. Since the truce was due to expire at four, the burial was a hasty and slipshod affair. More than 200 Union soldiers were rolled into a shallow trench and covered as deeply as time would allow, which in some cases was not deep enough to prevent arms and legs from thrusting through the dirt and pointing skyward like surfaced roots.

During the day the transport *Platte Valley* joined the two gunboats at the landing, and I was carried aboard it a little before noon, more unconscious than not. The three ships cast off their moorings and stood out into the river, the Confederates moved back into Town Ravine to burn whatever buildings remained, and the Battle of Fort Pillow was over — for everyone but Major Bradford, who had been captured, and was murdered by his captors three days later.

I was taken to a military hospital in Mound City, Illinois, where I remained for three months. My left arm was amputated at a point three inches below the shoulder; I was almost resigned to losing it, because after what had happened to it at Richmond, I figured it was jinxed anyway. My head injury was more serious — the ball had dug into my skull and opened the cranial cavity, but thanks to a good doctor and a merciful Providence, the wound healed with no ill effects.

Two months after the fall of Fort Pillow, I was interviewed in the hospital by Senator Ben Wade of Ohio, concerning the events of April 12. I have no idea whether or not he was aware of my actions in Washington during the Porter court-martial, but his behavior toward me was less than cordial. Maybe it was because I told him the exact and literal truth about the battle; the foolishness of the plan to rely on the *New Era;* the whiskey on the firing platform during the fighting; the refusal of the Confederates to accept the surrender of the black troops; the criminal depredations of the Irregulars during the night after the battle. Senator Wade heard what he wanted to hear. When the report of his sub-committee's "Investigation of the Fort Pillow Massacre" was published later in the year, it contained accounts of many Rebel atrocities, but no mention of Union whiskey.

In the late summer I received my discharge from the Union Army in Mound City, and took a boat to Louisville, a train to Lexington, and a buggy to Hazelwood.

Ellie's kiss was as sweet as fresh berries and cream. I pressed her as close as I could with my right arm.

"God damn — now I'm really going to miss that other arm. How am I am ever going to give you a decent hug?"

"I guess I'll have to squeeze hard enough for both of us." She did. "Oh, Hacey, Hacey, it's so good to have you home. Don't never let go, promise. Just hold me and hold me till we grow together like them two vines in the garden."

" 'And then they tied a true lover's knot — the red rose 'round the briar,' " I quoted, and kissed her lips again.

"Before you get permanently entangled, there are some other people who might like to say hello," said my mother dryly, and stepped out onto the porch, holding the hand of a serious-faced, brown-haired three-year-old boy, who looked at me unwinkingly from under level brows.

"Hello, Papa," he said gravely. "I'm Boone."

Another winter rolled slowly by, and then the end of the war was in sight. John G. Fee returned to Berea in the spring of 1865, and I rode down to the Ridge to join him three or four days a week. Lee surrendered at Appomattox, Joe Johnston surrendered two weeks later, the President was assassinated — and it all seemed less immediate than chopping new shingles for the roof of a schoolroom.

In the fall Ellie and Boone and I moved into our own home in Berea. By ones and twos, the other Bereans who had survived the war drifted back to join us. We cleared the brush before the first frost. By Christmas all damage to the school building and Hanson's sawmill had been repaired.

In January, 1866, Berea College reopened.

Three of its students were blacks.

Epilogue: The Old Lion

THE YEARS that followed the war were generous to me. Ellie presented me with three other children to keep young Boone company. Their names are Patience, Wentworth, and Falconer — three names as well broken in as a favorite old saddle. They all attended Berea College as students and then went out into the world to do what they could to improve it; Patience as a schoolteacher, Boone as a lawyer, Wentworth as a doctor, and Falconer as a Campbellite preacher. Mother lived long enough to see them all established in life, and then died in her sleep at Hazelwood in 1891.

In the years immediately after the reopening of Berea, two young men appeared as students and gladdened our hearts: Robert and Armisted Padgett, Ellie's younger brothers. They both did well in their studies — Armisted especially distinguished himself in veterinary medicine — and elected to return to the mountains after their graduation. They are a source of considerable pride to their brother Falk, who also returned to the Big Sandy country, where he now manages a successful hardware store in Paintsville.

The bushwhacker Champe Ferguson did not live to see

253

the end of the war. He was captured and executed by Union troops in 1864 — but not, I regret to say, by the First Kentucky Cavalry. However, Frank Wolford's troopers did accomplish their main mission. They captured John Hunt Morgan. It wasn't their fault that the "Rebel Raider" escaped from a Union prison camp and led a final campaign before he was killed.

Nat Crocker also did not survive the war. He was killed leading his black soldiers in the Battle of the Crater, before Petersburg. I like to think — no, I am sure — he found more purpose and more zest in his year and a half with his "Ethiops" than he would have enjoyed in twenty years of clerking for the War Department.

After an apparently hopeless fight for justice that lasted almost a quarter-century, Fitz John Porter was reinstated in the United States Army, with the permanent rank of colonel. At his own request, he was immediately placed on the retired list.

Thomas Wentworth Higginson carried on vigorously through the nineteenth century, and is now happily trying out the twentieth. He seems to spend half his time writing his memoirs and the other half receiving testimonial dinners. We have remained irregular correspondents, and I also keep abreast of his doings in the *Atlantic Monthly,* where his articles often appear. There is more mellowness than militancy in his writing now, and his nature is as sweet and his wit as buoyant as ever.

As I write these words, it is the year 1903, and Cassius Marcellus Clay has been dead six months. During the four decades since he left the field at Richmond, deprived of his chance for martial glory, he never for a moment ceased to be the protagonist in a melodrama of his own devising.

He returned from his Ministry to Russia in 1869, and he and his wife took up residence at White Hall. Two years later the prima ballerina of the Imperial Russian Ballet, heavily veiled, arrived in a carriage at his door and delivered his "Russian son" to him — a sickly, sad-faced boy named Launey. Clay took Launey into his home to raise him, and the boy's mother departed. Tongues wagged throughout the Bluegrass — tongues *usually* wagged about Clay throughout the Bluegrass — and Mrs. Clay packed up and moved into Lexington, announcing that she wouldn't raise her family in the same house with "The General's Bastard."

Clay and the little boy lived alone in the forty-room mansion for nearly ten years, with only two or three shiftless Negroes for company. Launey's health declined, and Clay, still haunted by the murder of his son in 1845, decided that one of the blacks was poisoning the boy. He drove the suspect off his land, the man returned and took a shot at him, and Clay killed him with the pistol he had been given by Abraham Lincoln.

He reentered politics on his return to the United States, but was not destined to play an important national role again. He supported Horace Greeley for the presidency against Grant in 1872, and Tilden against Hayes in 1876. He challenged both the radical Republican "Carpetbag" governments in the Southern States, and the Ku Klux Klan which opposed them illegally. In Kentucky elections he was more often Republican than not, and at one time marched eighty armed Negroes to Foxtown, to vote for a Republican candidate whose supporters were being intimidated by Democratic bullies.

Launey ran away the same year Mrs. Clay finally sued for divorce, in 1878. After that, except for the few blacks around him, he was completely alone. I would ride over to

White Hall every few weeks to call. I remember one conversation we had in his study, which was almost completely stripped of furniture, books and decoration. It must have been sometime in the middle 1880s.

We were talking about Boston before the war. "Did I ever tell you about the time I was at dinner at some abolitionist's house on Beacon Street, and was seated next to a runaway slave?" he asked with a smile.

"I don't think so, General," I answered, although he had.

"Well, sir, we talked all through the meal, and got on famously. Finally, as we were finishing our ices, he looked me in the eye, shook my hand, and exclaimed, with deep and vibrant emotion, 'Mr. Clay, yo' skin may be white, but I kin tell yo' heart is black!' "

I laughed with as much enjoyment as he expected. He chuckled with me for a moment, and then lapsed into silence, his eyes ceasing to focus on me. Idly he brushed the shock of white hair back from his still masterful brow. I waited for him to speak again.

"A black heart," he said softly. "He said I had a black heart. That was a compliment, you understand, Hacey."

"Yes, General, I know."

"And he was right. The way he meant it, I did have a black heart. I had the blackest heart in the Republican Party."

"The way he meant it, you certainly did."

He focused his eyes on me again. "Sometimes I wonder at the way things turned out. You hardly would have expected everything to happen that way, would you?"

"Not rightly."

"Hmm," he grunted. "You know, Hacey, last night I opened the upstairs windows and let the bats into the house to eat the insects off the walls."

"Why, General?"

"Just to have something alive around me."

In 1894 he took it into his head to marry the daughter of his tobacco tenant, a fifteen-year-old girl named Dora Richardson. Word of the approaching nuptials inflamed the surrounding neighborhood, and the High Sheriff of Madison County swore out a *posse comitatus* to rescue the girl from White Hall. Clay stood them off with Lincoln's pistol and one of the brass cannons from the *True American* office, and the Sheriff gave up the attempt, saying it would take an artillery company with two field pieces to succeed against the General.

Two years later Dora decided she wanted a divorce, and Clay gave her one, paying all the legal costs himself. The child-bride then married a young roughneck named Riley Brock, and, incredibly, the couple returned to take up residence with Clay in White Hall. This state of affairs continued as Dora became pregnant and bore a child, whom she named Cassius Marcellus Clay Brock.

Riley Brock began to drink heavily, and one night when he beat Dora in a drunken rage, Clay drew his pistol and ordered him from the house. Brock left, but returned late that night with two companions. All were armed, and determined to take Dora and the baby to Richmond.

Clay met them in the great living room of the mansion, now empty except for a few bags of apples on the floor. He fought all three of them by the flickering light from the fireplace. He gutted one and shot the second — the third escaped.

This last battle sapped his strength, and he went into a decline. I traveled to White Hall for the last time, to sit beside his bed and hold his hand.

"By God, I stirred them up, didn't I?" he asked.

"You did more than that, General," I replied.

On the night of the 22nd of July, 1903, as the most violent tornado ever known in Kentucky struck the cemetery in Lexington and smashed the statue of Henry Clay, his cousin Cash died in his sleep at White Hall. He was ninety-three years old. Behind him he left — Berea.

The college grew steadily during the postwar years, adding classrooms and residence halls, a store, a chapel, and quarters for unmarried male and female teachers. Enrollment increased each year, and included both young men and young women, both white and black. For the last few years the proportions have stabilized at, roughly, 60 per cent mountain whites, 40 per cent blacks.

Ellie and I shared in Berea's growth with high pride and great joy. We saw it send out its message of hope to the impoverished hill people and the confused Negroes of the Border South, and we saw their eager response. We played our part in replacing hate with love, purposelessness with ambition, ignorance with knowledge, in the hearts and minds of hundreds of young people.

In 1894, Ellie succumbed to influenza.

Since then, I have lived alone. But I have never been lonely. There are too many students and too many friends for that — and too many memories.

For every day I can look out to the South, across the Ridge to the blue mass of the mountains — toward Wild Cat and Lebanon, toward Beaufort and the Sea Islands, toward Fort Pillow.

And, remembering the pain and the blood and the dying, I yet can think, "That was a time to be alive. Thank God for it."

AUTHOR'S NOTE

I owe many debts for *The Way to Fort Pillow* and its predecessor, *Hacey Miller.* My greatest is to the late William H. Townsend, whose *Lincoln and the Bluegrass* is both the most informative and the most entertaining source of events and manners in Kentucky before and during the Civil War.

Other books I could not have done without are *Birth of Berea College,* by John A. R. Rogers; Eastham Tarrant's *Wild Riders of the First Kentucky Cavalry; Reveille in Washington,* by Margaret Leech; *The Celebrated Case of Fitz John Porter,* by Otto Eisenschiml; the Wade Subcommittee's *Report on the Fort Pillow Massacre;* John Allan Wyeth's *Life of General Nathan Bedford Forrest;* C. M. Clay's *Memoirs;* and, of course, T. W. Higginson's inimitable *Army Life in a Black Regiment.*

J. Winston Coleman drew me a map of ante-bellum Lexington so detailed I could imagine myself walking its streets; the late Cassius M. Clay supplied facts on the poisoning of his great-uncle's little boy and the subsequent trial; J. T. Dorris made his unique collection of Clay-iana (including bowie knives) available; and the libraries of Lexington, Berea College, and the University of Kentucky were more than needfully hospitable, as was the Newberry Library in Chicago.

The reader should know that the account of the events at Fort Pillow represents my own view of what probably happened. The official Northern version and the eyewitness reports of Southern officers and men of Forrest's command differ so widely that no one can say with certainty what really happened that bloody day and night. I have tried to reconcile elements from both versions, to form a consistent narrative; I can't swear it *did* happen this way, only that it *could have*.

Finally, I want to thank my wife, Nancy, and my children, Jim, Nancy Lee, and Jenny, for their enthusiasm and forbearance. Every writer who works at home should be as lucky.

J.S.